Awkward, hapless Marick is still s̶̶̶̶̶̶̶̶̶̶̶̶̶̶̶̶̶
his wife, his child and his faith when he is reluctantly thrust
into the position of chaplain at a large public hospital. Shortly
after arriving, he meets Hugo, a scientist and a man almost as
lost as Marick himself, who is working in a forgotten lab,
deep in the subterranean realms of the hospital. Hugo is
convinced that the bacteria he uses for protein production
have – unbelievably – begun to produce gold. Is it alchemy,
evolution, a hoax or even ... possibly ... a miracle?

In the meantime, Christmas is approaching, the number of
homeless outside the hospital is increasing, the Director of
Operational Services is pressing Marick about his weekly
KPIs, you can't buy chocolate in the hospital shop anymore,
and Marick keeps waking with nightmares at 4 am every
night. If ever a miracle was needed, it's now.

A tender, sweet, sad, gritty, slyly funny and unexpectedly
uplifting novel about family, friendship, faith, love – and
alchemy – *Tiny Uncertain Miracles* is a gift to all readers.

'This is a novel luminous with love and hope
that will change the way you see the world'

Kathryn Heyman

Praise for *Tiny Uncertain Miracles*

'Johnston articulates the biggest questions and the smallest human moments with rare beauty and precision. A stunning act of imagination and storytelling' – Robert Lukins, author of *Loveland*

'Michelle Johnston is a miraculous writer. Full of beautifully drawn characters, luscious language and gentle wit, this is a novel luminous with love and hope that will change the way you see the world' – Kathryn Heyman, author of *Fury*

'*Tiny Uncertain Miracles* is witty, profound and a joy to read. Johnston posits that believing in something is better than nothing, and that redemption can come from the least likely places. Invisible gods, alchemy, medical science – all have their place, but none tops the marvel of people, in their own weird ways and often, despite themselves, being pretty bloody marvellous' – Paul Dalgarno, author of *A Country of Eternal Light*

'Original, enchanting and ultimately hopeful, *Tiny Uncertain Miracles* is a dazzling tale that will get under your skin and into your heart, in the best way possible' – Ewa Ramsey, author of *The Morbids*

'Emotionally rich, profoundly absorbing and entrancingly unique, this is a book you won't be able to put down. Johnston's sentences dance, her wit sparkles and her power arises from her authority and audacity. Intellectually rigorous and achingly poignant, *Tiny Uncertain Miracles* is a virtuoso performance by a writer at the height of her powers. I have not read anything as satisfying and stimulating for a very long time' – Alice Nelson, author of *The Children's House*

Michelle Johnston

FOURTH ESTATE

Fourth Estate
An imprint of HarperCollins*Publishers*

Australia • Brazil • Canada • France • Germany • Holland • India
Italy • Japan • Mexico • New Zealand • Poland • Spain • Sweden
Switzerland • United Kingdom • United States of America

HarperCollins acknowledges the Traditional Custodians
of the land upon which we live and work, and pays respect
to Elders past and present.

First published in Australia in 2022
by HarperCollins*Publishers* Australia Pty Limited
Gadigal Country
Level 13, 201 Elizabeth Street, Sydney NSW 2000
ABN 36 009 913 517
harpercollins.com.au

A catalogue record for this book is available from the National Library of Australia

ISBN 978 1 4607 6271 4 (hardback)
ISBN 978 1 4607 1528 4 (ebook)

Cover design by Hazel Lam, HarperCollins Design Studio
Author photograph by Steve Wise
Typeset in Bembo Std by Kirby Jones
Printed and bound in Australia by McPherson's Printing Group

MIX
Paper | Supporting
responsible forestry
FSC
www.fsc.org   FSC® C001695

This book is dedicated to those whose love opened the door to a story about miracles — Anita, Isabelle, Jules, Richard and Marbles — and to the scientist with the key to it all, my brother Wayne.

As for the earth, out of it cometh bread: and under
it is turned up as it were fire. The stones of it are the
places of sapphires: and it hath dust of gold.

King James Bible, Job 28: 5–6

Thus you may multiply each stone four times and no more
for they will then become oyles shining in the dark and fit for
magicall uses. You may ferment them with gold and silver, by
keeping the stone and metal in fusion together for a day, and
then project upon metalls. This is the multiplication of the stone
in vertue. To multiply it in weight ad to it of the first Gold
whether philosophic or vulgar.

Isaac Newton, *Praxis*, c. 1693

Round about, round about
Lo and behold.
Reel away, reel away
Straw into gold.

Rumpelstiltskin, Brothers Grimm, 1812

ONE

Not a bone in Marick's body was suited to the church. When a man comes late to God, looking for answers, pulpits and hymns aren't always what he requires.

'It's not working out, is it?' The Deacon spoke with his back turned and his soft, leonine hands clutched together. 'We're happy to write you a reference. There's an opening at The Public over the road, we've heard. Hospital chaplain. Might suit you better.'

Marick reached behind one ear and wound down the tiny dial. Even if not in full proclamation mode, the Deacon's voice could scud off the stone of the high-vaulted church vestibule and cause Marick's hearing aids to squeal replies of their own.

It was working out, Marick wanted to respond, if working out meant refraining from bringing down the walls in a trumpet of doubt. Marick could promise to fall back into godly line, but he suspected the Deacon's mind was made up, convinced by the rumours and complaints whispered under archways. This, Marick realised, was it.

The walk from the church's basement to the hospital's administration block was short, and downhill. Marick took a breath in and set off – he and his stocky workhorse body, his eggshell hearing, his thick, dark hair that defied the meticulous middle part Marick aspired to. Organ-song faded out behind him, and several crows circled in the stilted summer air above, as though they were timekeepers on some great astronomical clock.

The white blast of daylight was a surprise, and Marick blinked in its glare. Under his arm was a cardboard box containing his belongings: a Bible, several notebooks, vestments. He filed through the cathedral gates. A car shot by, too fast for the speed limit and too heavy on the horn, and his step caught. He suspected he resembled a detective in a miniseries who had cleared out his desk in shame, and he hoped none of the clerical staff were standing in the church grounds, taking the opportunity to catch a few morning rays and watch.

Compared to the stately, upright angles of the church, the hospital was a casserole of architecture, all overhangs and crumbled curves. The front entrance was obscured by mushrooms of smoke rising from patients in concerted huddles, many in gowns and wheelchairs and accompanied by metal poles hung with intravenous fluids like lampposts, all of them puffing away in the cool shade of the *No Smoking* signs. Geometrically speaking, the hospital was a fiasco, and, once Marick had excused his way inside, it was not easy to navigate the corridors and dead ends to Employment Services.

There, in an air-conditioned office plastered with health and safety notices, Marick was asked a stream of questions. The clerk did not look at him and spent most of their encounter trying to determine if he would be eligible for parking. At no time did she ask him if he believed in God. He signed his name with his free hand, still clutching his box with the other. She produced a map, which looked to Marick like an electrical diagram, and drew a red ring around a square buried in the interior.

'Your office. Basement level two. Between Specimen Reception and Microbiology,' she said. 'And a pager. You do know how to use one, don't you?'

'Thank you,' Marick said. 'I was a payroll officer in a former life,' he added as if that explained things. 'So yes.' He hoped he sounded endearing, but her expression was a tomb.

He wanted to ask what was expected of him. What did the job entail? Were there others?

'Do I have a roster?' he asked.

'It's only you,' she said, blinking. 'Budgets,' she added, as though this was the one-sized answer that did for most questions coming across her desk.

Marick thanked her again and took the map and his paperwork, placing them on top of King James. Here he was. A neo-Anglican washed ashore. A defective man tossed up onto the sands of a job, with an employee number and a pager. A job it was though, with its forecast of possibility. He would have his own office it seemed, his diocese the heavy corridors of a hospital. Not what he had planned, but there were few posts out there for a man with a theology degree permanently under construction and no option to return to life as it was B.C. Everything in Marick's timeline he viewed as A.C. or B.C. − like a calendar in reverse. After, or Before, Claudia.

He consulted the map; each corner felt like an increment, a step, towards a future with promise. He had the sense that venturing through new territories might let him go a fresh round with God.

He came to what on the diagram was labelled Chapel, only to see it had been repurposed. The sign above the door declared *Day Transition Unit*. It was not clear who or what was to pass through the room now. It still had a vestigial thread of crimson shot through its décor, and he could make out nurses standing over patients and blood pressure cuffs going up and down like bellows. He loitered, leaning his head on the window, and he watched the industry inside, wondering where all the pews had gone.

Moving on, he tackled several sets of stairs, an elevator and a number of doors of various sizes. He became lost more than once and referred several times to the map, lining it up with what he could see in front of him. More doors appeared, some of which looked familiar. Marick wondered whether he had come this way before – a wayfarer's déjà vu. He descended. Eventually he found the room of his own, a small windowless office with a faded *Pastoral Services* sign over the door. He set his box down on a desk emptied some time ago. Poking around the vacant workspace, he wondered why the last chaplain had left. The drawers and the shelves offered up no ready answers.

He sat at his desk. He waited for his pager to sound, but it was silent. At one point he tracked his way over and knocked on the door of the switchboard, asking if they could check whether his device was functioning. They tested it for him, letting it yowl down the corridor.

'They'll call when they need you,' a woman said from behind a grille. 'That's how it's always worked.'

Returning to his office, he examined his pager again. Nothing. He walked up and down his little surrounds. This corridor was low-ceilinged and phosphorescent, and it had obscure departments opening off it like cave mouths. Later, when he began to explore the subterranean riddle of the whole hospital and discovered how many burrows snaked through the foundations, he wondered how the entire building didn't collapse on itself, imploding into plumes of dust and electrical wiring.

Marick's cloister down here was forsaken. Only a scatter of workers passed by, all of them lost in their own monologues. None seemed to notice the new chaplain.

He decided to arrange his room. He would make it his own, as he would the job. Standing his Bible next to the desk lamp, he ran a finger down the book's leather spine, catching his nail on the softening cracks. The book was loam brown and aged, its cover returning to pelt through constant use.

The office came with a computer. Its buttons were stiff, and he blew the dust off its top, booting the thing into wheezing life. After wrangling with a catastrophe of passwords, he found the Pastoral Services department information on the hospital website. It was rudimentary, offering little guidance on the business of hospital chaplaincy. He picked up the papers he'd been given and thumbing through them discovered a half-page document that was part orientation, part job description. It didn't say much. In essence he was to provide succour and comfort. Non-denominational if he didn't mind. Not too much religion was how he interpreted it. Fine, Marick thought. This would suit him fine.

When six p.m. came around and he closed the door of his office behind him, he emerged into the half-light of a day mostly spent. He stepped from the front entrance into the still of the city which, too, seemed to be dreaming of remaking itself. No sea breeze had arrived, leaving the dusk air dank. Early December and the great parch was underway, with everything about to turn an abrupt brown. Everything except, of course, the velvet church lawn across the road. This was maintained by a silent army to a shade of green that could be considered immodest. He glanced over at the limestone silhouette and was surprised to feel little sorrow. He could now permit himself to admire the building, with its brass parade of fittings and design. Marick thought he could have been an excellent priest if it weren't for God. If it were simply the rituals, the music (loud), the accessories. The stoneworks. The confidence. The afternoon light through stained-glass windows, and the possibility, abstract and hidden like a croon among its ancient pages, of forgiveness.

The number two bus swung into his stop, and Marick stepped on board. He lumbered to his usual seat, halfway down on the right, where he could cling to the yellow dimpled pole as the corners came at him. While the bus rumbled along, he watched the city undress to reveal its suburban skin. The houses flattened; the gardens grew. His own place came into sight, and he pushed the button in the pole, summoning the bus to a stop. He called it a house, but it wasn't. It was the triangular third of a triplex he had occupied for the last three years, moving in sometime after the divorce. It was a wedge-shaped apartment built of rough bricks, with a treeless courtyard out the front. Inside, the walls were painted a sunless colour. There was a single living area connected to a narrow kitchen, an electric Wurlitzer organ in the corner that he never played, and a print of Caravaggio's *Death of the Virgin* hanging in the hallway. A single photo of his daughter, Claudia, that he'd fallen into the bad habit of keeping next to his bedside. No photos of his ex-wife, Diane. No mementoes of a fourteen-year marriage.

Marick microwaved a frozen turkey dinner for one. He set a place at his small table – fork, knife, glass of juice – but when he cut into the meat, he discovered it was watery and soft, as if it had already been half-digested. He scraped it into the bin, even though it was a sin to waste food.

He pulled out his job description and reread the single sheet of paper. The date at the top declared it had been written seven years ago, as the millennium turned – that moment of hope. And now, this would be his. A role to celebrate the realities of religion – permission to be a practical man. Action would be his catechism. Comfort and succour indeed, with the expectation he could respond to the needs of others like a theistic chameleon. Some simple ministering. Providing gentle companionship to the unwell, that was all.

⋅\ä⁊ĺ⋅

But that was not all. Returning the next day, dressed in formal pants and crisp blue shirt, with a small gold cross pinned to his collar, Marick was engulfed. As though yesterday's solitude was a misleading prologue. He discovered a different God from the one floating among the sermons and the choirs up the hill.

His pager fired off as he walked through the hospital's front door, requesting his attendance in the Emergency Department.

Steady, he told himself as he followed the mammoth signs.

A nurse in neat scrubs ushered him down an aisle seething with workers. They reached the backblocks of the department where a crowd was milling around a door. A sense of something to be confronted inside threw Marick off balance.

She put a hand on his arm as they neared. 'Catholic,' was all she said.

He started. Non-denominational was one thing, but it was another thing entirely to feign the authority of the Church of Rome. Spilling from the entrance to the room was a clan, ten people at least, all of similar appearance. The women had long black hair and each wore patterned clothes of bright, primary colours. They were all shorter than Marick. As he was propelled through the crowd, they turned to him in unison, their faces contorted and gothic. Black rivulets ran down the women's cheeks and the men's pupils were dilated with rage. Hands pawed at him; voices bubbled through his hearing aids.

'Father!' they called. Their agony was obvious, the air awash with it.

'They're all family,' the nurse guiding him said under her breath. 'Filipino.' She summarised the story for him during those few seconds of transit, nailing the words into his head. Inside the room was a sixteen-year-old girl, raped and set on fire and left to die in the stairwell of an inner-city apartment building. 'There are some rough places out there,' she added, as though they were speaking the same language.

Marick's feet caught, and the nurse grabbed his arm.

'Are you alright, Father?' she asked.

He wasn't sure how to answer. He compromised with a nod.

'Her injuries, the burns. They were unsurvivable,' she said. He had not heard that word before – unsurvivable. 'Palliation was our only option.' Several women were rocking over the slight body like branches in a rough-edged wind.

Marick could feel his jaw hanging, slack on its hinges. The smell in the claustrophobia of the room was putrid, unplaceable. It was perhaps charred blood, petrified skin, the singe of hair. He could see motes in the light, performing some macabre dance. The perfume worn by the visitors melded to create something new, sickly, wrong, and Marick feared he would vomit. He closed his mouth and tried not to breathe. Next to him was an IV pole, standing unemployed, and he grabbed onto it. Sixteen. He didn't know sixteen. He'd not seen Claudia at sixteen.

'You are Catholic, aren't you, Father?' one of the family members asked. 'You have to hurry. She needs the last rites.'

He stared at the soaked bandages covering the girl's face and body. A tube appeared from a gap near her mouth, connected to nothing but the cloy of the air. Her chest did not quiver, did not move, did not rise. He sent an imploring look to the nurse. She reached over and whispered in his ear. 'She's already dead. You were all we could get. Just do what you can. We've been waiting until you got here to record the time of death.'

The stability in Marick's legs threatened to abandon him.

He made sure the family could not hear, and murmured to the nurse, 'The last rites aren't for those who've already ...' – he wasn't sure which word to use – 'passed,' he settled on, resorting to euphemism, the ambiguity of cowards. 'And I'm not ...' but where could he go from there?

The nurse shrugged. 'Hasn't been declared yet, so I'm not sure there's a difference. Look at them.' Her whisper was harsh and business-like, and she gestured with her head towards the women. Marick had flirted with Catholicism during his detour of a life A.C., while he was both undifferentiated and anchorless, but it hadn't had much time for him in return. It did mean he knew the words, the actions. But the true meaning, right here?

A prolonged note of despair keened through the group. He lay his palm on the woman closest to the girl – possibly the mother – trying to imbue in his gesture what he was incapable of producing in words. She calmed a little under his touch, which gave him enough to carry on. Needs must was as much justification as he could summon. His throat was dry, and the Eucharist stuck as it came out, but his memory did not fail him. Placing his hands on the bandages – shrouds, he thought, with their disturbing, tepid wetness – he managed to repeat the Viaticum, louder. His intonations were the only sound in the room. Towards the end he faltered – what was he doing for a girl already gone, whose final hours were unimaginable, worse than hell? He decided at this point his priority was to the living, and he carried through to the ritualistic last. The death felt unfinished, and there was little he could do to complete it.

It was then all over. Marick was escorted back out, winding through the small crowd. Several of the family nodded at him. Empty-hearted thanks and no, they did not need him to stay. Their regular, proper priest was on his way. He would be the one to provide solace during the long hours to come.

Marick took a last look. The nurse returned to the room,

and the family closed around her. He shuffled off, alone. The corridor back was long, the lights overhead brazen. Staff marched by him. He feared he smelled oily, of crackling, of death. Perhaps he could go home, take a shower. Why had it not occurred to him he would be faced with such things? What had he expected? Not to be part of the brokerage of death, that was for sure. Not to stand next to violence as its witness. And the familiar torment returned to him, that bitter reflux in his gullet. How was he supposed to find answers when all that appeared were more questions? What sort of God presides over circumstances such as this? If he couldn't make sense of Claudia, his poor Claudia, living out her days as a wraith on the other side of the world, what hope did he have of understanding things here?

Reaching his office, he realised somebody was inside. It was the Director of Operational Services.

'You're the new chaplain? Just thought I'd drop in and say hello. Welcome, that sort of thing.'

His name was Fraser and he walked around Marick's cramped office, picking up items, some of which still had dust clinging to them. He shook a stapler and wiped a hand across it. Marick stood tense and angled in the doorway and hoped he hadn't carried the scorched smell in with him.

'Just making sure you can log in to your emails,' Fraser continued. 'Good communication is paramount in an institution such as this. Any problems, get onto IT straight away. And we'll need your weekly KPIs too. I appreciate you've only just started but we have a strict policy about data being in on time. Hospital and health care standards.'

Marick's words over the dead girl had left ash in his head and he was having difficulty following Fraser's spiel. A lick of sweat itched the small of his back.

'I'm sorry, but KP ...' He wasn't sure if he'd heard right.

'Indicators, Father. Key Performance Indicators. You have them. I have them. We're all benchmarked by them. It's how a corporation of this size runs. There's no funding without KPIs. Now because you've started mid-week I can give you a grace period until next.'

Grace, thought Marick. The eyes of the girl's family stared at him, an after-image behind his own lids. In that moment he rued leaving the timeless fluidity of the church. Grace indeed, with its candles like butter, organ music from gleaming pipes washing between major and minor notes according to the swell of the congregation's hearts, intonations indistinguishable from dream-states – and the doors closed by nine. Here, he realised, there would be little grace. It would be the clutch and claw of fear, which was able to dissolve grace like acid. He understood fear alright.

Fraser was leaving, his hand on the door. 'Measurables, Father. Everything in this hospital is measurable. Even your faith.' And he was gone.

'Even what faith?' Marick asked the room.

TWO

The Public, named by committee and governed by forms, had its own chronology of crisis. Its history mirrored that of the city as they both shot up – each desiring to shake free their colonial origins, doing so in episodic shudders. The hospital was unfashionable, sidelined during election cycles, showcased once in a while under the pop of camera-flashes when a rare good-news story emerged from its depths. Mostly though, it was an inner-city mess, a necessary blight, a place best avoided. Executive staff didn't linger in its boardrooms, only staying for a little reactive planning and a few edicts, cobbled together in haste. The building grew in vagaries and spurts. New structures were stacked on top of old; successive chiefs preferring piecemeal redevelopment to useful policy.

On the floor below the chaplain's office, the light was dimmer. Things down there were older, creaking, forgotten. Items were transported in, rarely removed. The lights on the ceiling and walls had not been replaced in years and were thin, naked tubes of fluorescence, studded with long-dead moths. They emitted a corduroy glow and when they eventually quit, they did so with a drawn-out fizzle. Lining the corridor walls were seized-up wheelchairs, broken trolleys and a ghost-field of empty gas bottles laid out in an equipment graveyard, a cortege rusted to a halt. Sound was almost entirely absent, except for an occasional echo of the hospital's business above, thumping through the ceiling.

Halfway along the corridor, behind a non-descript door was a room. A tiny room, measuring a little less than three metres at its widest. It retained a memory of its former life, and still had a laundry feel to it, with a series of washer-dryers muscled in, shoulder-to-shoulder beneath the bench. The resemblance ended there, though. The room had been appropriated. On the benchtop, with space at a premium, equipment was lined up with naval precision: odd paraphernalia, an incubator, two microscopes, a centrifuge. A black voltaic cradle trailed electric cords from under it like a tail, groomed into place. A single fluorescent light on the ceiling hummed, intense and full of action, and the room smelled of brine and vinegar.

Silent and hunched over the largest of the microscopes was a man who had slipped away from his job in the laboratory near Marick's office on the level above. This man did not move, compelled as he was by the vision beneath the barrels. It was hard to tell with his upper body crouched over the eyepieces, but he was a tall man. He was tree-bark brown and had hereditary hair – thick and onyx-coloured, with a dawning of grey at both temples. His eyes were of uneven pigmentation and his muscles had gone a little soft from too much sitting and thinking.

His hands gripped the sides of the microscope. They had turned bloodless with the effort. He would remember this moment, which he would relay later that day to the newly employed hospital chaplain, as the one where Sandya's prediction, after so many false promises, finally came true.

·˙\ͷ˷·

On the floor above, there was no such conviction. Marick entered his office for the second day on the job, hung his satchel – containing a small banana and a sandwich wrapped in clingfilm – on the back of the chair and sat. He had debated returning at all. Yesterday's encounter had tormented him through the night, and nights for Marick were monstrous at best. It had been another where he was raked by talons, suffocated, strangled by his own thoughts, and when he'd attempted prayer in the inked hours, his words were little more than argument.

There was no time for further reflection. Marick's pager bawled as soon as he sat, and carried on clamouring through the morning. He struggled to answer all the messages coming in tiny text form in his pocket. Not all of them turned out to be requests to meet Death on his collection round – some were more prosaic: a chat, a non-sectarian confession, biblical advice, but a sizeable proportion were to sit beside the abruptly bereaved in the ruins of grief.

Maybe he could have prevailed if it was once or twice, but servicing those demands that flashed up on the small screen – *Family on Ward 12b request Chaplain. Mother dying*, or *Need Chaplain. Emergency Department. Distressed Relative's Room* – tore afresh fibres in wounds somewhere deep. The behests were relentless. He puzzled through the hospital's layout, sensing his heart beat a little faster with each corner.

The variety of enquiries did lead to Marick discovering more of the building. At one point, near the front entrance, as he issued forth into the light he found himself next to the volunteer's shop, a zestful hive tucked into an alcove. He peered through the window and the head volunteer – Dolly, her badge proclaimed, bowled out to meet him.

'You must be the new chaplain. Welcome to The Public.' Marick sensed a cluster of women watching from inside the shop. When he glanced their way, they looked down, resuming their business in a collective flurry.

Dolly was immaculate, a woman in miniature with perfect hair in sculpted aluminium waves and a pair of glasses swinging from her neck on a pea-green plastic chain.

'Are you settling in? Finding your way around alright?' she asked.

Marick and the truth had a brief debate. 'It's certainly big. And what a shop this is. Lovely.'

'It's wonderful to have a chaplain back on board. The hospital has felt rudderless without one. This place needs you. Otherwise, it's all meetings and despair.' She gestured down the corridor with a vague wave.

'Despair?'

'I'm kidding, Father. I really shouldn't. I am sorry. But please let me know if I can help you with anything. Been here forever, I have.'

'I did wonder ...' He thought he may as well ask. 'The last chaplain. Why did he leave?'

Dolly leant in to whisper. 'They say he went mad, but if you ask me, I think folks don't always know the difference between mad and broken.'

That was a line. He could take it for himself. Lock it away somewhere. Not for a sermon – he'd write no more of those – but to help categorise his mind's inventory of things broken that continued to grow despite what was supposed to be time's healing properties. Broken things defined him, he thought. It would be useful to start finding a few pigeonholes for them.

He wanted to ask more but a new sound screamed from his pager, one he had not heard before. It was urgent, and several people around him broke into a run, taking off in the same direction.

'You'd better get that,' Dolly said.

Marick did not have the physique for sprinting. He followed, struggling to keep up. Later he would discover he had been added to the group cardiac arrest alert. A new initiative, someone of unclear designation would tell him. Streamlines the whole process.

At one point, he lost sight of the mob. He must have taken a wrong turn. He spiralled down a staircase. His pager continued to harangue him, crowing as he rounded a bend. Another staircase, down. A sign on the wall designated this one as a fire-escape. A murmur of panic sounded in him, an atavistic fear of being lost, a distant nightmare checking into his day. When the stairs ran out, he opened the bottom door and peered into the depths. There was nothing but vacant corridor, barely lit, with a tumble of storage hugging its walls. No crowd. As he ducked back into the stairwell he caught sight of somebody several floors up, taking steps two at a time. The same sound squawked from her pager.

The woman stopped momentarily, looking down at him. 'This way,' she yelled. 'Ward forty-two.'

Marick laboured his way back up the stairs and caught her. He peered down but couldn't see the door at the bottom, as though it had only existed in his confusion. He was muddied by the layout, confounded by the stress of it all. Puffing, he and his companion burst through a doorway several floors up and tagged on to the posse that swelled in size as it turned corners and took further staircases. At least twelve people had joined, a charge of workers with stethoscopes clacking around necks and the staticky swish of synthetic fabric. The surge poured into a room on a ward he had not yet visited. Marick stood at the back and braced his arms on his thighs to reclaim his breath. If he kept his breathing quiet, he could remain invisible. He did not know why he was there.

The centre was all action and voice. A woman in police-blue scrubs stood at the foot of the bed, calling instructions while another person hollered out numbers.

'Twenty-nine, thirty, breathe!'

Bending to peer through, Marick saw a frail elderly woman, lifeless it appeared from his vantage point, recoiling in time with the count. A red-faced doctor above her was sweating and compressing. One of the patient's breasts, pale and empty, flopped to the side, and the exposed flesh accompanied the rhythm. Below, Marick could see her unheld, crypt-white hand swinging beside the bed.

The CPR continued like a freight train.

'That's a rib,' he heard someone say.

The scene was dense. It was both chaos — clashing voices competing with each other — and military in sequence as workers stepped in to have their turn on the chest. A queue had formed, ready to take over. Marick was ignored, a nobody at the back of the crowd.

The woman in charge asked several times for the medical records. 'Does *anybody* know her history?' she put to the air.

Marick thought she looked like a weary conductor, perhaps exhausted towards the coda. She had margarine-coloured hair, pulled back in a scraggly ponytail, and her scrubs hung from her without shape. As she spoke, she frowned as though the entire event was an existential one.

A clerk pushed through the crowd with a battered file and handed it to a nurse.

'She's eighty-one.' The nurse opened it to the first page. 'Cancer,' she read out.

'Right,' the doctor said. And with a few utterances that undulated through the room, all actions ceased. A final voice called out a time, which was recorded on a form in triplicate. The crowd dissolved. The room emptied. A dozen pairs of soft shoes padded out, leaving no echo. The only people remaining were Marick and two young nurses, who began retrieving equipment flung around during the tornado of attempted resuscitation — and the waxen patient. The old woman's toothless mouth hung open, her abraded lips no longer able to bleed. To Marick she looked as if she'd been wanting to call out stop from the very beginning.

'Do you need me?' he asked the nurses. They looked up.

'Oh, the chaplain,' one said. 'I don't think so. There's no family.' She pulled the gown back up to cover the woman's chest.

'May I?' he asked them.

They shrugged, and he walked over to the woman's inert body, laying a hand on her arm. Where he touched her whey-coloured skin, he sensed the warmth departing. He wanted to fold it back into her, keep her warm for a little longer. Surely they could have found somebody to come, somebody to weep over her, he thought. He clutched her hand, flexing it at the wrist and encompassing it in his, but the colour drained to a mottle all the same. And as she blanched she became more and more a shell, undignified in emptiness, on a hospital gurney. He was not sure what to do, standing there, connected by his palm to the surface of her, and he heard himself urging God to turn up, hoping there had been another witness apart from the workers, zealous as they'd been, but now gone. Trying to think of the best prayer to recite, he came up short, so settled on simply saying sorry.

'Excuse us, Father,' one of the nurses said, bustling around him.

Marick stepped back, looking once again at the woman's final expression. It was anguish. That's what it was. The face of another broken thing. 'Would it be usual, doing CPR on someone of this age?' he asked the nurse.

They both stared at him, then returned to their chores. 'She wanted everything done.'

The other nurse said, 'Some people don't ever want to give up.'

Her co-worker shook her head. 'No. It's just that nobody tells them what it will be like to die. Nobody describes this.' She pointed to the woman's naked limbs, the stains of haemorrhage, the violence of the light overhead. 'Their whole life, nobody discusses it. Then death comes as a mighty surprise.'

'Exactly. As though people don't understand what it is. Death.'

Whisking a white sheet up into the air like a parachute, the nurses held the corners as it settled down on the body.

'True. And here patients move from ward to ward so fast, nobody has the time to sit down and explain.'

'Speaking of which,' the other said, looking at her watch, 'we'd better get a move on. So if you don't mind, Father …'

Taking a last look, he said a generic line of prayer for this anonymous death and collected an identification sticker from the dead woman's file. What would he write next to it? Watched on with horror?

His mind returned to the previous chaplain. Maybe erosion of pastoral sanity was part of the job. An inevitable wage to be paid, payback for years of hymn-filled comfort and seclusion.

It was clear. He would return to his office. There, he would pack his things and leave. How could he continue? The misery quotient would be too high, the purpose debatable. In his search for answers, he had moved so far from understanding what the questions were, the angles from which he now viewed things rendered any insight opaque.

The gum of the sticker made his fingers tacky. It was evidence of his visits, the last physical thing of the patients he would hold. The reality of the stickers felt monstrous: gluey slips to be converted into lines on a spreadsheet. He was expected to take identification from every patient he visited. 'It's all about accountability,' Fraser had told him. 'Without a sticker, how will we know you've been?'

That spreadsheet's a menu of mortality and misery, Marick had wanted to reply.

Plus, Christmas was approaching. This was always a difficult time for Marick. Despite the baubles hanging from the ward doorframes, the cheer, the tinsel and the trees, the day was coming at him like a slow-yawing bullet. He could not go on like this. He would be crushed by the job, ground under by the brute weight of untended memory.

Before he reached the main hospital thoroughfare, he ducked down a side set of stairs into the catacombs. He had discovered a tunnel connecting the front entrance with basement level two. Nobody else took it, giving him the advantage of avoiding any human contact.

The walkway was like the engine room of a battleship in dry dock. There were low-hanging ducts and pipes, iron protrusions and jutting handles of unclear purpose. The walls were dreadnought-dull and the ceiling was dotted with rusted sprinklers ready to reticulate the place if anybody lit up.

You are a terrible chaplain, he told himself. Not even able to nod and say hello to strangers.

The smell of canned oil leached from the walls.

Where would he go now, though? Who would he spend time with? Little remained of his previous existence. His phone book was empty. His meals were eaten alone. It had taken the divorce to admit he had no friends of his own. Diane had tried to tell him.

'It's unhealthy,' she'd said years ago. By her tone, he knew she meant humiliating.

'But why do I need anyone else? I have you and Claudia,' he'd replied.

The years at the church had not provided the camaraderie he'd thought they might. He'd fallen into the job under the Deacon by odd fortune. He'd been on the brink of deferring his studies for the second time when he'd answered an advertisement found pinned behind several others on the theological college noticeboard. The Deacon had seen something in the rawness of Marick's questioning that had him taken on as the great man's personal assistant. 'And you're an exceptional listener,' the Deacon said. 'Undervalued quality in the church.'

But when the questions made their lawless way into Marick's public duties, and he mistook his own crisis for an opportunity to wage a muted war on God, a flood of unflattering surveys about him were submitted, and it was agreed Marick would be suited to somewhere more practical. You wanted me to be practical here, thought Marick – he had the spreadsheets to prove it. It seemed this was one of several things for which he and the Deacon had differing definitions.

The Deacon had asked, early on, what had compelled Marick to seek out a life of the cloth after spending most of his years relatively godless, immersed in paperwork and suburbia. Marick had lied to the great man, spouting the line he had heard others so often use: that he had simply been called.

The turmoil within – this torrent of questions heavy on condemnation and short on answers – had peaked again by then, and Marick had nobody with whom to discuss it. It was true, he listened with care to the words of his colleagues, but he found reciprocation rare. Social events were rarer still. He would turn away when some of the fully-fledged priests would pull up chairs together after a particularly rousing mass to share the last of the communion wine, rather than embarrass them by their lack of invitation. Faith, too, had begun to consider him a hollow companion.

As Marick approached his office, he could see a figure, a man by the looks, standing outside his door. His first thought was to dodge into a recess and avoid him. It would presumably be the Director of Operational Services, pestering him for his ecclesiastical data. But it was not Fraser and this man had spotted him, judging by the way he unwound from his slouch into a posture of anticipation.

'Hugo,' the man introduced himself, holding his hand out. Marick could feel tension in the handshake. Hugo, tall, haunted, looking as though he had seen the unthinkable, which, Marick would discover soon enough, he had.

'Have you got a minute?'

Marick nodded. What else did he have?

Hugo led the way down the corridor. They crept down a different set of stairs, one Marick was sure he hadn't seen before, entering an alleyway lined with detritus. Hugo unlocked an unmarked door with an old-fashioned key. 'I want you to tell me what you see.'

The room was tiny, stuffed to the hinges with strange pieces of equipment, most of which Marick couldn't recognise.

'My own square array,' Hugo said, as though this explained the place. He gestured to the microscope. 'It's in here. I'll focus it.'

Hugo settled himself over the top of the microscope and lowered his face to the lenses. He twirled a dial with his right hand, stopped, and remained motionless. He was transfixed.

Marick wondered if this strange man had forgotten he was there. The moments dragged by.

'Actually, I'll make a fresh one.'

Marick decided it best to say nothing. Hugo stretched back and reached into one of the dryers. Out came a large beaker, full of curdled liquid. The overhead light threw dancing shadows on the meniscus.

'What I'm going to show you may be hard to believe,' Hugo said, and pulled his glasses down from his forehead, replacing them on his nose.

He extracted a small slide from a cardboard box and selected a pipette from another. Clasping the device with four fingers and using his thumb as a trigger on top, he plunged the pipette into a bronzed seam of fluid. After suctioning out some of the fluid, he transferred it to the glass plate, where Marick watched it drop, spreading like a bloom of paint. Hugo laid a coverslip on top, slotted this new slide under the barrel of the microscope and lowered himself again to look.

'Incredible,' Hugo said. 'Just the same' – he gestured to Marick – 'tell me what you see. Be honest.'

'I'm afraid you might have me mixed up with somebody else,' Marick said. 'I'm not a scientist. I'm the chaplain.'

Hugo glanced up at him. 'That, Father, is exactly why you are here.'

When Marick came to know Hugo better, when the pair ventured into each other's history and were no longer harbourless men, Marick would discover much to explain why Hugo had said this. He would learn that Hugo remembered the day his mother told him he had the fingerprints of Fate on him – Hugo described the day with crisp clarity. It was the day they went to see the roses, Hugo said, conjuring for Marick the bite of the morning air, the way he turned to his sister and smirked, knowing that it was Hugo whom Fate had chosen over her. More would emerge later. Marick would discover Hugo refused to use the title doctor, that he visited his old university at midnight to wander its deserted colonnades, and he flipped to the horoscope pages before the political news – although he would hide this from Vivian, his wife. Unbelievable for a scientist, she'd said to him. The fragile truce at home? That took its time surfacing.

In this early phase of their friendship though, Hugo seemed content to catalogue himself as an overqualified pipette washer. He explained to Marick that he was a microbiology assistant in one of the factory-like hospital laboratories, where his role was to siphon bodily fluids out of pots that arrived through a decaying pneumatic system, in order to count off the cells and enter the results into a computer program that crashed with dispiriting regularity.

'Go ahead,' Hugo said to Marick, shifting aside.

Marick did not want to admit that his experience with microscopes was limited. Hugo was expectant, scrutinising him as though his opinion had worth. Marick lowered his head to the eyepieces, but had difficulty using both eyes at once, swinging his head side to side in the hope of catching a glimpse of what was underneath. After a few passes though, the ribbed beam of light caught and shone, soft as night onto the plate below. Shapes materialised. He stopped moving and held on to the barrels of the apparatus for better purchase. His eyelashes brushed against the casing as he blinked.

'What do you see?' Hugo asked.

Marick sensed impatience.

'Are they,' Marick asked, 'cells?'

'Bacteria, yes, but what do you see inside them?'

Marick turned the focus dial as he'd seen Hugo do. At first, he simply saw units in motion, short, stumpy tubes rolling and squirming. Colours, lights, glints. He looked harder. A few were twitching, some were still, but in all of them a glow, a pinprick.

'Keep looking,' Hugo urged him.

Marick did. He wasn't sure what normal bacteria would look like, but somehow he knew these were not going to be that – normal. As he continued to stare, watching one cell tumble, then another, he realised each had the same shining core. The light snagged on them, reflecting the minute rays in scatters.

Lifting his head, he rubbed the bridge of his nose and settled back over the microscope. There it was. In each of the cells, as they swam beneath him, was a tiny bead, the most microscopic of nuggets, the unmistakable glitter that could only be gold.

Marick was looking at gold.

THREE

'You know what this is, don't you?' Hugo was nodding at Marick in a way that suggested the answer was obvious. 'It's—'

Marick did not want to disappoint this man with his blazing eyes and heightened voice and something else inscrutable – something arising from this intimately shared experience. Marick had a choice to make, to say the word that should be said. *Impossible.*

He did not.

'A miracle,' Hugo said.

Marick flinched, as though the word was a strike. He swallowed. He hesitated while Hugo took control again of the microscope and became engrossed in the wild vision beneath.

Miracle. The concept might have been the bedrock of the book Marick had committed to, but the term in this laundrified setting rang like a gunshot. Marick had dissected the miracles in that book – the Bible that had never left him even during the periods when he couldn't bring himself to turn the pages. When the Deacon had suggested Marick's life was somewhat godless,

Marick thought the cleric might have been more accurate calling it erratically so. God had appeared a number of times during Marick's youth. Marick had tried telling his parents, but they had glossed over his explanations of dreams and odd visions, relegating them to the inventiveness of childhood. As a family they ventured through the jaws of their local church when guilt accumulated like scale, and a dutiful visit to a Sunday service was akin to a good scrub. Marick's mother, Deirdre, had been a fierce school administrator, a practical woman who took her mantra of self-reliance to extremes. She was dedicated to the well-being of her students, building a no-nonsense career in classroom politics for the ironclad benefit of education. But somehow, she'd missed a few important events at home, in particular a single vaccination when her only son was a year old. Marick's hearing was forever wrecked.

Marick's father was the absent type, an air-conditioning man who was away more often than not, living his life in the roofs of others. He was oddly pleased when Marick, still at school, talked of joining the church.

'The only way to disrupt things is from the inside, son,' he said to Marick, with uncharacteristic philosophy. Marick was not sure what he was supposed to be disrupting but was so warmed by the support he didn't ask.

His mother chipped in. 'Plus, you're not really the marrying kind.'

Marick had wanted to be the marrying kind. He had fallen in love with exhausting regularity but it was a sentiment never returned. He of the handwritten love letters, the riding of his bike into a parked car while waving to a girl he fancied resulting in a broken wrist his mother ignored for days, his school dance requests laughed off, the walks home alone. Then there were the reactions to hearing aids the size of additional ears. 'Look at the Paki!' his classmates hooted. He was confused by this label, being distinctly Caucasian, until he discovered they'd named him after a pachyderm.

It became easier to live life alone. His bedroom became a foxhole. With the door shut, he heard almost nothing of the world outside. It took him weeks to discover his father had left them. Marick emerged one morning to find Deirdre slamming washed dishes into the rack. He watched the suds dribble down the sides of the plates and glanced up at his mother's tear-covered face. It was too difficult to ask what was wrong. That was not how things worked in their family.

She spun around to face him. 'Aren't you going to bloody ask where he's gone?'

Marick froze. He had never heard his mother swear.

'Or don't you care?'

Her face looked like dough, swollen in places, sunken in others. He went to pick up a tea towel to help by drying, but she snatched it from him. She began to cry.

'Why start now?' She held up the tea towel, like it was Exhibit A. 'Did you think it might have been you?' she added.

Might what have been him? Marick stood fixed.

'Have you even been listening to what's going on? You just don't bloody listen.' She stormed past him, away to her bedroom, where Marick could hear, quite clearly now, the distressed sobs of somebody broken.

Later she would apologise, in stilted, controlled language.

'You don't understand the humiliation,' she said. 'I wasn't really blaming you.'

But the grenade had hit, and in the wound permanent scars of guilt formed. Deirdre returned to coping the only way she knew how, by closing up and getting on without words. Then there was nothing for Marick to listen to. He retreated again.

It was around then he became fixated not so much on miracles, but miraculous happenings, which he only realised later were very different things. By the end of primary school, he was obsessed by the possibility of spontaneous human combustion and took out every library book he could, looking for proof, unable to sleep with the thought that the spark of it might choose him in the night. After that it was the paranormal: UFO sightings like silver bullets in the night sky, spirits the only trace of which were grainy outlines on photographs, extrasensory perception.

Marick made wagers with the God who turned up at loud and unpredictable times in his head. He set challenges; he begged for his hearing to be restored and asked on a regular basis for some sign, any sign, of God's existence. He wanted to pray for the return of his father, but after six months of Deirdre's darkness, his mother surfaced and asked that they never speak of him again. 'Best thing that will have ever happened to us,' she said. 'A clean break's the best way. It means we can get on with our lives.' Again, Marick had no clue what she meant.

God came and went. Marick read the Bible from front to back, but had nobody to ask about the questions that rose from every page. He finished high school and sleepwalked into an accounting degree, after which he signed up to the first job that came his way. Eventually, God faded, featuring less and less in

Marick's days. And then, for a time, he considered Claudia the only miracle he needed.

'Is that,' Marick had to ask, 'gold?'

Hugo broke into a wide beam. 'Sure looks like it. Beautiful, isn't it?'

'I don't really …'

'Understand? That will come next.' Hugo pulled out the glass slide and held it up to the light. 'I thought they were dead.'

'Who were dead?' Marick asked.

'The bacteria. They'd stopped production.'

'I'm not sure I follow. But I'd very much like to hear about it.'

Hugo handed the slide to Marick. 'It's actually pretty simple.'

Marick peered around the room. Simple? He looked at the slide with its bland nothingness out in the open.

'*Escherichia coli*. Gut bacteria, but also living microbial factories,' Hugo said. 'They've been top-notch protein producers, this culture. Thoroughbreds you could call them. All I have to do is follow a recipe. My own, actually. I design the DNA script on a special computer program and email it to a laboratory in China. They construct the DNA and send it to me by post. I bring it in here, mix the DNA base with this master-batch of bacteria and my own culture medium, incubate them for twenty-four hours, blend it all down like soup, electrophorese the proteins out and there you have it. Bespoke proteins. Whatever you want.'

'You get DNA sent to you in the mail? Marick was used to watching people's lips while they spoke as a backup, but this conversation was so foreign he was not sure he was getting it right.

'Exactly. In brown envelopes, directly to my house. But this batch had been slowing right down. I thought it was all over. See this?' Hugo picked up a chunky black basket with cords trailing from it. 'It's a voltaic cradle. State of the art. Every day I come down here to check production. He held the box for Marick to examine. 'This is where you see which proteins you've produced. You send an electrical current through the gel plates and the proteins separate out. The molecules you want light up like a laser. They make a magnificent, lush purple line.'

Marick had questions fighting in his brain as to which would be first out. What he could see was a man, a scientist, speaking as though blossoming, describing the details of a new discovery. A man pulsing with truth. What Marick could not see was the steep price that would be charged, when all was said and all was done, by this truth.

'I see.' Marick was used to adding this into silences. 'But this! It's, it's ...'

Marick stiffened.

'Not protein,' Hugo finished.

Marick exhaled. There could be no more talk of miracles. Hugo was a scientist after all. Overhead were the dull clunks of messages and missives being sucked through the system of vacuum tubes, to be spat out somewhere unknown.

'Why are you doing this in a hospital laundry?' Marick asked.

'Here? It's a little sideline. An extra. Nobody knows about it except my contractors. And Vivian. And now you. But you're the first to see this.' Hugo took the slide back from Marick. He held it between his two hands with reverence. 'This wonder.'

Were Hugo's eyes glistening with tears? If the sight of the gold had not convinced Marick that what they were looking at was something phenomenal, Hugo's response did.

Who am I, Marick thought, to be in this room at this pivotal point? He wanted to ask why Hugo had come to him. Why seek out the chaplain when what he needed was a scientific pair of eyes?

But when Marick went to put his question into words the desire to know shrank. He had been asked. That was enough.

He pressed on, opening the door to Hugo's story.

It seemed Hugo had fallen far. Only a year earlier, he and his bacteria had been the talk of the university not far from here. Head of translational biotechnology research, Hugo was king of a hub that buzzed with intellectual desire. At the peak of his success, Hugo was corralling his special strain of *Escherichia coli* into producing a new protein every week: carriers for vaccines; mother-proteins entered into trials with the hope of finding elusive anti-cancer drugs; sculpturally beautiful proteins folded softly around themselves just for the aesthetic challenge; even the casein particles of cheese, so that Hugo was able to render great wheels of cheddar in the Biotechnology Department alone. It could have fed the world, he told Marick.

So many adventurous molecules. Such tantalising success. Each one produced a cheer from the team and drinks at the end of the day. At one stage the word Nobel crept into lunchtime conversations and it rode up and down the staff tables on a wave of fervour. He and Vivian drank champagne, planned an overseas holiday. Hugo was vertiginous with momentum. But somehow, the momentum morphed into over-enthusiasm – a PhD student, eager to be part of the zeal, recorded a few creative results that found their way into a landmark article published in *Nature*. An urgent retraction was required and the university was outed in self-righteous dispatches all over the country as tolerating scientific fraud.

Hugo's name was cleared on paper, but within a week all his staff were moved on and his equipment redistributed to more honourable departments. 'You do understand, don't you,' some nameless envoy from university administration told him over wet rice paper rolls in the cafeteria, 'how important the good name of the university is?'

'But we're in the middle of some very important work,' Hugo said. 'Our research is at full tilt. I have people depending on me. I can't just shut it down.'

'I didn't come here to haggle, Hugo,' the man said, standing and wiping his chin with a serviette. 'I'm just the messenger.' And he marched off, leaving Hugo to pay the bill.

Hugo agreed to his departure but took his master-stock of bacteria with him, cocooned in liquid nitrogen. He would recreate the protein-manufacturing process, and for the job he commandeered a tiny uncharted laundry, situated below the hospital lab that had taken him on as microbiological assistant. He planned to better the process, free from the constraints of the university.

Hugo had spiralled though, he admitted to Marick, from hope to disquiet, as his bacteria demonstrated a stubborn streak they had not shown before. Hugo could only coax his bacteria into producing a single, haphazard, heat-stable enzyme. Now he was not much more than an overlooked cog in a supply chain for a cleaning company who paid a small monthly retainer for a line of protein mistakes found to make an effective slurry when mixed with ammonia. There would be no Swedish prize-giving ceremony for his part in *Bio-Kleen!*

'But over the last week they began petering out,' Hugo said. 'Like their stamina was spent. The gel plates were getting drier by the day, until this morning they were completely empty. The bacteria weren't empty though.' His face again lit up. 'They were full of gold.'

'Are you sure that's what it is?' Marick asked. 'Gold? Could it be anything else? And how?'

'I've been asking myself the same things. Creation, contamination. Parthenogenesis, prank. Fusion, freaks. All I know is it's real, and the more I think about it, the more the first of those seems most likely. The bloody sublime.' Hugo looked up. 'Sorry, Father.'

Marick shook his head in dismissal.

'These are special bacteria, though.' Hugo pushed the large pot with its shimmering lattice of threads across the bench so that it sat between them. 'I do know how I could confirm it. If it's the real stuff.'

Hugo reached behind the front row of equipment, pulling out what looked like a rice cooker. He scooped a cup of the thick fluid from the main beaker and poured a little into a test tube, which he then inserted into the barrel. 'Centrifuge,' Hugo said. He pressed a button and the machine cranked up to speed, whirring away.

'Does anybody else know about this room?' Marick had a sense of the surreal, that they were sitting in this tiny hermetic space, discussing the unthinkable as though it had a basis in normality.

'No-one. Occasionally the Croatian cleaning lady who does this floor pops in, but apart from that, nobody else has a key.'

The centrifuge shuddered, a metallic sound clanking from its slowing insides. It beeped to notify Hugo it was done. Opening the lid with care, he pulled out the internal vat. Hugo poured off the top liquid.

'Supernatant,' he told Marick as they both peered in. There it was: a flashing layer.

Hugo shook the glittering sediment into a little plastic pot and screwed on the yellow lid. He passed it over. Marick held it up to the light and could see the glinting flakes, the reflected light, the lunacy. This was his moment to interrupt. Ask the hard question. He stared at the pot and did not.

'Bacteria producing gold,' Marick said instead. 'Really quite something, Hugo.'

'Isn't it.'

The two men remained motionless in that hemmed-in room. Marick waited in the hope that Hugo might come up with more explanation, but there was nothing but silence.

'I should go,' Marick said eventually. 'Business.'

'I'll send some off to the geology lab at the university,' Hugo said as though he hadn't heard Marick, and shook a tiny amount into an envelope. 'Give them some story about a research project. Perhaps I'll ask if they can work out which mine it's from.'

Hugo really believed, Marick could see. This was no act set up for whatever reason Hugo might have. The scientist had begun scribbling notes.

'I'll have to do all sorts of tests,' Hugo said. 'Observations. Reproducibility measures. Control groups.' He began to make

37

room on the bench, moving equipment. Stacking petri dishes and plates, he wrote on cards, numbering and naming groups, while Marick watched, silent. 'And I think we should keep this between the two of us, Father. Just for now.'

'Oh, that won't be difficult.' A smile came to Marick for the first time that day. 'But please, I'm not Father. It's Marick. I do need to get back to work, though, if that's alright.'

'Will you come by tomorrow?' Hugo asked.

Marick did not want clarification as to why. He would come by, of course. He departed, leaving Hugo focusing on the plates and the curiously coloured liquids and odd machinery, ready to set the whole circus in motion.

The hospital deaths had lost some of their bite.

FOUR

The remainder of the afternoon held wall-to-wall entreaties. Marick wanted an interlude to process what he'd seen, but the wards had other plans, and he tramped up and down stairs until his thighs ached. Even with his map, the sources of the various requests continued to be challenging to locate. The layout of the hospital appeared to have been designed at a thousand different desks, with none of their owners on speaking terms.

By five o'clock, the calls petered out, and he dedicated some time to staring at his spreadsheets.

Before hopping on the number two to go home, he wandered over to the cathedral. Skirting the church was the ragged fringe of city. Among it were lank, weedy parks and a few graffiti-strewn bus stops, but these were woven between shiny apartments, raucous cafes and wine bars yammering with trade. It was a place confused. Was it a city on the decline or the mend, Marick wondered.

Looking back at the hospital, he surveyed the befuddlement of signs. The building was flanked with them; great flashing squares laden with information about parking and no parking and emergencies and directions that contradicted the next sign along.

Marick stepped away from the neon, through the filigreed iron gates and into the gilded silence of the church grounds where he could finally address his thoughts. He plodded across the lawn. The word miracle had left behind a chalk outline in his head. He needed some walking time to process it all.

The colours of sunset were rich, aged, with the departing sun lending a caramel to the limestone walls. Not too far from him, where the last gasp of day was slipping through the metal fence, one woman sat alone, eating. Perhaps this was an early dinner in a transient ceasefire. Marick recognised her as the leader of the day's failed resuscitation. She was silent, spectral and tired, as though even the act of sitting there cross-legged was cumbersome. A tiny chirruping bird, a black thing with a jaunty tail, hopped onto her knee to steal crumbs while she stared off elsewhere. She looked like she was willing into existence a short spell of peace, Marick thought, and as he watched, she scrawled a few words into a notebook on her lap. The bird flitted away.

She looked up. She and Marick locked gazes. Something indefinable passed between them for an instant, but it disappeared as quickly, and the woman with *Emergency Physician* tattooed on her top dropped her attention back to writing. Marick felt strangely exposed and turned away, walking back to his stop just as the next number two belched in.

After letting himself back into his unit and unpacking his satchel, he knew he was not done walking. His steps so far had not achieved what he'd hoped.

Marick's rental was in an unpopular part of the city, not yet claimed for fashion or money, and the small print filed away in council submissions said it never would be. Developers had glanced over the divided lots and moved on to more hopeful areas. It was too swampy or too far from services, or simply too awkward. But in its favour was its winding proximity to the river, if you knew which laneways to take.

Marick changed into more comfortable clothes: a t-shirt he loved for its softness and old track pants. The evening was again still and warm, and Marick wondered if this was what the climate planned to do here as it changed – melt the place to a final halt. There was no breeze to cool the walls and the dirt. Everybody would be complaining tonight. It was un-Australian not to have some degree of sea breeze to sluice away the day's heat.

Marick reached the path that hugged the river and set along it. In the distance, columns of smoke rose from fires burning somewhere north.

The river had many faces. This evening it was a weary brown, but only days before it had been shingled with sunlight. On mornings when the wind whipped at it, it was carpet-rough and foreboding. A promise of something, even if Marick did not know what. Walking conditions were not pleasant tonight, but he persisted. From the blind curve of the road ahead, he heard the thump of car speakers, a commuter's anthem. As the car came into sight, he saw heads hanging from windows, young men who looked like they were full of the joy of something. Of life. Of the evening. Of togetherness.

The car veered close, and Marick felt the visceral sound of the thud shift shape. He waved at the men, a good-hearted greeting to match their cheer. Passing in a swerve, the men poured forth a stream of obscenities, directed with unequivocal threat at him. Marick could make out the words despite the wail of the song. From the back window, a beer can was launched, arcing towards him. It tumbled, a thin stream of dirt-amber liquid flywheeling around it. Marick ducked, and managed to miss being struck, but caught the tail end of the fluid as it streaked down his pants.

The men drove off. The music faded. He picked up the beer can, crushed it a little more and deposited it in a nearby bin.

The thump of his heart settled. Keep walking, he told himself. Gold. Gold. That's where you are. He shuffled through his memory for all the times gold was mentioned in the Bible. Breathe. Walk. It was present in the very beginning, he knew, in the river flowing out of Eden into Havilah, and it was there at the End of Days, when God promised to make a new earth, a new Jerusalem, paved with it. The intervening chapters had gold wending in and out of their verses. A false prophet here, of heavenly value there, but always the most revered of metals. A divine gift. A gift, he thought again, not a miracle. Never a miracle.

Several families were picnicking on a bare patch of lawn that hugged a crescent of the river, sneaked between clumps of leggy reeds. He heard their normality, the shouts, the balls being thrown to siblings, a champagne bottle uncorked. Normal had such a strange sound to it, he thought. Strange and foreign. He wondered if he ought to warn them about the hooligans, but presumed normality would not attract such target practice.

The city was visible through the haze across the river, and the buildings looked like models, scattered childhood things dotted with random lights, the whole skyline thrown together without much bother for order. Perhaps an anti-city, unwelcoming to those not included.

The beat of music thumped closer again, the car returning, and Marick slipped behind a tree. They drove by. He remained hidden for a few more minutes. From here, the view of the river was unimpeded. This river, he knew, was ancient. Its own history was born in dreams and stories, and the land fed by it, soaking in it, was even older. There were things untouched, unknown, below his feet. Aquifers and blind animals and sacred burial grounds. Bones and antiquity, scars and excavations. Vaults and textures nobody thought to see. Past visitations of fire and ice. Borders. It was a question that never let up. How did the God of Rome square with the epochs of existence, the spiritual history below the soil here? It was a conundrum, overwhelming in its immensity.

At the same time practical truths were just as hard for Marick to come by. No question there was much on this earth yet to be discovered, particularly in the subterranean layers over which he now strolled, stepping away from behind the tree and onto the path. He was always reading news of finds being dug up and extracted from strata below, finds requiring the local history books to be rewritten. So why couldn't there still be other minerals, microbes, physical laws as yet unknown? It occurred to him that he hadn't asked an obvious question. Where does gold come from? Just the ground, he'd always presumed, but what sort of answer is that? No better or worse than blind faith.

Marick did not consider himself a scientific man, but when he arrived home, he did his best to frame the mystery into a simple question: *What is the origin of gold? Can it be made?* The answers were not in his paper and leather, and he got nowhere. He knew it was absurd to look for them in ink, rather than the pages of Google, but he couldn't shake the faith he had in the printed word. He had volumes and volumes of history books, lined up in order of eras. If he was ever asked, which he wasn't, he would say his hobby was human history. One of his great follies was trying to gather in one place an understanding of a communal past so he could somehow find a home for the myths, but his books were pitifully short on modern science.

He had an old laptop that he used for writing out sermons he never gave and storing his tax documents, which were becoming fewer by the year. It had troubles with connectivity. He persevered, and his online search turned dizzying. He cycled back through crackpot sites run by backyard alchemists selling secrets and raw ingredients to set up a home laboratory. These days the internet was not much more than an advertisement-clogged, delusion-filled sump of lies, he thought, with its foundation prejudice and its purpose obscure. In theological college the warnings had been clear. The Bible, they had been told, was truth. Beware all others who try to wear the same clothes.

Searching on, the origins of gold began to make themselves known, and Marick wondered why he'd never thought to ask the question before. Gold was not simply made, nor did it belong in Hugo's *Escherichia coli*. It had cosmic origins. There was some kind of cataclysmic serendipity in gold finding its way onto the planet in the first place.

He stood and stretched, decided he needed tea. Filling the kettle, he realised he could smell stale beer. He should change pants, he thought. With his head beginning to entertain the fact he knew next to nothing about the elemental origins of Earth, he made his way to the bedroom. Sitting on his bed – neatly made that morning – he pulled one leg from his track pants and caught sight of Claudia. The photo, in its thin black frame; her hair, no longer golden itself. When she was five, her curls had begun to lose their burnish. They were a mahogany-colour when the photograph had been taken, or that's what he'd called it. It's brown, Marick, Diane would say. He sat for several minutes, adrift, before forcing himself to turn away and finish the job of getting changed.

On opening the narrow chest of drawers, he saw his choice was limited. He extracted a green pair of polyester pants, hideous really, but folded neatly in an otherwise empty drawer. He then dropped his soiled track pants in his 'bachelor-sized' laundry basket.

No more Claudia. Not today. He had science to acquire. He returned to the kitchen, made an Earl Grey tea (not his favourite, but it had been on special). Back to the computer. Gold. He needed to know.

Billions of years ago, the process had begun. Billions, he read again. In the wake of a celestial collision, an accidental crash between lost, circling stars, it was among the beauty of nebulae – luminous, rippling, towering clouds of stars – that gold formed. A deeply improbable event, an explosion of light and neutrons caused atomic spume to spray out to the edges of the nothing. As they whizzed, particles clumped together and these newly gazetted atoms of gold hitchhiked their way to Earth on stray rocks.

Marick sipped his tea. It was already cool. He read on. Once the gold hit Earth, it rested, glorious and undisturbed until the molecules, now a metal, were scoured out of the ground and fashioned into greed. Improbable, he thought, but here it was now, adorning fingers and bank vaults all over the world. There was mention of other processes: nuclear processes, fusion, fission, concentration, but the details went further than a man dually trained in theology and accounting could follow. All he felt was lost.

He tossed his pen across the table. Was this going to be some sort of test? Another where he would not understand the rules? For much of his life B.C., he was convinced he was gaining the ability to look inside people, understand their hearts. He'd heard that when you lose one of your senses, the others heighten. This had made him wonder whether because his hearing was only damaged, not lost, that his other organs of perception might grow in equivalent fashion, infusing them with metaphysical power. He had been wrong. Diane proved it to him. She'd provided the challenge but withdrawn the interest in the result. But today he'd met Hugo. He knew Hugo was telling the truth. Felt it in the triumph of his words. Truth was such a violent act. The strongest truths were unmistakable. He collected his pen, a little embarrassed by his petulance.

Time had creaked on, becoming the hour for bed. Now comes the trial, he thought. Every night he hoped the horrors wouldn't crawl into his bedroom, dragging themselves in like beasts from a bog, dripping and ready.

They did though. Every night. At four. He no longer needed to check his clock. Sometimes he'd be ready, and the scenes playing would not take him by surprise, events he'd managed to suppress from spooling out during the daylight hours. Occasionally it was not a scene. Last night, after his first shift at the hospital, it had been a figure he presumed was the Devil, or an accomplice of sorts, standing at the foot of the bed as though waiting with patience for him to awake. 'You know I'm real,' the shape had said in a low voice, 'so stop trying to pretend.'

In the damp hours tonight though, it was Claudia, well and riding her first bike. She was seven. The bicycle had been a point of contention, raising an argument about gender expectations that had blindsided him. All he had done was agree with the woman at the bike shop that a seven-year-old girl would love a pink basket and streamers flying out like bugle-song from the handlebars. Diane brought it up every time Claudia ventured out riding.

'Plus, do you think a bike is safe, all things considered?' Diane had asked. 'I don't really think it's a good idea for her to be out of sight.'

Marick had shrugged. They had to let her be independent at some point.

The reel tonight was downhill, Claudia on the wing with the pedals going round so fast she would lift her feet with a child's abandon, bending her knees until they almost knocked her chin. Those mahogany curls, catching the light, turning back to gold. And then a sudden, visceral black, full of accusation.

It seemed the more beautiful the memory, the more painful the awakening, and while the rest of the city made no noise, Marick sat up like he was launched, his skin so saturated with sweat it hurt, his sheets bulldozed into great piles. He slapped the photo of Claudia down. He couldn't bear to know her face was smiling at him.

The hours then progressed as was routine. He'd given up on prayer during these times long ago. Meditation did not work either. He simply succumbed to the firestorm in his head without fight. This time felt no different, although at one point he realised his mind was saying a single word to him on repeat. Alchemy. Alchemy. He switched on the lamp, troubled by the shape and the power of the word, and reached over to the bedside radio. When things were making no sense in his head, he liked to listen to talk-back radio, hearing people dialling in opinions also formed in the coal-heart of night. People like him. They provided the comforting froth of human chatter.

Sometimes, though, he found kinship difficult with his nocturnal tribe. This morning provided a welter of callers, incensed by the rollout of a new telephone network. He heard the same arguments all over again: nanotechnology, radiation, phone towers, cancer – always cancer – population control by government, and then the platform was given over to a young woman described as an influencer, who encouraged people to rise up against health officials trying to pump their children full of chemicals.

'Do you mean vaccines?' the radio host asked.

'That,' the caller replied, 'is a dirty word in our house.'

Marick would almost have preferred the Devil. He turned the radio off and lay on his crumpled sheets under the thud of the ceiling fan, the blades rotating in the dense air until the first throb of morning, and the delicate light was again east born. Again. Yes, he would visit Hugo again today.

FIVE

The route for the number two bus was under review. Several stops had been cancelled altogether, and the one Marick used near the hospital's front entrance was shrouded in council-regulation tarpaulin. This meant he had to alight down the hill on the thinning edge of the business district, and as he filed up past the platoon of towering city buildings, he had both the hospital and the church looming in his sights. It wasn't clear which was in the shadow of the other. Walking this way also took him past the fig tree in front of the hospital's executive block, a craggy leviathan which looked biblical itself, as though it could play stand-in for its ancestor in Eden.

'It was an apple tree in Paradise, Marick,' one of his clerical mentors had castigated him when he said as much to a focus group while they were whiteboarding ideas for an adolescent outreach program.

'But you do know Michelangelo painted it as a fig tree on the Sistine Chapel?'

Marick had tried to push the point. He had stood under those painted vaults, spellbound, and couldn't believe there wasn't some greater meaning in the symbolism.

'The fig tree motif is Judaic, Marick. It has no place here.'

'Michelangelo was not God,' another of his supervisors had said, and Marick had been put into another period of remediation.

This arboreal implausibility, however, stood huge and real. It challenged the pavement, its roots picking up bricks and resettling them where they ought not be, tripping people who ignored the warnings on signs. Its long branches reached out in all directions – over the fence and up to the hospital's roof – and its leaves were as thick as sandwiches. Ripe figs dropped where they pleased and in places the path could not be seen for fruity sludge. The administration staff had been unsuccessful in their bid to have it tamed, as it had managed to attract the label of protected.

'The branches are crawling through the vents and roof spaces,' someone exasperated had claimed in a submission. The city's Ecological Protection Chapter had not been moved. Nobody had any idea of the tree's age.

The tree had another use. Its green and tormented canopy, daylight mere pearls in its gaps, formed an arcade of protection. Underneath, a primordial huddle of people without rooves to call their own gathered to spend their nights, and often their days as well. The roof-top forest dovetailed, quite conveniently, with the western eaves of the hospital, which themselves were long and cantilevered, and the mishmash of covering structures provided near perfect shelter from the elements.

At ground level, in the tree's lilac shadows, were water fountains and window inlays and long wooden seats. There was a permanency to the arrangement of sleeping bags and shopping carts and recycled belongings, and Marick suspected real estate was pegged out quite formally.

Marick clipped past the small crowd of homeless people. The greetings between itinerants and chaplain were jovial enough (others weren't so lucky), but although he knew many by face, he knew none by name. The group had a testy relationship with the church and were the reason a set of very handsome iron gates had been erected in a hurry several years earlier, complete with a swinging padlock which was clanked shut earlier and earlier each night.

'Very complex,' Marick was told at the Community Integration Working Party when he had asked what the parish could do about this societal failing, and to his shame he had never followed it up.

He stood on a fresh fig and his shoe sank into its doughy heart. Its smell was released, rich and ripe like wine. Funny that the smell, too, took him back to Rome. All roads, he thought, with a brief smile. All roads leading, of course, not only to Rome, but to Diane.

He shouldn't have gone then – everyone agreed. He'd only just begun his second year of tertiary education. But if he ever had a calling, it had been to Rome. A break from university, extending into autumn. The university was desperate to keep people in its accounting degree, and so was prepared to forgive him missing part of a semester. That first year of business information systems and regulatory law had seemed so vague to Marick, so dimly lit, he had thought now or never, and bought a sturdy backpack, booking the cheapest airfare he could find.

Asked later, he proclaimed he had wanted to see Christianity in its original clothing, if not the flesh. Really, it was the word of it – Rome – the meditative journey of a single word that had hooked him. The Eternal City, with its terracotta-domed sunrises, the steps – unpeopled in the winter mornings – the fountains, the twinkling vitality of the lights and drinks of an evening. A scooter. Spending his first night with a woman, not knowing he would have to pay her afterwards. Going back to her a second time despite it.

Most days he lined up with the tourists to shuffle through the Vatican. He would stop at the Sistine Chapel, staring at the ceiling until his neck hurt and he was pushed on. He latched on to the back of walking tours to hear the history of the place, the persecution of St Peter, the lives lived out on the very ground on which he was walking. Until then he'd had no concept the figures in the Bible could have ever been real, that they were men and women who lived, with loves and gout and breath and hunger. That Christianity itself could also have been a real thing, a historic event, tangible.

Conflated with this new, raw passion, though, was Marick's discovery of Caravaggio. He scoured the city to find every one of them, checking them off in a notebook, his mind split wide with the wild light, the sharp edges, the anarchy of the painter's energy translated into perfect brushstrokes.

In the Borghese Gallery, at the top end of a garden hung with shadows like lace from every tree limb, he bought tea in a paper cup from the cramped, steaming cafeteria, and pored over the gallery's guidebook. Behind him, he heard a woman with the familiar Australian accent, disagreeing with her friend about how long they had left to stay at the gallery before they had to check out of their hotel. Marick turned to investigate, and that was how he met Diane.

'I can walk you back,' Marick offered, when it became clear Diane wanted to simultaneously see the *Boy with the Basket of Fruit*, have her friend return the hotel key so they would not be charged extra, and not have to walk back alone through the circuitous park and down to street level.

'I'm Australian, too,' Marick said, as if that made him the automatic best choice.

In the warmth of the gallery, underneath the chiaroscuro of Caravaggio's aching works ('It means light and shadow,' Diane told him, which he already knew but did not speak up, fascinated as he was with her appetite for explaining artistic techniques), Marick recognised this as a profound juncture in his life.

While they walked through the rooms together, Diane pointing out the richness of the colours in the masterworks, the way you knew they had to be Caravaggios when you compared these works to his students' hung next door, and giving Marick a rundown on the painter's wild and felonious life, all of which Marick was aware, he decided that any iteration of love he had experienced before had been mere pretence.

'Have you ever seen anybody paint fruit that way? The most exquisite basket of them in history,' she said. They stood under that painting for so long, Marick was surprised the seasons hadn't changed by the time they exited the gallery.

'I wanted to go to art school,' Diane told him, 'but my parents wouldn't let me.'

She had a way of speaking that was so fluid it bypassed his ears altogether, flooding deep into his mind.

'You'll never get a proper job, they told me. Which is why I'm doing interior design. But you know, I love it now. I can see myself creating grand designs, knocking the socks off anybody back home.'

She described at length the ideas she had about uprooting the decorating world, reducing it to ashes, pushing boundaries nobody had before in their parochial little town. The same city! They both lived in the same city!

After three days, Marick couldn't believe she still wanted to keep seeing him. 'I've never had anybody *listen* to me like you do,' she said while they ate gnocchi at an outside table under lamplight well into their second carafe of rosé. Diane had told her friends the day the pair met that she was not leaving Rome after all, and she would catch up with them in Florence in a week's time, where they had a tour pre-booked for the Uffizi.

'I wish you could come,' she said to Marick. When he'd expressed a wish to do so, she had said that her friends would kill her. This was supposed to be their girls' trip, paid for by their parents, all of them making up for some familial guilt the girls dissected in detail every night. 'No boyfriends,' Diane said.

Boyfriend. She said boyfriend. He watched the way she twisted her earring in her right ear in absentminded thought, or examined her fingernails at length, all in ways seductive that Marick could not explain to himself. The way her pinkish blonde hair swept across her face – perfect light and shade with its dark roots. Her faultless nose, her short, unlined neck, the artistry in her clothing choices … and his mouth became dry.

They met up each day and trailed their fingers along crumbling, storied walls, stepped over ancient stones, ate melon in hidden-away piazzas, discussed the benefits of a senate, walked under fluttering washing strung up in narrow alleyways. They exchanged details. 'Write to me,' he said. 'I want to hear everything.'

Marick cut short his trip to come home. He'd planned to jump from train to train, wind through the Alps, visit the museums of Amsterdam, see snow, eat wurst, but there was no Diane in those parts of Europe, and no letters turning up in the post offices he said he'd be at, so he changed his ticket and returned to a grateful university. He bought three medium-sized canvasses and a box of oil paints only to discover he had no talent for translating light. It didn't matter though, Diane would be the artistic one, and he gathered up the courage and called her.

Figs. Figs was where he was. He scraped his shoe at the hospital's main entrance before entering. He checked his pager and was relieved to find its little screen empty, despite it being in range. Taking advantage of the morning quiet, he thought he might do some more digging around. The internet had not shone the light he needed onto this strange intersection between bacteria and gold, and he wondered whether he might find some truth in reference books. He could try the hospital library.

On impulse, Marick decided he would buy something to eat. He'd missed breakfast with the disarray in his head, but now he wanted a little kick and was not keen to go with the ham sandwich he'd made that morning, which would have undoubtedly already grown soggy inside its plastic wrap. He veered into Dolly's shop, which was sparking with the energy of the volunteers.

'Father!' Dolly called out. 'Welcome. What can I get for you?'

'Don't judge me, Dolly, at this time of the morning, but can I buy some chocolate?'

Dolly's expression twisted into something dark. 'No. You cannot. Not my doing, Father. Six months ago, the executive here put out a *decree*. Allegedly chocolate is a health hazard, category two. At first we had to have it hidden away in locked cupboards, like we had to do with the cigarettes. Now we're not allowed to sell it at all. The hospital needs to be an example of health, we were told. We trade in low-sugar sweets and toothpaste now, plus these dreadful bean and tuna combinations. As you can imagine, custom's dropped horribly.' She picked a can off a shelf nearby and thrust it towards him, her lips curled. 'I've had to lay off some of the staff. Only six of us now. But the best volunteers you'll ever find.' Her expression recovered and she turned and waved at her troops. 'Eight metal joints between us, but a more dedicated group you'll never find.'

'Then I'll take whatever you recommend.'

Dolly fetched a small stepladder and placed it close to a shelf. She was quite short, he noticed, but decidedly spry as she climbed the first step. How old must she be?

'And that's not the only thing they've foisted on us.' She stepped back down with care, placing a bland packet of confectionery on the counter. 'See that information booth at the front entrance? That's for the meet-and-greeters. Now those girls are something. They know the hospital like nobody's business. Got their own version of The Knowledge, they have, and they spring guerrilla tests on each other to make sure they're up to date.'

Marick nodded, content to be fed Dolly's stories.

'But they tried to get rid of them recently,' Dolly said. 'Did you hear?'

He hadn't, but a response was not required.

'First we knew about it huge screens appeared overnight. Ogres on big metal legs.'

It was clear she was raring for a tale. Marick had time; his pager was quiet.

'Aggressive things they were,' she continued. '*Touch me*, the screens said, *and I'll tell you where to go*. The nerve.'

Dolly punched a few numbers into a flat grey till. She shook her head, deleted what she'd put in, and typed something else. 'I'll give you a discount, Father. Anyway, they popped up all over the hospital, with their self-congratulatory maps. People deserted the girls' booth in droves. But the hospital hadn't banked on us. Multipronged attack, it was. My role was to go around turning the machines off early in the morning and hide the power cables. A bit of orange juice on the screens and there you have it. Job done.' She wiped her hands on her pinafore. 'I needn't have bothered, of course. The machines couldn't get their button brains round the routes in the place, and so many people missed their appointments the screens were taken away quietly one night and never replaced.'

Marick counted out some coins for her. 'Thank you,' he said.

'Humans, Father. That's the only important thing. Flesh and blood. But you'd know that.'

'You're all quite extraordinary, Dolly. The hospital should consider itself lucky to have you.'

Dolly appeared to ponder this one. 'I do have something to ask you, Father. Perhaps you could come by another time?'

'Of course, Dolly. I'd be delighted.' And he would. There was something sympathetic about the atmosphere in the shop. It was a welcome mat for the hospital, a place apart.

As the reprieve from the pager appeared to hold, Marick deposited his satchel in his office, taking out his sad food so it wouldn't be further squashed, and wove the path to Hugo's laundry door. He knocked, but there was no answer.

This non-descript door was contradictory. A contradiction within a paradox. Look at it there, he thought, a divide between the evidence, the KPIs, the unhappiness out on this side and the transcendental, the mystical, and, well, Hugo beyond. Again he knocked, wanting in with a desperation. Nothing.

After a few minutes, Marick's pager, perhaps tired of him straying, resumed the score from its insistent song-sheet. Unravelling the contradiction would have to wait.

SIX

It was late morning before Marick was able to set foot in the library. His pager had solicited from him several visits: one to a woman dying angrily in the respiratory ward, another to a man who had spent the last week in a coma and was keen on regaining lost time. 'A few prayers if you don't mind, Father,' he'd whispered. 'I missed them while I was under.'

At least Marick could feel he'd been of vague worth. After his duties were done, stickers collected, notes made, he looped down through the crevices and hallways. He had not been to this section of the hospital before. It was a creaking dustbowl in an ancient part of the whole scramble of building.

Marick approached the librarian at the front desk, whose lips pursed before he even heard Marick's request.

'Oh, nothing important,' Marick tried to sound nonchalant. 'Just references on the medically mysterious, or the occult. Perhaps the historically misunderstood.'

The librarian frowned and pointed towards the back stairs, returning to the paperwork in front of him without speaking.

Marick was supposed to feel embarrassed by the response, he realised, and he duly did.

The library was from another age, transplanted. Marick would not have been surprised to see gas lamps. In its forecourt the smell was evocative: of brass polish and wax. Dust particles waltzed in the slants of sunlight piercing the high windows. Any noise was soaked up by the felt-lined shelves, which disorientated Marick further. As he passed through the main atrium, he looked up to the mezzanine above, with its shelves of heavy books bound in rich colours, held in by railings of beaten iron. The ground floor was populated by medical texts and journals: a solemn repository of knowledge. These were not what Marick was after.

Down the back steps, stone and worn and curling, he entered the damp stillness underground. There was little order to the titles arranged in an epic sprawl here. Perhaps there was a system in place, but books about obsolete medical equipment stood next to obstetric journals, technical manuals alongside newsletter collections. There were a few fiction titles with vaguely medical themes and several decades' worth of the Guinness Book of World Records.

Marick browsed, picking out volumes at random, flicking through them and returning them to the shelves. He pulled one out that he thought might have some useful leads: *Bacteria: Friend or Foe?* He thumbed through to the section on *E. coli*, but there was nothing that spoke of the alchemical. A book across the way described new bioengineering techniques, but there were no surprise elements. He wandered down one aisle, then another. His eye caught a book with dust in the creases of its spine – *Medical Curiosities: Untangling the Unexplained* – and he hauled it from its place, bringing it back to a dingy table in one corner. Inside the front cover were several disclaimers. Not medical advice, it said, but all the articles had been peer-reviewed and referenced. It was many years old, he saw.

He ran a finger down the table of contents, and his chest heated. There was a title, ridiculous in every word of it, but there all the same. *The Gold Excretors of Plymouth*, it said, with a footnote apologising for the vernacular. In the middle of the book, flanked with references and recommendations for further reading, was what read like pure fancy.

Late 1600s. A cluster of families. A tiny village. The nascence of a colony and the beginning of a nation. Marick looked around to see if anybody might be observing him, reading the preposterous. A marvel. All of a sudden one, then two of them, then the whole clan, began, quite simply, to excrete gold.

Gold, Marick thought, of all things, in their bowel actions. The claim was outlandish, but the authors assured the reader the episode was researched as best they could, considering the wash of the years.

This went on for several generations. The family members would take turns harvesting the gold, which they'd sell for an impressive sum. They built a swathe of magnificent houses with the proceeds, which were well secured for the era, surrounded by spikes and hunting dogs.

Marick remembered what Hugo had said the day before. *Gut bacteria. Living microbial factories.* He read on. Sentries from the village were posted around and were paid handsomely. The families were tight-lipped – no outsiders were allowed into the fortress – and they grew richer and richer. Suspicions unfolded, as could be expected, and several of the women were dragged off and tried as witches.

None of those involved spoke in public about it. All theories back then were about magic. No concrete evidence survived.

At some point, a little way into the next century, it all just stopped. The family members reverted to voiding their bowels like the rest of the world. Debts could not be repaid, houses were boarded up and the cohort slunk back into the obscurity of colonial America. Nothing remained to back up the story. Except, the authors of the book went on to say, there have been rumours of sporadic and similar occurrences in the backwoods of the planet, never lasting long, never officially documented or investigated. As though some families are chosen, and then the phenomenon disappears.

Marick could feel a curdling inside. As though it could all be an elaborate trick. It was like reading that a certain part of existence had been fabricated, without giving away which one. He flicked back and forth through the pages, hoping to find it was fiction, made up, a joke, but all the chapters were referenced and credible. It was hard to understand why he was thrown off balance by reading this. What did it mean for Hugo's discovery? Was it some cycle of science now returning, finding a man fated, or was it dangerous distraction? But alchemy? Surely as a concept, this was a pagan dream, one that neither a scientist nor a man of God had any business suggesting. He had to get back to the laundry.

'I'm so glad you're here.' Hugo ushered him in when Marick appeared at the door. Hugo's face was flushed, close to glowing. 'There's more.'

'More what?' Marick asked.

'See for yourself.'

Marick had arrived determined to face reality. Hugo appeared to think the same.

'The things I've discovered,' Hugo said to him as he hunched back over the microscope, slotting a fresh slide underneath for Marick.

Marick adjusted to the perspective change created in the tunnels of the microscope. There was, indeed, more. Every cell was aglitter. Tiny chips and granules and knobs of gold.

'I've been reading,' Hugo said.

Marick would wait till he was done.

'Things I'd heard about during the course of my undergraduate studies, but which only now make sense. Take Deadwood, for example.'

'Deadwood?' This would not be the first time Marick would ask Hugo to repeat words, labels which sounded out of kilter from any conversation he'd ever had.

'Homestake Mine. Out South Dakota way. There's a whole bunch of research going on there. Secretive, but government sanctioned. They've got an astrobiology team who shimmy down into its depths to study the intraterrestrials.' Hugo was almost breathless as he spoke. He didn't wait to be asked. 'Intraterrestrials, if you want to know, are organisms that live deep underground in what are essentially alien ecosystems and biospheres. Some of them eat nothing but rock, and don't require even an atom of oxygen for respiration. And you know what the amazing thing is?'

Marick shook his head.

'Homestake? It's a burnt-out old gold mine. That's where the intraterrestials are thriving. Best seam of gold in the whole area. Those aren't normal microbes, Marick. Like the sulphate reducers.'

'Sulphate reducers?'

'Yes. You see, some bacteria are so ancient they were around before atmospheric oxygen came into existence, so they had to breathe something.'

'But this still doesn't mean—'

The laundry was lit up with Hugo's excitement. 'And only recently discovered. Seabed nodules! Seabed nodules, Marick. You're never going to guess what they are. Mounds of precious metals – cobalt, copper, manganese, covering the abyss of the ocean floor – that need bacteria to make them. These are bugs that weren't even known about when I was at university. Found in the deepest oceans, where it's blacker than our minds can fathom and strange beyond the imagining. Microorganisms that can extract trace metals from the seawater, turning them into solid metallic nuggets. But my boys have gone one better, Marick, don't you see? Gold de novo. We're on the cusp of a biological revolution. And I'm right there, Marick. Right at the front. I can't begin to tell you how big this is.'

Marick watched Hugo as he paced the few steps up and down the laundry, after which he walked over to Marick and clasped onto both his upper arms.

'It's happening,' Hugo said.

Marick did not have an opportunity to ask what *it* was.

'Just think, Marick. Think of Leeuwenhoek, the first to see animalcules under a ground glass lens. A drop of water was all that man needed. He saw it all: alive, bottomless, alluvial. Consider Robert Hooke, Pasteur, Koch, all of them firsts in their fields. The greats.'

'They are amazing. What you have here is amazing. You are amazing,' Marick took a breath in, 'but I don't think any of them were suggesting,' he would simply have to say the word, 'alchemy.'

'Ah, but that's where you're wrong, Marick. Before then. Who was the greatest of all scientists? A man who conjured up scientific truths from his notepaper as effortlessly as breathing. Isaac Newton, Marick. Not only did he rein in the laws of nature but while doing so he wrote the work of which he was most proud, his treatise on alchemy.'

Hugo paced again. Four strides up, four strides back. Marick knew a man in the grip of certainty when he saw it. Something in the set of his jaw, the focus of his eyes.

'Is that your phone?' Marick asked. A trill was coming from Hugo's pocket.

'Oh yes.' Hugo pulled it out and looked at the number. 'It's from the university. I'll put it on speaker.'

A weary sounding assistant from the Geology Department was on the line.

'Your results,' she said with a sigh.

The tension in Hugo's fingers was obvious. His knuckles bulged white around the phone.

'It's just plain gold,' she said. 'All the mines produce the same type. Which, of course, you can read about in any textbook.'

'Is it?' Hugo asked.

'Is it what?' Her irritation with the inane research projects students did these days was clear. 'Obvious?'

'Gold,' Hugo said.

Silence on the line. Perhaps she was used to the doziness of university researchers, and she spoke with slow, clear words. 'Yes. The gold you sent us is gold.' She hung up without saying goodbye.

The air settled. Hugo's breath slowed. 'It's gold, Marick.'

Marick watched him. It was time to share his own library find. As Marick relayed the wild story from centuries ago, Hugo nodded the entire way through, as though counting up points earned by his theories.

'You're going to think this strange, Marick, but my mother predicted this. I've never been able to tell anyone about it, even Vivian.'

'I'm listening, Hugo.'

Hugo leant against the bench, clutching one of the small pots of gold against his chest. 'You will only get one chance, she said to me. I remember it perfectly. She was waiting for me to be old enough, I think. It was the day we went to the Rose Garden. My mother Sandya knew things. Could see beyond the senses. It was in her blood. She was from Agra, a city of marble and dreams she used to say, and she fled to London in the blackness of an Indian night to be with my father, Wing Commander Albert Francis. They'd met while he was on leave on his final tour. Sandya thought she was marrying for love, the Wing Commander for duty. He made it his job to stamp out her Indian-ness, but a burning core of it remained. That day, among the roses, I remember. We'd taken the tube to Hyde Park. We never went into the city, it was always too expensive or too far, but my mother wanted to see the gardens, which had only opened the year before. We walked the circular paths. *China Rose. Tea Rose. Queen Elizabeth. Golden Beauty,* she read out. I remember the smell being so sweet and thick it was difficult to breathe. Sandya got angrier as we walked, and neither Penelope, my sister, nor I knew why. "You know Vishnu's Arbour was laden with fragrant roses," Sandya told us. "Our Gods were growing roses before these people knew what they looked like." She waved her hand at London. "So much taken from us. Even our magic," she said. I remember scoffing. After all, Penelope was younger, and it was important I make it clear I was the mature one. But Sandya grew fierce, all at once, and gripped me by the shoulders. "One chance," she said. "Fate will come for you, my boy, and you'd better be ready. Ganesh has his eyes trained right on you. And when that time comes, and even I don't know when it will be, you will not be able to tell the difference between Fate and magic.'"

The silence in the laundry following this was an omnipresence. It filled every space and square. When some words come out, they cannot be returned, and the world tilts on its axis a little.

'No difference at all,' Hugo repeated.

'Is your mother, is Sandya, still around?' Marick needed to wrestle the conversation back from the cliff edge.

'No,' Hugo said. 'It wasn't too long after that she died. Dropped without making a sound in the bathroom while rubbing her chest with liniment for the pain that had dogged her the last few mornings. After that the wing commander moved the three of us to Australia. Why, we never got out of him.' Hugo rolled the pot with the gold flakes in his hands as though he was warming it.

'For a long time, I thought she meant the discoveries at the university, that those proteins were my destiny, my moment, but now this has happened, I think, Marick, her words make sense. This thing,' and he looked down at the pot holding the gold, the gold grown like seedlings inside his bacteria, 'which straddles two worlds.'

Hugo handed it to Marick. 'So can't you see? This is not so much alchemy, but the new alchemy. The inanimate inside the biological. The mineral arising from the animal. The old finding balance with the new. The known meets the unknown.'

Revelations meets Genesis, Marick thought.

Just as Marick had the realisation this was no confession, but intimacy masquerading as conversation, his pager went off. They both jumped.

'Tomorrow? Will you come again?' Hugo asked. 'I need you, Marick.'

Marick found it difficult to reply. Of course, of course he would.

SEVEN

Marick's next few days played out to a similar tune – he churned through his jobs, peeling off stickers and chancing further into the depths and the impasses of the hospital. The sounds he heard, the stories, the secrets and the bargains, continued to weigh into his nights. Many of the hallways were claustrophobic, with elegies in their corners and openings. The walls of the wards had deaths fossilised in them like rubble, deaths for which he worried he had negotiated no peace.

His antidote was Hugo, and Marick did not tire of the thrill of walking into that laundry with its buzz of life and Hugo's excitement and his latest thoughts on the discovery, which Hugo was convinced would be a scientific coup beyond imagining when it was revealed to the public. Hugo would pull Marick over to the microscope and implore him to watch it all again. Marick played audience to the splendour of the microbes cavorting, dividing, pulling apart their DNA in raging, lustful yawns.

They had agreed on a secret knock for Marick so Hugo could let him in without suspicion. They did more than talk gold. Over the days, Marick heard more about Vivian, Hugo's wife. She worked as a counsellor at the university where Hugo's research lab had been. She had weathered the scandal pretty well, he thought, although sometimes he would catch her glaring at him in inscrutable silence. She loved books. They had a fairly average marriage. They hadn't had children, not for want of trying.

'You must meet her one day.' Hugo said.

Marick would also drop by Dolly's shop most mornings.

The week before Christmas, he stepped in to buy the daily newspaper. She was busy doing a stocktake but halted all activities to hustle him into a corner.

'Father. There's something I want to talk to you about.'

'Of course, Dolly.' He had stopped adding, *I'm all ears*, long ago. It surprised him how many people thought he was making a joke and took the opportunity to make a painful quip back.

'It's about hearing God,' Dolly said.

'Go on.' They were in a side recess. A trolley trundled by.

'I've had a bit of a disappointment recently, and I'd like your advice on how to make sense of it.'

'I'll do what I can for you, but I can never guarantee—'

'My kidney,' she interrupted.

'Oh.' An organ. Not what he'd expected.

'I've been rejected.' She pulled a crumpled envelope with the logo *The Public's Organ Donation Program* visible in the corner. It had been opened many times. 'They don't want my kidney. I've been hoping to donate one for years, but I can't get past the first hurdle. They say I'm not suitable.'

Marick wasn't sure how to reply. She must be at least seventy.

Although Dolly looked externally pristine, who knew how things were winding down inside.

'It was my chance. My life will be done soon enough, and I wanted to make the last part of it count.'

It sounded a little extreme. 'I'm so sorry to hear, Dolly, but why don't you donate blood, or something else,' he asked. 'Why a kidney?'

'Because God told me to. In a dream.' She folded her arms as though she knew Marick could have no comeback. 'Who am I to defy God?'

She had a point.

'But surely you already volunteer your time, give so much of yourself?'

Dolly looked around to make sure nobody was listening and moved closer, to talk in a whisper.

'It's hard to define,' she said, but went on to do a very good job of it. Some indescribable feeling she got, she told him, every time she saw a young person hooked up to a dialysis machine. Once a week she took her turn with a mobile trolley containing a selection of confectionery – 'Low fat, Father,' she said – and a few discreet toiletries, and she tootled it through the wards. She always took a deep breath when entering the renal unit. The chronic kidney disease patients have it the worst, she explained to Marick. Their bodies have betrayed them, leaving them half-alive and sitting in miserable matrimony to a hulking, clunking machine, trying not to watch as their bodily fluid coursed through the thick snaking tubes. Whenever she walked in, pairs of eyes, frosted, yellowing and slow, looked up at her, distracted from hell for a moment. The noises from the machines were never synchronised. They gave off a ratcheting sound full of pain while the monsters rinsed those poor people's blood like a long cycle on the washing machine.

'It's horrible,' she said. 'So when Our Father came to me one night, suggesting I give up one of mine for them, it seemed obvious. Maybe my life might be worth something after all. Mervyn would have approved.'

'Mervyn?' Marick asked.

'My late husband,' she said. 'Great moose of a man. Great reader. House full of *New Scientist*. I haven't been able to bring myself to cancel the subscription. Fifteen years it's been, God rest him. Mesothelioma. Awful.'

'Yes, awful,' Marick agreed.

'But they don't want it. My kidney. Which is what I'm trying to get to the bottom of. I am quite healthy, Father. In every way. Never smoked. Never drank. There is no doubt I'd have the bloodwork of a much younger woman. So I thought I would ask you. What do you think God is trying to say here? Should I persist? I could pull some strings.'

He wanted to tell her he was as ill-equipped as a translation service as he was a curate, that he hardly knew what God might want from him, but was saved by one of Dolly's co-workers calling her back in to locate one of the less common tuna and cracker fusions. She sighed.

'An abomination they are,' she said, 'but the staff all complain when I don't have them in stock. Do get back to me when you've had a chance to think about it, Father. I'd appreciate your help.'

Marick bypassed his own office to visit Hugo's makeshift one. Dolly's request felt like a faint choke in his throat. Yes, he could get away with sounding authoritative to strangers on their various cusps, but it was another matter altogether to hold dominion about God's wishes over someone like Dolly.

He rapped on the laundry door; three slow, two quick; and tried to appear casual, uninterested in the response, as a woman, presumably one of the cleaners, clattered behind him with a bucketful of sprays and brushes.

Hugo opened the door a crack, eyeing Marick for a few seconds as if he didn't recognise his friend, then let him in.

'I've been putting feelers out,' Hugo said. 'Joined an internet chatroom, anonymously of course, mostly full of other protein producers. See if anybody else has come across this. Most of them are calling it crazy. Loudly. Which always makes me suspicious. The pressure's on, Marick. I'm going to have to get results out there soon. So I've got hold of an ordinary bunch of *E. coli*, ordered in from a lab interstate. I'm letting them go head to head with my boys. Same culture medium, same atmospheric conditions.'

Marick was not following. 'Aren't yours ordinary *E. coli*?'

Hugo busied himself in a notepad of numbers. He picked up a pencil and chewed on the end of it, crossing out few lines and scrawling something over the top.

Marick waited. Hugo didn't answer.

'Hugo?'

'Hmm?' Hugo peered at Marick over his glasses.

'Your bacteria here. I thought you'd said they were ordinary.'

Hugo hesitated. He stared at the pencil and took his time answering. 'Well, it depends on how you define ordinary.'

The centrifuge pinged its completion note again. Hugo fished out the tub.

Hugo added, 'Maybe I haven't been as open as I could.'

After all this, Marick thought.

'So where did you get the original strain from?' Marick asked. 'The ones producing the gold.'

'Didn't I tell you?' Hugo asked.

Marick shook his head.

'China,' Hugo said.

'China's a big place.'

'I guess so. Different lab from where I get the DNA. The thing is, these lads are gene-edited. Kind of frowned on here, but nobody knew. Nobody needed to know at the university.' Hugo rolled the pencil back and forth between his fingers, with small nervous motions. 'I'd rather that didn't get out, if that's alright.'

Who would I tell, thought Marick?

Hugo continued. 'Doesn't detract from what they're able to do, though. In fact, it makes them more remarkable. This single strain.'

Marick was on the outside of something, he knew, as though knowledge was a smooth sphere from which he kept sliding, no matter how he tried to grab on.

'But you believe me, don't you, Marick? I know you do. You're the only one who's seen what they're capable of. What these bacteria can produce, no matter their origins.' Hugo opened a low fridge and pulled out a pot of rosé-coloured fluid.

The vinegary smell in the room grew stronger. Marick experienced a brief wave of nausea. He did not understand what he was being asked. Was he expected to believe the bacteria or believe Hugo? He wasn't sure he could trust himself to ask for clarification.

'I'm sorry, Marick. I really thought I'd mentioned it. But you have to understand, a little gene editing is not going to create bacteria that can make gold. They never did this back at the university. There are much bigger processes at play here. Occurrences that I don't yet understand but are undeniable.'

Hugo turned to Marick. His gaze was clear. Marick knew he was looking into the eye of truth.

'Yes, Hugo, I have seen it,' Marick said. It was a relief to voice it, as if declaring an end to a battle. He picked up one of several pots lined up along the back bench. The scientist and the chaplain stared at the enigma inside. 'I believe you, Hugo. I'm with you.'

Hugo exhaled.

Marick's pager beeped, clamouring for attention.

'I'll have to get that,' Marick said. 'I'm sorry.'

'Before you go, Marick, I told Vivian last night. About the gold. She's going to take a little convincing. I wondered whether you might consider coming around to our place for dinner tonight. She'd believe you, Marick. She'd trust a priest.'

'An invitation?' Marick castigated himself for saying this aloud when it should have been in his head. His heart gave a single dull thud. Early in his theological training he'd been told people often feel uncomfortable asking the clergy to social events. 'They don't want to joke with you around,' a superior, somewhat of an advice enthusiast had told him. 'It's like they feel exposed in front of the Almighty himself.' It had been so long that he thought he may no longer be capable of pulling off even the most low-key of social events.

'Absolutely. Six o'clock? Vivian will try food out on you, but don't worry too much.'

Marick found it difficult to focus that morning. Free-floating anxiety caught him each time his mind tried to move to other things. It was not just the test of the gold out into the open. It was the going around to a house. Conventionality. Conversation with a wife.

•٠\̖٢٠̣٠•

When Marick returned home from his European trip, he tracked down Diane before he unpacked. She was enthusiastic on the phone.

'I thought you were going to be away till next semester,' she said. 'This is wonderful! Let's have dinner.'

She was more striking than before, and Marick found it difficult to swallow the tagliatelle they had ordered to recreate the experience of Rome. The food may have fallen short, but that didn't matter. He heard about every detail of her trip, her words nutrition enough.

'Florence was marvellous. Very *Room with a View*. Our pensione was in a tiny square, with cobblestones like a mosaic. Every night we went to the markets and drank mulled wine from polystyrene cups to keep our hands warm. There were lights everywhere. Like Pointillist lanterns. Yes, that's what they were. God, I want to go back. Maybe the two of us could. An art tour of every city in Italy.'

She smiled so both rows of her teeth were exposed, with her head on a tilt, which Marick would later learn meant she was joking or worse, goading him into saying something he didn't mean. But at that wobbly table covered in a plastic cloth with a fake red-check print, his mind emptied of anything but the vision of them standing hand in hand, looking up in wonder at every Great Master that existed. *Pointillist lantern.* Nobody else he knew would have said this.

'I'm not sure my parents would fund another trip though,' Diane said.

He had asked about everything, hungry to know each detail from the moment he had last seen her. They talked late into the night, until the chairs in the restaurant were stacked around them. He discovered they were turning twenty-one within a month of each other.

'We should have a combined party,' Diane said.

•¹⁄₂⁷⁄₂•

No flush remained when Marick remembered back to his days of courting Diane. He thought the intensity of the recollections would last forever, but although they still snagged him when he came across a fragrance that was undeniably hers – musk, vanilla, hairspray – those memories had moved house in his head and now resided in a less favourable part of town, the wrong side of the tracks, along with litter and guilt and regret.

But tonight he would have dinner with his friend and his wife. He tried out the word again. Friend. He wanted it to sound natural if anybody asked, unlikely as it would be.

His pager tugged him back. Good. A job. It was what he needed to rebalance. The Palliative Care Unit required his presence. To get there, Marick needed to navigate a plexus of corridors and exit one building before stepping into another. The weather was not too fierce – the air outside was pool-calm. As he walked inside the next block, the peacefulness continued. He had grown to like this ward. Here mortality was more brother than enemy. There was less recrimination and last-minute bargaining.

The room his pager had asked him to attend smelled sweet. There were open jars of honey, and jellies and jubes and toffees were strewn over the bedside table.

'My husband's never been much one for God, Father, but we thought it might not be a bad idea to hedge his bets. Which is why we hoped you might come. They say he's going to die today.'

It looked like the woman – Annie – haloed in the light and attentive by her husband's side, was right. The man's breathing was forming eddies, turbulent at his lips, although it did not appear to be distressing him. He was white-haired and serene.

'He's had a fair bit of morphine,' Annie told Marick. 'The sweets were just a send-off. I've been so harsh on him the last few years. Doctor's orders, you see. No sugar. Now I feel guilty. He loved them so.'

Marick smiled and sat on the bed. He picked up the patient's hand and ran a thumb over the broken strands of his veins.

'Anything in particular you'd like from me?' Marick asked.

'Whatever you think would help, Father.'

Marick covered the man's spindly hand with his own. Whatever Marick found troubling in this untethered period, mostly from his effort to understand how God figured in these liminal moments and what form he took, his stalemate was not what this couple deserved. He settled on simple talk.

'A few days ago, I was walking to my bus stop when I saw a red slash of graffiti on the wall. *Repent or Burn*, it said. I wondered who would write that, how angry they must be, how unsure of their God.'

The sunshine streaming through the window was as light as lithium and sparkled over the scrunched lolly wrappers. It created a subtle vision of hope, fleeting but intense, as Marick gave this quiet oration, a minor character off in the wings in a great drama, the footlights warm enough to encourage him. There was such peril in doubt and darkness and blessed release in the light of faith – how comforting it was to surrender to belief, even if transiently.

Annie looked thoughtful. 'Do you think there's a chance, any chance at all, he'll end up in some sort of hell if he's spent most of his life not believing? He went to church once in a while, but I don't think his heart was in it.'

'No.' Marick may not have understood much, but this he knew. 'He won't be thrown into some pit of fire. God may be difficult to fathom, and not always easy to hear, but He is neither vengeful nor vindictive.'

She smiled and leant across to whisper into her husband's ear. Annie said something Marick couldn't catch. Then she turned to Marick. 'Thought so,' she said.

'If there's one thing I know from my time on this planet,' Marick said, 'it is this: if something makes little sense, it is unlikely to be true, no matter what you've read in hallowed books or are taught from the dais.'

He heard himself speak the words. Listen to yourself, Marick. Bookmark this, he thought, this place of safety. Somewhere to come back to later.

The man, most of the way out of the world now, took a breath only once every minute or so. His lips, mostly hidden under wisps of white hair, were a gentle dusky colour, and his hand inside Marick's was weightless, emptied of any strength it may once have possessed.

'So you see,' Marick continued, 'your God for this afternoon is the God you need. He is the God of amazement and of new life and of goodbyes. The God that is grateful you had time on earth.' He recited a brief prayer, a few sentences only.

Annie wiped a tear from one eye. 'Thank you, Father. Don't feel you have to stay. You must be a busy man.'

Marick reached over and lifted her hand, connecting it with her husband's.

'I'd like to, if that's alright.'

He wanted to be there for the final moment. To experience exactly what happens. He wondered whether he could find something in that juncture, a flicker of understanding. He peered with intensity at the man's face as it was powering down. Those eyes were closed, with the occasional dart beneath the lids. Was the man dreaming? Imagining his body walking free? Perhaps finally breaking bread with a God denied to him in life? His heartbeat entering a black hole, his soul soaring on thermals? It was trance-like for Marick the observer, while anything was possible, while death exchanged positions with life.

He had no concept of how long he watched, unblinking.

Annie tapped him on the shoulder. 'Are you okay, Father?'

Marick looked up.

'He's gone,' she added.

Marick looked, closer. She was right. Her husband's breath had finished on a sigh. Nothing. He saw nothing. Life unravelled, no sign at all.

'Thank you for your words, Father.'

He looked up at her, a little taken aback. 'Were they alright?'

'Perfect,' she said.

He took a deep breath for himself, large and alive, filling every sac of his lungs. He remembered to take a sticker.

'Merry Christmas, Father,' Annie said, and she lay over her husband's body as though she were funeral drapes.

Leaving the floral and candy light of the room, he notified a passing nurse and made his slow way back to his office.

EIGHT

At five o'clock, Marick pushed his chair back and rose. He had worked out the timing to the minute. He would have preferred to go home in the interim, change into something more – well, he wasn't sure what he should change into. The best he could do in his office was loosen his tie and smooth down his hair. Glancing at his watch again, he made his exit. His stomach contorted. You're being ridiculous, he chastised himself. It's only dinner.

Having factored in time to purchase an offering, he dropped into Dolly's shop. It did not help his apprehension.

'What would you recommend I take as a gift for a dinner date, Dolly?'

'Chocolate, obviously. Failing that, why don't you take one of those nice cyclamens in pots I have out the back? They're very stylish. But a date, Father. How lovely.'

'No, it's not that sort of date, no. I mean …'

'It's fine, Father, really. You can buy chocolates from the delicatessen down the road. I never thought I'd hear myself say that – they've always been the competition. My selection was the pride of the hospital.'

Dolly proceeded to tell Marick how she had studied chocolate. Knew it like nobody else. She explained that when Mervyn's piles of *New Scientist* magazines grew barstool high, she rebelled and proclaimed she deserved a periodical of her own. With a little research she came across *Candy Central*, a monthly publication posted out of a small town in Nebraska for which the airmail cost was greater than that of the magazine itself. But what an edge it gave her. There was not a confectionery debut of which she was unaware. It had articles on everything from the chemistry of sweets to wrapping design, helping her decide how to arrange the shop, as though the diversity of colour on the shelves might make up for the failings of society outside. She did make allowance for another of the volunteers to order the savouries, as long as she could check the order before it was submitted. Especially those tuna and cracker combinations, which she couldn't abide.

'But I've already explained that to you, haven't I, Father? I mean, who eats tuna from a can?' According to Dolly, who grew up with the sea lapping at her door, tuna meant dense slabs of meat, smelling of the deepest ocean, oily on the fingers and tender on the tongue. When it had been pulled up and smacked to death on the deck right in front of you, and if you were given a morsel, if your dad would let you because he was feeling generous that day when the fish were biting big and the price was sitting pretty, you could let the tuna melt in your mouth like fairy floss.

'Sixty years ago, Father. How does time do that? But I'm getting carried away. Who's the lucky lady?'

'No, no. I'm having dinner with a friend and his wife. One of the scientists who works here. Dr Hugo Francis. From microbiology. Maybe you know him?'

Dolly frowned, appearing a little insulted she didn't. 'I'd imagine he hasn't been here for long. Under the radar perhaps.' She walked out the back, returning with a small pot containing wilting stems topped by a flight of ruby petal butterflies. 'But now you've mentioned it, there are a lot of people coming and going on staff here. Like nomads. Not like the old days where people had jobs for life. What sort of a relationship with a hospital is that? What sort of administrative staff has no allegiance to their people? So much unhappiness here. I wonder if the writing's on the wall, to be honest.'

'That's a funny saying, isn't it,' Marick looked at his watch. Still a few minutes before he had to leave. 'Did you know it comes from the Bible? The Book of Daniel?'

'Well I never, Father. Do tell.'

'It was at a great feast for Belshazzar, the young and decadent king of Babylon. He'd invited thousands of guests, and it was a party to end all parties. But he was vain and proud, and probably rather drunk, and he ordered the drinkware to be brought forth from the royal cupboards – only they were gold vessels stolen from the sacked temple of Jerusalem. God, furious at this blasphemy, turned up and began writing on the walls with an unseen hand, prophesying that Belshazzar would meet a grisly and rapid end. Which he did, ending up slain before the next sunrise.'

'Goodness. And all for the use of the good gold,' Dolly said, smiling.

'The gold leading to the writing on the wall,' Marick said in a quiet voice. 'I must go.'

'Yes, I mustn't keep you, Father. Just updating the telegraph, then I'm off myself.'

As Marick picked up the cyclamen, he watched Dolly retreat to her window to move a few of the notices around. The front glass of her shop was plastered in notices: most handwritten with phone numbers and requests. A trading post for anyone in the hospital to advertise wares and services, furniture, babysitting, lost pets, soccer sign-ups.

'Enjoy your evening, Father,' she called as he left.

After popping into the delicatessen on the way to the station and selecting the more expensive brand of chocolate, with pot-plant in hand, Marick jumped on the 5.28 train as the doors were closing. The carriage was not air-conditioned, and he worried the chocolates might soften in the heat. Dustings of the plant's dirt had already left their own bouquet of residue on his shirt.

Australian trains had little on their European counterparts, Marick thought. Here they were dull boxes, sliding back and forth between flat suburbs. No steam. No slowing to sound horns through tunnels or clacking over ice-cracked waterways. Diane described those train journeys as sailing through meridians, bisecting mountain tops covered in arcs of snow which were like backdrops painted for plays. Their whole first year together, they always came back to discussing Europe. Australia was parochial, backwards, a cultural badlands for two restless students.

They never had their combined birthday. Diane's parents threw a party for her at a hotel bar with a dress code in the city. Marick was just happy to be invited. It was the first time he had met her friends. Most were in design, or photography. Some were studying art. He had never believed art was something to be studied at university, straight out of school. These people were intoxicating. The music was loud, with a bass beat so explosive you could feel it in your chest.

'So you're Marick,' said one of Diane's girlfriends as she toppled over to him and draped herself on his arm. He had to stare intensely at her lips to have any idea what she was saying. That, and a few negronis from a fountain, meant much of the conversation was lost on him. 'She's been rabbiting on about you,' she slurred. 'She really likes you.'

Marick was scared he might have misheard. It seemed too fantastic to be true.

'She says nobody has ever listened to her the way you do. She's gone.' She strung out the *awe* sound until it faded on her breath. And then she, with her piercings circling her ear like train-tracks themselves, was gone too.

It was another six months before Diane brought up introducing Marick to her parents. The prospect of doing the same with Marick's didn't arise. His mother lived on the other side of the country now, having chased the sun for an early retirement, and Marick rarely spoke to her. Estranged, he told Diane over coffee, although he knew the word did not go any way towards explaining the relationship. Diane didn't ask why. The subject of his father never came up beyond a throwaway comment on the divorce. He had Deidre's line branded in his mind, that they'd been better off without him. Not once did Marick mention the responsibility he felt for his father's departure. That was stored somewhere deep. Within the month his father would die in a flash flood, trying to drive his Land Cruiser home from a night at his local men's shed, but Marick would not find out about this for years, and when he did, the knowledge brought with it a mystified lump of grief he would never shift.

'I know they'll love you, Marick. My only advice is don't say too much. Dad likes to hold court. But you're good at that, so I wouldn't worry.'

Marick took whatever advice Diane doled out. They were seeing one another every day by then. Although they were studying at different universities, they had a printout of each other's timetables so they could eat, drink and slowly find their way into bed together. Marick's heart was unfurling, as though leaf by leaf, letting raw sunlight into his newly unguarded core. He never missed a lecture, though, never failed an exam. Diane wasn't always as devoted, and she'd put off the parental introductions a few times so they didn't blame him for her lapses.

When they did meet, Marick arrived at their house empty-handed.

'You're supposed to bring something, flowers, anything,' Diane admonished him afterwards.

Diane's mother was showing Marick an old picture of her own mother, who had trailblazed her way into medicine – unheard of at the time. The photograph was so aged and cracked it looked like lightning had feathered its merciless way over it, and Marick was peering closely for any likeness to Diane, when her father bowled in and took over the evening.

Diane's father was exactly as described. He wore his authority lightly and with élan, like the jacket slung over one shoulder when he arrived late to dinner and they were already seated. He'd stayed for one last round at the yacht club.

'Accounting, you say, son. We're always looking for people with accounting skills at the firm. Internships, that sort of thing.'

Marick did what he had been advised, and only spoke when asked a direct question, using as few words as he could get away with.

'They think you're great,' Diane told him later, and they returned to their feverish exploration of each other, an ecstatic state Marick would never have imagined ending.

<hr />

The train jolted. Marick craned his neck, making sure he was keeping an eye on the stops. The Francises' house was in one of the older suburbs he'd never visited, and he had to be careful to stay orientated to the foreign street names. He was nervous enough, without missing his station, and he had to keep reminding himself it was only dinner with friends, not meeting anybody's parents.

Arriving at the house in perfect time, at five minutes to six, Marick wandered up the front path, trying to brush the dirt off his shirt. His only success was smudging it into odd Rorschach shapes, as though his clothes could now pass for a psychological test.

The front yard was overgrown, with weeds spraying like fountains from borderless garden beds. Clumps of lawn had been liberated by the looks, seeding themselves in random places among the paving stones fallen out of formation, surrounding the letterbox, creeping up tree trunks like tentacles. Quite a bit of shadow, not much light. He ducked under a tree, letting loose a flutter of birds that squawked at the inconvenience. There was little breeze. The air was humid, swampy.

Marick rang the doorbell and waited. He thought he could hear raised voices inside, transported out on what little draft there was. Panicking, he prepared apologies in his head. But when the door opened, it was done so by a woman who looked serene. When his eyes adjusted, he saw she looked more than that. She had a soft corona of hair, and somehow appeared liquid-limbed, fluid while she moved.

'I'm Vivian. You must be the priest.'

'Oh, I'm not a priest. I'm a chaplain. Never got as far as priest, I'm afraid.'

And instead of making comment she opened her mouth and laughed, her white teeth visible. Marick felt guilty, as though he had somehow seen inside her.

'Come in. Hugo's out the back.'

They passed through a house that was a tumble, refreshing in its mess. There were books, piles of unfolded laundry, printed material and fake fur throws on lounges. Every corner looked like somewhere to sink into. They reached the back door, and Vivian pointed to a verandah. 'He's out there,' she said. 'I'm making cocktails. Can I get you one?'

'Just a weak one, thank you kindly. Oh.' He had forgotten he was carrying gifts. 'These are for you.'

'You lovely man. Thank you. I'll bring the drinks.'

The backyard was also in disarray, neither of them having much love for gardening, Hugo explained.

'I'm so glad you're here, Marick. Sit down.'

Hugo dusted off one of the chairs for him. The outdoor furniture was cracked and weathered. Gnarls of uncut branches dangled overhead. Along the back fence hung a row of sheep skulls.

'An amazing online find, apparently,' Hugo said when he noticed Marick inspecting them. They were arranged in stepwise fashion. 'Like fifties flying wall geese, but with soul, Vivian claims. She's a bit bohemian like that.'

'I'm not bohemian, darling.' Vivian walked out to them with a tray of sea-green cocktails clinking with a melange of fruit and ice. 'This is the extent of my decorative talents, I'm afraid, Marick, and this place is such a shambles we never have people out here to appreciate my inadvertent outback aesthetic. I, we, do apologise for the mess. But it's so hot tonight I can't bear to stay indoors.'

There was something unusual in the way she pronounced 'darling'. As though the first syllable was in conflict with the second, the word a challenge rather than endearment, but then what would he know. He could not recall the last time he'd even heard it used.

'Oh, not at all, I'm just so grateful to be asked.'

You could be a bit cooler yourself, Marick, he told himself.

Vivian handed round the drinks. Marick could smell her perfume. Like monsoons and wilted blossoms. He had trouble with his glass – the fruit kept knocking on his nose. The drink, however, was syrupy and delicious.

'I hope you don't mind, darling, but Leonie and Paul are coming over later. I promised them ages ago.'

Again, that word, although it sounded more natural this time. What was he doing, analysing Hugo's wife's speech? He felt his mind fog a little and wondered if the drink was stronger than he'd requested.

'God, really?' said Hugo. 'I wanted to talk about what's going on at the lab, you knew that.'

'She's my *sister*, Hugo. I am sorry, Marick.'

'Oh, goodness, I don't mind at all.'

'We'll have dinner first, though. If it works. I'm trying something new. It's been cooking for ages. Who knows when it will be ready?'

Hugo made no response, taking another long draught of his drink.

'I've got starters, though,' she said. 'Another experiment. Let me get it.'

Vivian breezed back inside.

'I want you to persuade her, Marick,' said Hugo.

Marick was momentarily confused. Why was he needed to persuade Vivian of anything? What authority could he possibly bring?

Hugo's wife returned with a creation on a platter. 'Retro,' Vivian said. 'Food as pop-art.' She laughed again. 'Oyster terrine. God, it looks awful.'

It did. It was an oval of sepia-coloured mousse surrounded by crackers and pale, dry lemon wedges. Dotted over the top like a chess play were tinned oysters. It had already started to melt in the heat, and the oysters had flattened, leaving faint yellowish trails seeping down the side like lava.

'Don't feel you have to have any. I'm not sure I will.' Vivian smiled.

'I was just quoting Einstein to Marick,' Hugo said.

Was he, Marick thought? Had he missed it?

Hugo spoke as though doing small-town theatrics. '"The most beautiful experience we can have is the mysterious," Einstein said. "It is the fundamental emotion that stands at the cradle of true art and true science."'

Hugo had unquestionably rehearsed it.

Vivian set the platter down. 'I don't think Einstein was referring to the unfeasible, Hugo.' She turned to Marick. 'What do you think about this gold thing? Hugo tells me you've seen it.'

The ground moved beneath Marick. He could not grasp the tone and was not sure where this was heading. His best policy, the safest route, was honesty.

'Yes,' he said. 'It's been utterly consistent. Every day, Hugo's bacteria …' Marick's hesitation stretched into the heat of the night. Hugo was nodding with brisk, sharp movements. 'Well, they make gold.'

'And this isn't in his usual lab, right? The one he's paid to work in?'

'I told you, love. It's the separate one.'

'I'd like to hear Marick say it, Hugo.'

'It's in the separate little laundry, yes, the one he uses to make the proteins for the cleaning company.'

'What cleaning company?'

'*Bio-Kleen!* darling. I've explained this before. Where do you think that extra bit of monthly money comes from? I'm on a retainer.'

'And you are talking about,' Vivian turned back to Marick, 'gold as in eight hundred dollars an ounce gold? Gold with value?'

'Not quite,' Hugo took over again. 'The value is scientific.

And it's only minute quantities. They're bacteria, Viv, not an open-cut mine.' Hugo upended his drink, finishing it. 'It will take a while to get any decent data out of it and we shouldn't tell anyone else about it until we have.'

'People are going to have a hard time believing you when you do, anyway Hugo. After what happened at the university? Being sacked for academic fraud doesn't put you in the most reliable of positions.'

'God, Viv, I wish you wouldn't use that word. You know I did nothing wrong.'

The two of them stared at each other for a long time, until their expressions changed into a grievance Marick did not understand. Neither of them flinched.

Vivian stood. 'The dinner will burn.' She walked back into the kitchen, her summer dress swinging. Marick couldn't help noticing her legs, which seemed as smooth as polished ivory – long, pale, muscular.

'That's why Marick here is so valuable,' Hugo called out after her. He rubbed his forehead. 'Jesus, I'm sorry, Marick. Can I get you another drink?'

Marick had only half-finished the one in front of him, which had turned a watery lime colour. He shook his head.

'She's got a point, you know,' Hugo said. 'It was a pretty bad business. And the *Nature* debacle wasn't the worst of it. Hang on.' He went to a small outdoor fridge and pulled out a bottle of wine. He uncorked it and poured a large chug into his cocktail glass, creating a yellow-green mixture with the remnants of the liqueur. 'Drink up, Marick.' He sat on his chair and leant forwards. 'It was Melanie, too.'

'Melanie?' Marick asked.

Hugo lowered his voice, glancing towards the kitchen. Marick, again, remained wordless, while Hugo told him Vivian had suspected something.

'It was ridiculous, but that's how women are sometimes. You might not know, but they are,' Hugo said.

A something, which Hugo assured Marick, was nothing. Melanie, his PhD student at the biotechnology laboratory, the only one he had confided in about the bacteria's origins and their unique genetic makeup. Melanie was doe-eyed and diligent, an exceptional doctoral candidate. Compact and Korean.

'"I'm a Hyundai!" she introduced herself to me,' Hugo told Marick. 'She dreamt of becoming an actress. She was auditioning for the university performance of Ibsen, she told the team.'

Hugo continued, explaining how Melanie got caught up in Hugo's bullish enthusiasm, particularly when they stayed later and later, designing proteins that seemed destined to install them on the world biochemical stage. They just had to hold the distance. When a small delegation from the university's Academic Department marched down, past the chill of the rugby fields and the cricket pavilions, further along from the carparks and the waste disposal centre, down the concrete steps and into their laboratory, they expressed, in terms not at all uncertain, that although the work he was doing seemed be finding favour among some academic circles, unless there were publications in high-impact journals with major outreach indices, and soon, they would be forced to cut Hugo's budget. Publish or perish, one of the envoy added, enjoying the cliché. Fine, Hugo thought. We can produce anything we want, and faster than any lab in the world with our *E. coli* at full run.

'I was ignoring the gong sounding in my head, Marick. And my mother. I could hear Sandya talking. *Do not direct Fate. She will set the timeframe.*' Hugo swirled the remains of his drink, finishing that one as well. 'I'm not proud of it. Of what happened.'

Hugo paused a little longer before continuing. Melanie had not only followed the protein creations from the spark of idea to the graphs of their success, she also trailed Hugo. When Hugo explained to the team, late at night with takeaway Chinese food in boxes, that they needed to put in double time – the world was waiting for their results – Melanie went at it. She used an inventive timescale for the data, knowing how thrilled Hugo would be with the optics. He never checked it. Melanie confessed in tears the night of the reckoning, when the fraudulent paper was exposed. As her tears tailed off, and Hugo sat with her, in a way understanding what she'd done, she looked into his eyes, and moved in to kiss him.

'I didn't know what to do. I could see the whole thing in slow motion. I turned my head away. God, Marick. I'm a happily married man. I know these things happen in labs all the time, but not to me. I was shocked. But because I'd turned away from her, she kind of connected – it was awkward – with my ear. Those seconds felt like forever, but then she just upped and walked out of the lab. My problem was, though, for an instant I'd wished I hadn't turned my head. I wished I could have experienced what her lips felt like. That was what got me into trouble with Vivian, Marick. I felt guilty for imagining it. I never saw her again; she was gone. But when I walked back into this house, Vivian read me like a book. She knew.'

Marick spoke. 'Hugo, my friend. You did nothing wrong. You should be proud of yourself.'

They looked up with a start as Vivian returned to the verandah, bearing the next tray of food.

'Another disaster,' she exclaimed with an air that appeared to be delight. 'I am a hopeless cook. An intrepid experimenter, but useless in the kitchen.'

'That makes two of us,' Hugo's expression was forced, and he stood to help Vivian with her load.

Vivian did not acknowledge her husband's admission. 'Hugo, would you mind getting the plates from the kitchen. Wine, Marick?'

Marick shook his head. His head was already lighter than he would have liked. He found little joy in drinking. Although it would be easy to use his clerical role as an excuse, the truth was he felt lost in alcohol's grip. Where others found comfort in its invitation to mild oblivion, Marick was disorientated and flung to sea. And he realised he had some sort of job to do here, even though its intricacies he hadn't yet worked out.

'It's supposed to look like a trout,' Vivian said, peering at the dish. 'Kind of a gastronomic joke, according to the recipe. Chicken mince and vegetables, a few festoons, shaped into a fish. Christ only knows what this is.' She looked up at Marick. 'I am sorry. We do blaspheme quite a bit here.'

Marick laughed and could hear the sound as though he had speakers inside his head. An unfamiliar sound, but welcome. 'Do not worry in the slightest. I've been known to do it myself.'

They both beamed.

The verandah must have been set on a slight elevation because

Marick had a clear view out to the west. He looked up and was surprised to see the sun sinking in furious glory. Time had slipped away while they were sitting there. It was great brass band of a sunset. He said as much to Vivian, and she grinned again.

'Yes, isn't it lavish,' she said. 'You're right.'

'It's like seeing the inside of colours themselves.'

'Indeed,' she said, looking at him. 'Now watch it purple up. It always does.'

Hugo returned, transporting plates, cutlery, wine glasses.

'Oh my Lord, Viv, what's this?' Hugo pointed to her main course sagging on the serving plate. The three of them laughed with easy joy, a novelty for Marick, and a delight.

As Vivian was suggesting they should order pizza, the doorbell rang.

'Hell, they're early,' said Hugo.

Vivian made a complex gesture Marick couldn't quite read, a sort of one-shoulder shrug and a close-lipped line, and she headed off to get the door.

'I shall predict how this will go,' Hugo said to Marick, his voice quiet. 'Paul will bring in two bottles of red that he'll brag about getting on the cheap from his wine club. He does something with building development, which he'll tell you about within minutes. Leonie, that's Vivian's sister, will be whining about something that's gone wrong with her day: a customer, a failed delivery, the boys. Vivian will be a saint in return. Paul's face will turn the colour of his drink before they leave, and the pair of them will argue about something to do with money. Check me on this Marick. I'll bet I get a hundred per cent.'

And at least in this, Hugo did get all the facts correct.

NINE

One year with Diane became two. When he could not have imagined it possible to learn any more about another human, she would reveal more of herself. Physically, this translated to finding new parts of her, discovering fresh ways she experienced pleasure. He had taken a while to find any rhythm, but one day things were simply in tune. She admitted to having had a 'string' of lovers (her words – at no time did he ask), but none had taken the time to investigate what made her hunger for air while making love.

'It's like you listen to my body as well, Marick.'

Together they went out to pubs, listened to bands, discussed movies, talked, albeit with fading energy, of re-visiting Europe.

'Let's throw it all in, Marick. Open a bookshop. Maybe I could work for a chocolatier, or we could buy a market garden,' Diane said during a drunken night at a local hotel where the music was loud and possibly awful or wonderful. Neither of them could tell.

'Or get married,' he said. He thought he'd timed it for a break in the music.

'What?' she yelled.

'Nothing,' he shouted back.

But the thought had taken root. It was meant to be, he knew it. They went back to his flat and tore into each other. He made her climax again, and then again. He was too drunk to make much of a go of anything else, so was happy to be in her grip, with her hands clenching his hair, half-losing his mind between her thighs. On the third time, she called out, 'Oh God, Oh God!'

He didn't remember what he'd said to her in return, but Diane reminded him the next morning.

'I don't know,' she said. 'It's just prudish. You don't really think there's a God listening to us have sex, do you? I should be able to shout what I want. It spoiled the whole mood, like you were my dad, telling me off.'

He babbled apologies. Apparently, he'd reproached her for invoking God's name during her complex battle cry of sexual rapture.

'You don't even go to church,' she'd chastised him. 'Why should you care?'

He hadn't told Diane about his school-worn appetite to join the clergy. It now felt little more than an intellectual exercise, but he would like to study theology at some point. Take a night-school course. Go deeper. Understand the relevance of a significant part of their northern history. Work out, with an analytical brain asking for the hand of faith, what, who, how, in this fleshly life, is God?

He did attend the occasional church service though, and he wondered how it was Diane didn't know.

But more than that, he would ask again, in the sober, sparkling light of an autumnal day. With a ring this time. Why wait? Diane was the one, and he would never be persuaded of anything different.

❧

It was as though Leonie and Paul walked in surrounded by a cloud of noise, decibels swarming around them like insects. They were loud people, Marick could tell straight off. Paul, who did introduce himself to Marick as being 'in property', was liquored already, and banged his fist on the table after sitting, declaring all democracy was an illusion.

Leonie, who had wiry hair and was a little stocky – nothing like her sister – plonked herself down in one of the plastic outdoor chairs.

'I'd love a drink, Hugo,' she said. He poured her a generous glass of white, which she tipped down like water. 'What?' she said, glaring at Vivian. 'It's hot.'

'Have you had dinner, yet?' Vivian asked. 'We haven't eaten, and I've failed at my culinary creation. We thought we might order in.'

'Sure, as long as it's cold. Honestly, what is it with the weather? We haven't had a breeze in weeks.'

She had a point, Marick thought. The night was as warm as blood. Everything was sticky to the touch.

Hugo brought out more wine. 'Are you sure you don't want any?' he asked Marick.

'Marick's a chaplain at the hospital where Hugo works,' said Vivian.

In unison Paul and Leonie turned to him. 'A chaplain?' Paul said, as though Marick might be a zoo creature, invited to dinner on a chain. 'Bloody hell.'

'Please don't waste the dinner you've cooked, Vivian,' Marick said. 'I'll bet it tastes fantastic. It doesn't matter what it looks like.'

Vivian smiled back, and it was radiant. She made Marick think of an advertisement – for what he didn't know. A fragrance perhaps, or a travel destination. He had no idea why Hugo hadn't told him she was so beautiful.

The others had returned to a deep and theatrical conversation while Marick's attention had floated off.

'You're having a lend of us, surely.' Paul sat forward. His face was precisely the colour predicted by Hugo, and a sweet volatile smell poured from his mouth as he spoke, like paint.

'Hugo, I thought you didn't want anyone else to know yet,' Vivian said.

'We're family,' Leonie said. 'It's only right to share it with us.'

'It sounds like you've unearthed a golden goose,' Paul roared. 'We want in. Leonie's right. Family first, as they say.'

Hugo was riding high, Marick could see. He poured another glass for them all and raised his own.

'But Vivian's right. Keep it to yourselves until I get some solid proof. The experiments are going on as we speak.'

'Fucking alchemy, eh?' Paul said.

'Watch your language, Paul. There's a priest present,' Leonie said.

'Well, I'm not really a—'

'We've always thought you were talented, Hugo,' Leonie added.

Vivian looked at her sister, her mouth twisted, demonstrating that was not the case, and never had been.

'Biological gold,' Paul said. 'Can you imagine the take on that? Everybody will want a piece. You're going to need some good people around you, Hugo.'

'What are the experiments you're doing?' Marick asked, thinking that if he could bring the discussion back to the scientific, they might be able to skirt around that word, alchemy – it made him so uncomfortable. No matter how Hugo might explain it away, the word still implied that at its soul was magic.

'I'm glad you asked, Marick. They will be what proves it. Same conditions, different *E. coli*. I'm culturing a batch of the most boring *E. coli* you could imagine. *E. coli* B21 DE3.'

'Hugo,' Vivian said, 'that means nothing to any of us.'

'It's been watertight so far. My master-batch, there's gold in every one of them. Minute amounts sure, but I've recovered a gram so far. And not a twinkle in the control group. It's unbelievable.'

Somehow, they didn't eat dinner, Vivian's or otherwise. The stakes continued to be raised. Vivian repeated the word unbelievable, several times, and Marick knew she was working from a different definition to Hugo. More bottles of wine were drunk and the empty ones began to form an ominous pile in the yard. Paul grew louder. Leonie spent some time crying in the kitchen, and Vivian went in to console her.

'Just the usual,' Marick heard Vivian say to Hugo when she came back out.

'God, she's not at it again, is she?' Paul said and stumbled trying to get out of his seat.

'Go easy on her, Paul,' Vivian said. 'She's pretty stressed.'

Paul shook his head and punched some numbers into his phone, beckoning a taxi. 'Sure she is.'

Within minutes, a car horn sounded out the front.

Paul shouted, 'Call me!' as they departed, leaving blessed silence.

'I'd better go too,' Marick said. 'Thank you so much for inviting me.'

'But you haven't eaten anything,' Vivian said. 'You must come around again. I want to cook properly for you.'

'Yes, Marick,' Hugo said. 'Please.'

Marick could feel his face heat up, and when he hopped back on the train, rattling his way back, he imagined quieter dinner parties with just the three of them, and he whiled away the stops, lost in a pleasant fiction.

TEN

As Marick went to transfer from the train to the bus, he realised he'd left his housekeys at the hospital. He scrabbled through his pockets, but he knew they would be sitting in his satchel which was hanging on the back of his office chair. With no spare, and no other way to get into his triplex, he peered at the timetable pasted to the bus stop to figure out the best way to track back.

The night remained stolid. Nobody else was moving about in the suburbs. He was startled by a strange bird whistle, jumped at a dog barking. When the bus appeared, swinging round the corner, he exhaled with relief. Any magic the evening had held had dissolved, leaving a residue of faint disquiet. They were still a long way from understanding the happenings in Hugo's laundry.

Alighting from the otherwise empty night bus, he reached the front of the hospital, discovering the whole place had geared down into a more menacing mode. Although the moon glowed in an unassuming pocket of darkening sky, the air closer to him was full of blacker noises: the screech of horns, a lone shout, a truck reversing, police sirens. A queue of ambulances was lined up to offload their human cargo. He crossed the road, walking on the other side of the snake of vehicles, edging along the outside fence of the church. In the dark he did not see a pair of lonely figures up against the gates until he almost walked into them. They were hospital workers.

'I'm sorry,' Marick said.

One was a nurse, a heavy man with skin so dark his eyes made an incandescent contrast, white and downcast, as he leant against the fence, one leg bent behind him. He was smoking, concentrating on the cigarette as though deep in conversation with its wilted, disappearing form. The smell was acrid and bit the insides of Marick's nose. The man grunted and pinched the last of the cigarette to his mouth. Marick saw the pair were not together, but arranged separately like socialist statues past their time, forgotten and ignored where they stood.

The other was the doctor he had seen before. She sat on the curb, stone-still. Her shoulders were slumped and she was staring beyond the bitumen, beyond everything. Marick wanted to walk on, but he recognised pain when he saw it.

'Are you alright?' He spoke to both of them. 'I'm the hospital chaplain. It looks like you've had a bit of a time of it.'

The man tossed his cigarette butt to the path and ground it underfoot.

'The Devil's been dealing cards tonight,' he said.

The doctor made a half-laughing sound, brief – and cut it short. 'Pretty big hand,' she said. 'A lot in there. Car crash, no seatbelt. Ruptured spleen.'

'Methamphetamines,' he returned. 'That caged-animal roar.'

'Myocardial infarction, arrested coming through the doors.'

'That broken leg in a one-year-old. Bruises from days ago.'

'Nana from the nursing home, with no veins and no advanced orders.'

'Ace of spades,' the man said. 'I can't breathe.'

'Oh God,' the doctor said, and sunk her head into her hands.

Marick wasn't sure he'd be capable of hearing the stories behind any of those leads, but he swallowed anyway, and asked. 'Do you want to tell me? About any of them?'

The doctor smiled. She was so worn through, she seemed transparent in the thin light. 'If we got started, we'd never finish.'

'And we're both due back,' the nurse said. 'They're going to wait for no man.' He gestured with his head to where two more ambulances were rolling into the driveway.

'Thank you anyway,' said the doctor. 'We appreciate it.'

'Well, if you need to talk, you can always find me. I'm on pager.'

He knew, though, that nobody bleeped a pager when they needed to get things off their chest. A thought came to him. What the hospital needed was some sort of centre, a casual place, a haven for people to drop in and offload some of the pain of their days.

As Marick walked on, he heard them carry on.

'The Devil's won this round,' the nurse said.

The hospital, too, had changed its tune. Inside was a blast of noise layered over nothing. Near the front entrance a carpet-cleaning machine with a cyclonic roar was being driven by a man wearing headphones, creating damp circles as he moved from spot to spot. Dolly's shop was shuttered and dark.

He thought about those emergency staff out the front, preparing to go back into the unimaginable. They saved reams of people on a daily basis. He wondered whether he would ever get the chance to save a single one.

Marick swiped through the necessary doors, down, down, and retrieved his satchel. As he returned to the stairs to climb back out to the known world, he hesitated.

Biological gold, Paul had said. The sound of this made the already baffling even stranger. Marick slung his bag over his shoulder and asked himself the question in a different way. Was this his own chance here, a gift unexpected? An opportunity to be part of something greater? He needed to understand his role in all this. He had an urge to view the bacteria unwitnessed. Just him and their gold. He counted past the doors to find the alternative stairs to basement level three. He had to count – every time he had not, he'd taken a wrong turn, despite being sure at the time he finally had the route in his grasp.

Again he wondered whether this was one more problem that condensed into faith. Faith had always seemed to Marick to exist at the point where the answers finally ran out. As though it offered a bridge – convenient, he thought in his worst days – between the physical world with all its comprehensible machinations, and God on the other side. But this exposed the circuitous nature of the argument and its fibrous core, its knot. Without the bridge, there could be no vision of God, and thus, perhaps, no God at all.

This was where, for Marick, the questioning became unbearable, even nihilistic. Faith is the absence of questions, a depressed lecturer at theological college had told him, a man Marick had rather liked but whose contract was not renewed.

The revolving notion of this argument undermined his footing, a physical spin as he walked. The stairwell opened out near Hugo's laboratory. Surely though, he thought, faith does best when furnished with as many facts as possible, despite how it's advertised. He found the door. The threshold. Knowing it would be locked, he still tried the handle. He put his ear to the wood. It was not to hear what was going on inside, it was more to feel it. The thrum, the scuttle, the pulse. The sound, translated into the tangible, of possibility being cracked open. And then a sound from behind, a clank and a heavy accent.

'I help you?'

Marick spun around. Standing in front of him was an older woman, conical in shape, wearing a mango-yellow dress that was stretched over her humps and curves.

He stammered an excuse, embarrassed to be caught out like a cut-price thief.

She held a tarnished bucket with a long mop disappearing into its muddy depths.

'I let you in, if you like.' She glanced up at him. 'I clean down here. This whole block. All mine, like a kingdom.' Marick could tell she was smiling. She had an odd way of speaking. He, who was used to watching people's lips, could not see hers – she looked at the floor while she talked and her voice was muffled. The words he could make out were smothered in thick European vowels.

'It's alright. I'm just the chaplain,' Marick said, as if that made any sense.

'Lilyana, Father. Pleased to meet you.'

'I'm just leaving. You're working late, Lilyana.'

'Always, Father. I ask you something? Are you Catholic?

'Here I'm all denominations, Lilyana. And here for anybody who needs me.'

'Catholic is what I need.'

It was hard to see her face but Marick could sense her disappointment. He commiserated with her. Join the club, he wanted to say.

She shook her head, dismissing the conversation.

'I'm going home,' he added. 'I hope you get to do the same soon.'

How shameful it was to be creeping round somebody else's door, late at night, seeking fuel for his festering doubt. He wanted to trust Hugo. Deeply. And there was nothing to suggest he couldn't.

'Goodnight, Father.' Lilyana shuffled off, disappearing into the corridor.

During his trek home, doubt again joined Marick. It was his grim companion, rarely leaving, although it would often sit at the back somewhere, on slow boil. At one point during his theological studies, he had become obsessed with Nag Hammadi and the story of biblical doubt unveiled in the modern world, hauled out into the light. They had studied this episode in a breakout class, in Middle Eastern History, a subject he had come back to time and time again. Nag Hammadi was many things, but it was the unravelling that Marick had been drawn to, the narrative of it. The discovery of the lost gospels and codices in a cave in Egypt in 1945, which, instead of being shared and incorporated into the teachings of the Bible, were traded on the black market until they finally came to rest and were authenticated. Among the writings was the gospel of Thomas. Thomas represented doubt – he was its embodiment. And those newest of new testaments were all about doubt. If faith was supposed to be a foundational thing, solid and held together by religious roots, doubt was something buried far deeper, sealed in earthenware jars.

Two sides of a tumbling coin, Marick thought. Faith and doubt. But what else was alchemy if not a similar abstract concept? The making of new things from old? The mutation of bland to glittering? Illness to health, poverty to wealth? The dead inside the living? Transformation. Biological gold.

By the time he got home, Marick had decided the house of proof and reason may well be part prison instead of liberator. Marick let himself back in and prepared for four o'clock to come.

⁕⸝⸾⸝⁕

He asked again. Diane said yes.

There were disagreements about the ceremony. Marick had pictured a church wedding; none of her side agreed. 'They are paying for it,' Diane reminded him.

In the end it was glorious. There was a band, vows exchanged under a gazebo on a pier beneath an apricot sky, and speeches full of promise for the years to come. Diane's father booked out the entire front room of the yacht club for the reception; her mother didn't get a say in the decorating.

'This is my thing, my moment,' said Diane. And it was. The theme was white. Huge elaborate bows tied to the back of every chair, bevies of lilies on each table, curving their necks like swans. Balloons, muslin over chandeliers, and a flock of bride-

110

white doves released when Diane and Marick stepped outside for the waltz.

Marick's mother Deirdre had suffered a series of small heart attacks in the month leading up to the big day, so could not come across for it. Much later, when Marick was cleaning out her things, he discovered she had bought a special dress and matching hat that still had *mother of the groom* written on the delivery box.

Just before midnight the newlyweds were whisked away on a launch owned by a friend of Diane's father and secreted in a budget hotel, where they ate cold chips ordered from a fast-food eatery next door because they'd been too excited to eat during the reception. Marick sifted through the layers of her clothing, and then explored her afresh, like she was his own over-decorated wedding cake.

'What's this?' he asked, discovering a frilled band of lace around her upper thigh, wondering if he'd uncovered some type of amulet.

'It's a garter, Marick. Surely you've seen these. You're supposed to remove it with your teeth.'

Marick obliged with joy.

She fell asleep, but his heart was going like a snare. He got up and stepped outside. The night sky was tinsel, the air perfect, and he wanted to bay to the wind. He knew nothing would feel this good again. Something inside him had cracked open, split like a sunrise. The stars could drop from the sky and he'd still celebrate.

They ordered room service breakfast the next morning and spilt crumbs through the bed.

'Dad meant what he said, you know. In the speech.'

'That he hadn't thought you'd settle down so young?' Marick asked with his hand tucked under the warmth of her hip.

'No. About the job. He wants you at the firm. He'd be so proud. You'd be able to start straight away. You've only got another semester and it would mean you'd be earning from the get-go.' She rolled over and kissed him with unhurried care. 'A son-in-law and a colleague, he said.'

Marick had no problem with it. He liked Diane's father. He was a man who spoke his mind, plain and clear. Not a man who'd ever skulk away without word, Marick was sure. In certain moments, he would reveal a bitterness about the world, as if their family had missed opportunities that were never mentioned, but otherwise, his spades were well and truly called spades. Marick had no other plans for employment, so was happy to roll into whatever Diane's father planned for him.

They took their time getting dressed. It was as though their lovemaking was a measureless theatre to which they had front-row tickets. Diane screamed at her peak again, and somebody next door banged on the wall to get them to pipe down. Eventually, when presentable, they went walking, hand in hand around the river path. Marick felt bloated with happiness. The daylight was brilliant, torch-lit by a thousand suns, and had the drunken smell of gardenias and eucalypts. The gardens themselves were detonating with joy. It was such a strange feeling, at once a warm lethargy, walking with nowhere in particular in mind, and his insides on some sort of eternal cliff face. It was delicious, and exhausting.

The river was pond-flat that day. Boats played like toys on the water, birds lazed in the sky above.

'Let's talk about you.' Marick lifted her hand to his mouth, and kissed her knuckles, one by one. 'You'll be finished soon enough too. Where do you think you'll be applying?'

'God, I still don't know. All the jobs for interior designers seem so dreary in this town. You're just another cog in a corporate chain, working your way up until you're a bigger cog.'

'You've got such talent. You should be doing something amazing.'

'I know. I want to live my life on the leading edge. Be the tide. Do something incredible.'

'And you will. I have no doubt at all.' In that instant, Marick felt clairvoyant. She was exceptionally talented. He'd seen her sketches, heard her talk through her ideas. 'You shouldn't let anything get in the way of your dreams.'

'But how would I do that? Not working for the man?'

It became clear to them both at once. She would have a diploma, qualified to design. She would strike out on her own, straight from the outset.

'I feel sick with excitement,' she said. 'Of course. It makes sense. If you're earning money already, we can easily get by on a single income until business takes off.' She spoke so fast, Marick had trouble keeping up. 'My own place. A cute shopfront. Grey and white striped awnings. Hamptons style,' she said, although Marick did not know what this meant. When he did find out, he wondered when Europe had lost its place to America. 'I'll bet Dad will help us with a loan. I could do both – have a design-consulting service with a studio, and sell furnishings in the front, to complement my plans. Oh God, Marick. I can see it. I can hardly wait!'

They turned a corner and the sun shone into their eyes. It was fractal, shimmering, immense. They turned to each other and kissed, and Marick could feel his stomach leaving, his internal organs disappearing.

'Let's go back,' she said. And they did. The bed was still warm, and the pillows had remembered the shapes of their heads, and they didn't check out till evening.

ELEVEN

Word, true to its nature, got out. Marick should have guessed this was coming.

Perhaps it was the internet chat groups Hugo abandoned when he found them of little value, leaving them to bud off into small, propagating branches, or Paul's careless conversation during drinks with the boys later that week, or simply that rumours of such wildness were like water, finding any crack in its relentless reach to the ocean. However it happened, news of a man practising alchemy in the basement of a tired, inner-city hospital spread.

It was slow to begin with. Marick hoped it could be contained. As he strode past Dolly's shop in the morning, she barrelled out to meet him.

'Father. Have you heard? What's happening in our very hospital?'

Dolly relayed the sequence of conversational events that had reached her ears and finished with the news that somewhere inside the bowels of their great institution, a scientist had discovered bacteria that could make gold.

'Gold, Father! Can you imagine?'

Marick shook his head. 'Hard to, that's for sure.'

'What do you think? Is it a miracle?'

Again, that word. 'I wouldn't—'

'It's occurred to me, Father, that this is probably a sign.'

'A sign of what, Dolly?'

'I'm very attuned to signs, Father. A sign that says if a miracle can happen right at this precise moment, it means another chance might have opened up for me.'

'I'm sorry, what chance, Dolly?'

'To hand on my kidney. I've spoken to the Pathology Department this morning. I'm going to get my bloods done today. You don't work at a place like this for twenty years without accumulating a few favours.'

Dolly's cheeks were flushed in ruby patches. Marick did not have the heart to question her. But he would regret letting the talk of miracles go unchecked. He would fail at many things during the following week, but in retrospect this was, he was quite sure, the seed.

She had a hand to her hair, smiling in victory, and, unable to find much else to offer, Marick murmured, 'Good on you.'

'Thank you. I'll keep you posted. And I keep meaning to ask, Father, have you decided where you're going to give your Christmas sermon?'

'Sermon?' Marick asked. This had not crossed his mind.

'It's a tradition,' she said.

Marick scrabbled for an excuse but came up blank.

'I can organise the amphitheatre for you,' Dolly continued. 'Will you be wanting audio-visual equipment? A lectern? I'll advertise it for you, make sure you get a crowd. It's only three days away, but my telegraph is very effective.'

Marick backtracked. 'I didn't know there was such a place here.'

'Amphitheatre's a bit of an exaggeration. It's the grassed area behind the psychiatric unit. Excellent spot, shady all morning, lovely acoustics. It's where we've held our little concerts and such over the years.'

He didn't want to give a Christmas sermon. He didn't want to give any sermons. Certainly not to a crowd. His working life was now supposed to play out in the quiet of cubicles and rooms, with personalised words and nobody looking over his shoulder.

'Perhaps you could talk about miracles in our midst,' Dolly added. She may have winked as he turned to leave.

Marick bypassed his office and took the circuitous route through the greying tunnel to get to Hugo. He used his knock, twice, but there was no answer. The corridor was empty and the absurd piles of discarded equipment seemed to have grown overnight. It occurred to Marick that Hugo might well be upstairs in his proper laboratory, working at his official job. He often forgot his friend even had one.

At the front desk of Specimen Reception, a secretary looked up from a matted pile of forms.

'Hugo Francis? I'll check.' She punched a number into her phone and pressed the mouthpiece that curved off her headphones to her lips. On her desk were several plants in pots, in one of which was a small sign. *No rubbish please. I'm alive.*

'Hugo is always so hard to get hold of,' the secretary said. 'I never know what he's up to. And I've had a whole lot of people ring this morning for him. Been like Grand Central for phones. Hang on, he's answering.' She turned her head away. 'Hugo? You've got someone come to see you. It's the chaplain by the looks.'

People always knew. Even without the gold cross, he suspected they'd know.

Twenty seconds later, Hugo appeared in front of him. For a moment, Marick thought Hugo was embarrassed to see him there.

'Let's go elsewhere,' Hugo said, grabbing Marick's arm.

'How long will you be gone?' The secretary called out. 'We have quotas, you know.'

They disappeared through the fire door.

Inside the laundry, the familiarity was comforting.

'It's out, you realise,' Marick said.

'I do,' Hugo replied, leaning back onto the bench and clutching his neck in his hands. 'I've had some chap from the Australian Association for Alchemists ring me this morning. Who would have thought that is a thing. They're mainstream now, he told me. Brian, the alchemist. Go figure.'

It was a precipice. Marick knew he had to dive. 'Hugo, if this is going public, we will need to be very sure …'

He wanted to repeat the sentence using the singular – *I need to be very sure* – but Hugo had begun pacing, tricky in the confined space.

'What I need,' Hugo spoke in rapid fire, 'is to speed up the experiments. Make sure the data is watertight.'

'Do you think' – Marick was tentative – 'that perhaps getting an independent scientist to come in and watch, or verify or do whatever they need to do might help validate your research?'

Hugo stopped and stared at Marick, his eyes wide.

'Don't you believe me?'

'Hugo. Of course, I do; that's not what I meant.'

'That's what you're here for. Well, not just that; Marick, you are my friend too. My ally in all this. I know the discovery feels crazy, but you've seen it, Marick. And besides, another pair of hands in this tiny room? I can see the whole delicate thing being messed up.' He threw his arms wide to demonstrate something, perhaps how small the room was in comparison to their ideas. 'But,' he said slowly, 'maybe you've got a point. When it comes to credibility ...' Hugo's face looked like a squall, his brow twisted.

'Perhaps help me understand more then, Hugo. Tell me about these bacteria. Where they really come from. What they truly are.'

'Let's get a coffee.' Hugo exhaled. 'It's a bit of a story. Let's avoid the big cafe. How about the one behind the art gallery?'

The hospital had two cafes. One ruled the main walkway, serving standardised coffee from an automated machine charging overinflated prices to the desperate. The other, hardly patronised, sat behind the tiny cultural centre of the place.

'An art gallery. In a hospital. How have I not known about this yet?' It still surprised Marick to learn of territories he had not to date discovered.

'And the coffee's better,' said Hugo.

They walked down a ramp on the western side of the hospital and into an empty enclave. Marick dropped a gold coin into the gallery donation box at the front. The antechamber was deserted and they progressed into the gallery proper, an ancient hall with old-fashioned, elaborate cornices. It had a few spider webs, looped like snowy vines in its corners. There was a single wall of faded paintings – all done by patients the plaques boasted: chrome-yellow flowers, orange flickers on white, depictions of sickrooms with daubed representations of equipment, ash, bursts of night sky, amateur landscapes with box-like renditions of the church across the road painted from top-floor windows. Most of the works had a melancholy about them – the seclusion of the sick.

'They're not Caravaggios, are they,' Marick commented as they passed through.

The coffee, as Hugo had predicted, was excellent. They vacillated for a bit, chatted of nothings, as though they might delay this possible reckoning. Marick confessed his unease about the Christmas sermon. Hugo made a snide remark about Vivian's catering, about which Marick felt oddly affronted, although he made no comment. Eventually they got to the crux.

'So, the bacteria. What's going on, Hugo? Where, exactly, did you get them?'

'That's the thing. I didn't.'

Marick sipped his latte.

'Maybe you won't believe me, but it's true,' Hugo continued.

'Have you spoken a mistruth to me yet?' Marick asked.

Hugo replied immediately. 'Not once.'

'Then I shall continue in the same vein, my friend, of trusting what you tell me.'

Hugo reached out and gave Marick's arm a squeeze. It was such an intimate gesture in this indifferent space, but Marick understood. Trust like this is rare and precious, it signified, and we are fortunate to have it.

'Hunan Province. Just outside, actually. In a little hamlet. I'm going to need another one of these.' Hugo indicated his cappuccino.

'I'll get it for you.' Marick paid for a second coffee, and returned to their small table, out of earshot of the scatter of other customers.

Hugo settled into his story with vigour.

During his early days at the university, he told Marick, while Vivian and he were first dating, when Hugo was just another burden on the research grant application calendar, when he couldn't decide whether to branch into eukaryotes or prokaryotes, proteins or antibodies, health or disease, he read several vague papers about a super-charged strain of *E. coli* in a tiny laboratory in rural China.

'Everybody knew what super-charged meant back then,' he explained to Marick. 'Gene-manipulated.'

Hugo glanced around. Nobody was close enough to hear. He continued.

'This was pre-CRISPR days, you have to understand, Marick. It was close to impossible to do, but not entirely.'

Marick slotted the words he did not recognise into his memory so he could look them up afterwards and not interrupt Hugo mid-flight.

On impulse, and surprised he managed to secure funding, Hugo had organised a trip with the excuse of presenting one of the university's own papers on improving bacterial culture milieu.

Hunan was like nothing he'd ever seen. Hugo had rarely travelled, not even getting to India and the storied city of his mother. Every experience in China was a cumulative shock. A dense, richly hued shock. He'd always pictured China as concrete and smog, but his destination was anything but. He reached the village by rickety train, travelling abreast a rain front. The steep slopes into the valley of the town were consumed by billowing green vegetation, thick as dream jungles, and the whole place was hung with mist and foliage. The river flowed like mercury along the village floor and itself appeared green. This was illusion though, a reflection of the onslaught of trees, leaves, lichens, moss and shrubs. Compact farms were tucked among paddies, lush in deep green tiers. There were stone bridges and shanties down to the water line, curling smoke and the smell of steaming buns. Hidden temples. Sacrifices to deities left anonymously on the winding streets. Music. Incense. He experienced it all as a type of love, an inexpressible emotional connection from the second he hit the ground.

The laboratory team, however, was not expecting him, and had no intention of discussing their bacteria. The papers he had read were preliminary, and none of the publications' authors worked there. There was a collective frown and a shake of heads when the words 'genome-editing' were mentioned.

Hugo roundly misread the social cues and somehow managed to bumble his way into an invitation back the next day, and the next, and then a sort of friendship, with the wonders of *E. coli* at the core.

They warmed to an enjoyment of each other's attempts to explain the commonalities of a laboratory life – the shackles of bureaucracy in scientific endeavour, the nuances of nucleic acid sequencing, the push to publish. Their English was excellent.

Hugo did his best to learn as many Xiang words as he could, which he sounded out loud at night in his room. He tinkered with one of their computer programs and solved an annoying translational bug by illegally accessing his own university's servers, and gave them passwords they could use to download anything they wanted from the Biotechnology Department.

On the last night of his visit, he and his new friends found themselves at a local bar serving shot glasses lit with opalescent flames, which were slid down the benchtop, only permitted to be consumed if caught and drunk while still alight. At the end of a succession of emptying slugs of the abrasive baijiu down his throat, he told them of a dream he didn't realise he'd had until that moment. He wanted to enable the humblest of all organisms to change the world. *Save* the world, he remembered upping the ante. His friends raised their glasses. 'Stop Sepsis,' one exclaimed. 'Cure Cancer!' another shouted, and they downed one more. Two of the men ended up sleeping the night on the floor of Hugo's hotel room. They said a stilted goodbye the next morning, and when Hugo got to the airport he discovered his wallet was missing. But on arriving home and unpacking his suitcase, he found a battered box wrapped in brown paper containing an airtight tub with what was to be his future. How the bacteria had managed to survive the flight he did not know – perhaps it had been the chill of the aircraft hold. But survive they did, and Hugo had them growing and dividing within the day. He tried to contact the boys in the lab about a fortnight later to thank them but discovered the phone disconnected and the emails he sent bounced back.

'Fate,' Hugo said, looking Marick directly in the eye. 'Hard to imagine it was anything else.'

'And you've kept that batch going the whole time?' Marick asked.

'I have. They had an incredible edge when they were producing proteins. But you know, I've never looked too closely into them. Never sequenced them out. There didn't seem to be a point; they could adapt to any DNA request I gave them. It felt like it would be tempting fate, and I don't use that expression lightly. The DNA I fed them was nothing special. Everybody was using those sequences. It was these particular bacteria that were the magicians.' Hugo peered into his coffee. 'Of course, they were still only proteins I was producing in the lab. Plain, boring proteins. Nothing like an entirely new molecule.'

Hugo ran his hands through hair, stopping halfway through to grip his skull.

'That seems like millennia ago though, instead of eight years. God knows how I've gone from that to having Brian, a man from the Australian Association of Alchemists, on my case. And the hospital executive office has been leaving messages for me. I'm to attend a meeting. I need you there, Marick, when I go. Be my third rail.'

'I need you there,' Diane said to him. 'I can't do it without you.'

Opening night for Upstate Downtown had been postponed several times. Diane's mother said it was a good thing. It stretched the celebrations out this way, she said. But Diane was short with her and told them she could not face ringing the caterer again. It was the awnings holding the whole process up. The fabric wasn't what Diane had in mind, and she was clear about starting her brand as she meant to continue. In the end, she went with a pale duck-egg blue in the stripes. 'It's not the same,' she complained, but nobody else noticed anything amiss.

Around eighty people had been invited, most of them Diane's school and university friends. Diane's mother had her tennis girls and book club, and her father the yachting fraternity coming. 'It's like a wedding again,' her mother said. 'Who are you inviting, Marick?'

Diane's mother meant well, but they all knew her question was rhetorical. Marick had been working hard at her father's firm and was well liked by everybody, but not quite enough to crack the Friday drinks or Sunday barbecues. One of his co-workers had slipped it to him that this was because of the boss's son-in-law thing. Diane's father could be a bit of a tyrant, and everybody knew you didn't mix business with pleasure with family, or something like that.

In the end, though, it was a great night.

'Where else would I be, but right by your side, honey?' Marick said in response to Diane's plea.

There was an open bar, with plastic cups for the cider and chardonnay, and the caterer's teenage children sailed round with platters of salami and olives to a soundtrack chosen by Marick. The speeches were upbeat, the future exciting. A great night until Marick realised he couldn't see Diane. By eleven o'clock, when her father was roping some of the younger folk into stacking furniture and cleaning up to save money on getting cleaners back the next day, Marick found Diane crying in the bathroom.

'Sweetheart, what is it?' He pulled her close, trying to make a cocoon for her, wrapping his arms around her shaking ones. Tears trickled into his shirt, seeping through until his shoulder was wet. 'The night was a raging success, honey. Everybody loved the shop. Your ideas. And your friend who's going out with the journalist was there. Cannily done, I say.' He kissed the top of her head. 'Great publicity.'

She held out a flat plastic stick for him to see. Two little windows in it. Both with a bright line inside, shining in the tiled room as though they were backlit.

It took some time for the enormity to sink in. Marick stared at it. Diane watched him while he did.

They were pregnant. Marick was standing with his clever wife, in the bathroom of her own business, their own business, looking at a line which would change the trajectory of every other line of their own from here on.

'My God, Diane. This is … But how and why are we seeing this now?'

'Lisa.' This meant nothing to Marick. 'She brought it in for me. Said she'd had her suspicions for weeks.'

'But it's wonderful! Amazing! We're going to have a baby!' Marick knew he was sounding like an information-drunk fool, but he didn't care. He grinned until his jaw hurt. There would be three of them now. Three.

※

There were not many grins over the next week. Marick was lost, twisted.

'I have just opened my own business; how do you *think* I feel?' Diane shot at him in response to his questions. It was difficult to find the right thing to say. The conversation, as he had begun to fear, turned to talk of abortion.

'There'll be plenty of other chances. We're so *young.*'

'I'm twenty-five. Not that young.' Marick was desperate.

Marick was unsure when his night terrors had begun, but they had started to shape themselves in high school. One that featured early in his unsleeping brain had been triggered by nothing more than a school play. In his final year, a seventeen-year-old student had been hauled out of school to abort a pregnancy. He only knew because when she came back, she wrote repeated stories about the ordeal in their English classes, going so far as to spring a surprise performance at one of their assemblies. Her stories had been so visceral the details stuck, images which flared back at him while he and Diane were discussing the possibility of their own – his fellow student having to walk past a parade-ground of women with neat, blonde children in tow, shouting inches from her face and holding up signs. She'd described the chill of the thin gown, the antiseptic vacuum of the room, the doctor standing over her like a judge, the comments he made about her as she grew grey with sleep – words she couldn't distinguish, whether he'd said slut or shut – and the murk that looked like dirt in her underwear for weeks. The teachers intervened at that part and manhandled her off the stage. Not long after the play, she was taken out of school altogether, and rumours whipped around the school that she had suffered a mental breakdown and was having electric shock therapy.

It wasn't that he was against abortions. Marick believed strongly in the autonomy of women and their bodies. It was just this one. Their baby. Their own miracle. Something from nothing.

By the time Diane had an ultrasound, they discovered it was too late anyway. She was seventeen weeks gone. They could see the baby's face. And she was a girl. Seeing the tiny, curled fists on screen, the insistent throb of the heartbeat, the perfect eyes, changed Diane in the space of an appointment, and from there on they eased into sedate, shared anticipation.

Diane's father had agreed with Diane. 'You're so young,' he said, but Diane's mother was ecstatic. Diane had an older brother who lived in Ecuador, working for an obscure mining company, and everybody knew without saying a word that he would never produce any children of his own.

It was agreed; Diane's father would underwrite her business expenses, keep it ticking over. Marick would help out of course, in any way he could.

Diane grew large and radiant. Upstate Downtown was mentioned less and less. Marick scrambled over to her abdomen if she said the baby was moving, so he could lay his head on her, hoping for a kick to the ear. They painted a nursery and spent evenings thinking of names. Claudia, they both agreed on after crossing out pages of unsuitable ones. Claudia.

TWELVE

Marick was happy to accompany his friend. He was the wingman, Hugo's fraternal support – yes, his ally.

The executive offices were in an area he had not yet had the chance to see. The pair needed to take a specially designated set of lifts which set the tone from the outset. Silver doors and brass buttons. There were no others like them in the complex.

'What do you think they'll ask you?'

They both presumed it would be related to the discovery, but neither could predict which way the meeting would turn.

'I don't know. Vivian thinks they'll be testing the waters. If they truly knew what is happening downstairs, they would have organised a search party. Vivian is always right about these things. Comes from years of being a counsellor. She can see into the hearts of men.'

Marick had thought about Vivian a good deal since their dinner. He imagined she would be an outstanding support for students trying to find their way into adulthood. It was perhaps the openness of her face, her pale skin and wide-set, yellow-green eyes. She was non-judgemental in appearance alone, with her aura of respect, of kindness. Hugo was a lucky man.

'And talking about Vivian,' Hugo said as the lift pinged, 'she wants me to ask you over for Christmas lunch. I told her I'm sure a priest has more spiritual things to do on the day of our Lord and all that, but she insisted. Not that I don't want you to come. On the contrary.'

The two men stepped inside and pressed the button to take them to the top.

'As it happens,' Marick said, 'I am free. Just the brief service here at the hospital in the morning,' – he tried not to make a face at the prospect – 'and then nothing planned. Normally I would,' he added, worrying, not for the first time that Hugo would think him pitiable, a loner not by choice, 'but this year's been a bit of an upheaval, what with the new job.'

They stepped out into the quiet of plush carpet and jarrah-panelled walls. A few tasteful sprigs of tinsel were dotted over the cornices. Down the corridor, they could see the walls were hung with portraits; a collar of thirty or so deferentially photographed men's heads.

Marick read a plaque that ushered in the parade. 'All the Executive Directors.'

A prim receptionist asked them to wait, and they took seats on the least uncomfortable-looking chairs.

When they were ushered inside, it became clear Vivian was correct. It was all fishing, little substance.

'June,' the woman at the head of a long, mirror-shiny table said, standing to shake Hugo's hand. 'Program Director. And this is Fraser,' she gestured to the man sitting next to her, 'Director of Operational Services.'

'Aren't you the chaplain?' Fraser looked at Marick. He turned to ask June, 'Why is the chaplain here?'

June was impressive on her feet. Professional from head to toe with muted pantsuit and organised hair. Taller than Fraser.

'No idea. I didn't invite him.'

'He's here as my support,' Hugo said.

'Do you need it? I'd thought we were here for a preliminary chat. What do you think we're going to do?'

Hugo glanced over at Marick, not finding an answer for June.

She launched. 'Preliminary, as I said. There are rumours, Hugo, and I'm sure you understand we don't like rumours here, that you are conducting some research on the premises, which is not in an official capacity.'

'Our premises. Our coin,' Fraser's voice had risen a little.

'I'll handle this,' June said to Fraser. 'I'm sure you're aware,' June continued, 'that we have strict policy about these sorts of things. So I'm going to give you the benefit of the doubt, and simply say that whatever might be going on, and wherever it is, it can't continue, and I hope we don't have to have any further conversation about it.'

Marick could sense what Hugo was thinking. *They aren't even going to ask what it is.*

'Does that sound reasonable to you?'

Hugo nodded. 'I understand.'

'Excellent. That's it then.' And she stood.

Marick and Hugo made to leave, but Fraser spoke up.

'It's just that these rumours are quite unusual.'

The conversation turned to fishing with a very sharp hook. Fraser said he had been fielding some odd phone calls, including one from a United States pharmaceutical company that had a branch in Australia and was keen on having a meeting. Into novel arthritis treatments, they'd told him.

'Whole world's trying to cure arthritis, and we're trying to stay ahead of the curve, they said, so they'd like to meet the man in question. What man in question, I asked them,' Fraser said, 'which was where your name came up, Hugo. When they explained what they were on about, I had to laugh.'

Fraser did not look like a man to laugh.

Hugo was positioned at an odd angle. He had begun to walk out but had stalled when Fraser began and he remained motionless, as though without movement he might not spark any further discussion.

'Because it is laughable, isn't it, Hugo. Notwithstanding that using gold for rheumatoid arthritis has been out of vogue since the last sacking of a governor-general – my clinical mates assured me of this one – but these guys want to come and see, all the same. I set them to rest though. Because gold, and I really want you to correct me if I've got the wrong end of the stick here, never has been, and never will be, produced by bacteria.' Fraser's face had a look of distaste, as though he could smell something unpleasant.

June flashed Fraser a look, as if to say, *We discussed this.* She piped up. 'We do not want any scandals here, Hugo. We're a proud institution.'

Hugo's face was as white as a knuckle and he appeared to have lost the ability to speak. Marick stepped in. 'Thank you so much for asking us along. You don't have anything to worry about.'

'I'm glad to hear that,' June peered at his badge, 'Marick. Here's hoping this is the last we hear of this, yes?'

They retreated to ground level.

Hugo was lost somewhere in his thoughts as they walked. Fair enough, too. So was Marick. Just once, he wanted to hear Hugo say he was going to get an independent scientist in on this. He could not ask again – already he felt he'd pushed the point too far.

Hugo had regained his colour, buoyed when he finally spoke. 'You know what this means, don't you, Marick?'

Marick – and this was the least of everything bothering him – did not.

'It means somebody big wants what we have. If we are smart about this, go about it the right way, I bet we could secure some major funding. But when I say smart, I mean genius smart. Retaining absolute academic control. I've been thinking how we could scale up production, but it would need some seriously heavy-duty backing.'

Marick turned to his friend. 'Hugo. This feels too fast. There's so much about it that you, that we, don't understand.'

'Marick. That is the problem with being a priest.'

Marick could tell Hugo was trying to make light of what they were saying, but was somehow missing, glancing off the side.

Hugo elaborated, 'You're all so hung up on the *why* of things,' he continued, 'when in science all we have is fealty to the *how.*'

'But Hugo. You don't even have that yet. One step at a time. Your words.'

The thought of an American multinational glaring into the intimacy of the laundry made Marick feel stripped of clothing, of armour. As though he not only had allegiance to the first man he had called friend in many years, but to the delicate organic process budding in the layers beneath them.

As they emerged into the main thoroughfare, Marick's pager reminded him he had more conventional things to do, and the two men parted ways. Their farewell was a little stiff.

On a small ward, through the back of several less frequented outpatient clinics, was a sunny balcony built in to make more bed-space.

'It was only supposed to be temporary,' a cheery nurse told him as he was escorted out there. Marick was wanted to sit beside a frail, lemon-yellow man with terminal liver failure, to witness a will alteration.

'Are you sure it's me you want?' Marick asked. 'Aren't you supposed to do this in front of a Justice of the Peace? Or a lawyer?'

Most of Marick's knowledge of wills came from movies.

'Anyone can, Father, as long as they're trustworthy,' the nurse said. Marick took a minute, considering how valid this might be right now.

Marick waited for the man to form whatever words he needed to get down. It was slow going, but he finished off a sentence he had been working on and signed his name with a flap to his hand so vast, his pen hardly stayed on the page.

Marick had never seen someone this yellow. If it was lemon, it was over-ripe. He was almost green, and the whites of his eyes looked stained, a permanent colour of bronze.

'Are you clear about what you want?' Marick asked. It appeared that he was signing away his life's possessions to a charity for abandoned dogs, removing a distant relative from the deed.

'Couldn't be more certain, Father. I haven't seen Peter in years, and now I'm dying he sends flowers every day. I've never liked flowers.'

Apart from the floral aversion it all sounded entirely reasonable. Marick sensed his phone buzzing in his pocket but he ignored it to give his full attention to the issues at hand. The man with the swollen belly and the thinning hair and the veins snaking like tentacles down his neck and underneath his gown assured Marick he was entirely orientated, coherent and competent to understand the ethics of what he was about to do.

Marick counter-signed, and as he was asking whether the gentleman would like anything spiritual, a deep thud – a single bass note with a brief reverberation – shook the window to the ward. A bird.

'Excuse me,' Marick said, and strode outside. After all the bottled-up concern of the last few days, he had a sudden and urgent need to save something, anything. He remembered his father saying that when birds fly into windows they can get winded, or concussed, baffled by the rudeness of glass, and need a helping hand to make sure they get breathing again.

He turned corners, found an exit door, arrived at the foot of the window and saw the bird was not hurt, but perfect in death. A small robin-like creature with pearly feathers on its underside, was upended and its clawed feet stuck up like antennae, at skewed, unnatural angles. There was no sign of injury. No blood, no jaundice or loose skin or the bruises he was now accustomed to seeing, an animal not swollen with medicine or shocked by the injustice of finality, just the shimmer of feathers, white like surrender, unmoving.

135

He squatted next to it, adding it to the list of dead things with an invitation into the vault of his own skull. The poor, tiny thing. He pushed it, to be sure, but there was not a breath, not a movement. And then he found he could not get up. Nothing in his own body moved. The weight of the recent days became solid on his shoulders. His eyes felt like they should be watering but his tear ducts had seized up. He wondered whether he was having a stroke, and the word itself, usually a thing of horror and blame, seemed for the first time a kind of blessing. He would suffer it too. He found himself rejoicing. Of course, this was how he should end. It would be fitting. He deserved it. He would no longer have to face the rift between what should and should not be. Another release. He loved Hugo. He was sure of it now. Never had he felt so trusted by anyone whose neither pay nor path to salvation depended on it. But it still tore at him, this need to know, the truth of what his friend was cultivating in that tiny room. And all of it, right now, was too much.

He beheld the bird, taking in its piercing details: its olive-black eyes dull and stuck forever open, the pencil-shaped beak, skin that could have been ancient – the colour of coffee grounds – wrapped in whorls and folds around its stick-like legs, its brawny little wings laid back like interment robes, its serenity in death. But as he took in the magnificent details of the tiny world of a body, the liminal moment passed. His circulation returned to him in spindles. Marick understood he was not having a stroke. This was not karma, neither was it reprieve. He could feel his fingertips again and he hauled himself, with a little regret, to his feet.

Scooping up his broken charge he walked towards an emaciated garden bed a little further on, the still-warm creature cupped in his hands. This one at least he could bury. Nobody would inch him out this time. The concrete-rimmed bed of dirt and dried stalks and neglect was at least out of the way of the main thoroughfare. He would deposit the bird there.

As he exited the block into a turn of weather, now a dense humidity, with the sky sliding into gun-metal, almost silver, he remembered the missed phone call. Managing to dial his voicemail and hook his phone between ear and shoulder, he listened to the message.

It was Vivian.

'Marick.' She sounded breathy on the phone, and he held it so close to his ear it hurt, 'I've been thinking, wondering really, I would love the chance to catch up, to chat. Just the two of us. It's all so strange, isn't it? Would there be any chance at all you could drop by? I have tea,' she said, and something else he didn't catch, no matter how many times he replayed the message. He dropped the bird in the nearest bed and tossed a little soil over it. His hours were done for the day, so why not?

As Diane's due date grew closer, Marick lost some of his equanimity. He felt tidal, diurnal, washing from tender concern for Diane's ankles, or her heartburn, or her nutritional intake, to poring through books about what might go wrong. Diane, on the other hand, became calmer.

'I've written a birth plan,' she told him. 'As natural as possible. Epidural only if the labour is prolonged. Skin to skin straight away. See if you want to add anything.' She showed him the dot-points written in curling script on her own stationery they'd had made for the store.

'I just want two healthy girls,' he said, kissing the insides of her milky wrists. It had surprised him to watch Diane change. Early on he had been convinced she would have wanted the least thorny path — but she had shifted into a woman who talked about experiencing the time-honoured rites of her ancestors.

'Pain is part of it, Marick. They all managed, so why can't I?'

She spent hours stroking her drum-tight belly and playing classical music to their unborn child in the hope it would improve neuronal development.

But in a single doctor's visit fear swept in like a riptide. He used words like 'bed rest', 'blood pressure', 'intrauterine growth retardation' and 'proteinuria'. Diane was ordered to the couch while Marick was sent back and forth to the chemist to fill scripts. He took extra time off work, which his father-in-law, after some persuasion, agreed to.

'We should schedule this one to come out early,' one of the obstetricians said. 'Things will only get dicier from here.'

Diane remained confident. 'Let's just let it go a little longer. I'll bet I can do this.'

She couldn't. When Diane broke into a dull, slow labour, the midwife, after one look at the monitoring trace, called the obstetrician in the middle of the night. Diane was whipped into the operating theatre while Marick scrawled his signature on a consent form he didn't get the chance to read.

'General anaesthetic,' the anaesthetist said as he closed the preparation room door in Marick's face. 'You can't come in.'

There was no skin to skin. There were only bubble-like visits to the neonatal intensive care unit where little Claudia (could he do that, Marick wondered, name her while Diane was still in a haze of opiates and confusion?) sucked oxygen into her fluttering white chest. All he could do was wash his hands again and again in the hope he could hold her, only to be told, 'not today'. Tubes were changed, tiny ones for breathing, tinier ones for fluids, one for feeding that came and went over the week. There were serious conversations, not a word of which Marick remembered.

This was when prayer started back up – his rolling, begging bargains. Night and day, with desperation. The God he had put to the side was called back into action. Each morning Marick woke feeling like a bomb had gone off inside him – the china smashed, sparrows flitting through holes in the rafters, wind blowing through the rents of him. There's been a complication, he was told when he fronted up one morning. A small brain haemorrhage, a collapsed lung. There were more tubes. An operation. Diane was still away in a fog. She had an infection somewhere and it was proving difficult to shift. He took to prayer so hard he could hardly start a thought in his head without prefacing it with *Oh Lord*. In the end it became a simple pact. *Let Claudia live.* Marick's side of it was easy: a ready promise to live a godly life.

And within days, God arrived.

'They're resilient little buggers,' a paediatrician said with a smile.

Diane, as Marick discovered later, became a textbook case. It could have been an equation. Thwarted expectations plus an intensive care stay, milkless, absent contact plus the fear of mortality, with a few other variables thrown in for good measure.

'Does your wife have a history of depression?' Marick was asked at the clinic.

Diane required extended admission. One week, then two, then three. There was talk of electro-convulsive therapy.

'Sounds barbaric, I know,' her treating psychiatrist said, 'but effective.'

Marick learnt it all: formula feeding, nappy changes, car capsules, grow-suits and reflux and bone-aching fatigue. He ended up co-sleeping with Claudia, as it was easier to calm her that way. Diane's parents were distraught but unhelpful. They did bring the occasional dinner but baulked at looking after Claudia. Marick suspected they had a mortal fear of something so tiny and so clearly breakable. After a while, he didn't mind. How many modern fathers, after all, got to have this sort of experience with their newborn daughters?

The paediatrician warned him it was too early to know whether there might be complications from the haemorrhage. Marick hardly understood the shopping list of possibilities he was presented with: seizures, developmental delay, personality problems – or maybe nothing at all.

'We're all just slaves to time,' the doctor said.

The months shrank. The days swayed. Marick's unquiet slumber was his new earth. Everything changed, and nothing did.

THIRTEEN

Marick peeked around the side of the house.

In a formal exchange of text messages, Vivian told him she was going to do some gardening, try to get the place cleaned up before Christmas Day, so not to bother with the front doorbell. The temperature had crept up every hour, so that by three o'clock it was close to hitting forty. Nothing moved, the sun had staked its claim in the now glass-clear sky, branches had begun to wilt, and the birds did not have the energy to sing.

He found the side gate and felt for the latch, running his fingers over the rusted loop. As he hooked his fingers underneath the bolt, he was arrested by the sight of Vivian kneeling and bent over in the garden. Strands of her hair, honey-coloured he would guess to call it, were damp and stuck to her neck, with the rest piled up in haphazard fashion on her head. Her face, of which he could only see a fraction, was the red of mild exertion, more a flush than anything else. She wore loose, flowing pants and a singlet top. One of the straps had slipped from her shoulder, leaving the whiteness of her skin exposed to the sun. She wore no hat, no defence against its sadistic rays.

The yard was clotted with weeds, and the place breathed vegetation, a faint rotting odour of loamy fertility that he couldn't distinguish from death. He felt faint, boxed in by the smell, disturbed by the sight of Vivian's bare, mannequin neck curved over in toil. He blamed the heat. She was pulling out straggly, stringy weeds and tossing them into a pile in a corner of the yard. She sat upright at the sound of the gate.

'Marick. I'm so glad you came.' She rose from the ground with grace, barely using her hands to help her. Not for the first time, Marick wondered how old she was, and how it was she was so strong and muscled.

'I've made some lemonade. Home-grown lemons. Squeezed them myself. Will you join me?'

She brought out two glasses to the table. It was at least in the shade, so all they had to contend with was the sullen, slothful air. Well, that wasn't all. Vivian leant forward and passed him his drink, and he could again smell the spice of her perfume. It made him feel thick-headed and slow.

'Please don't think it strange I've asked you over here without Hugo. I am full of questions, and the poor man is so tied up with what's going on he can't field a sensible answer.'

'I can certainly try,' Marick said.

'I'm going to come out with it, Marick.' She took a long draught – nearly half the glass was gone when she placed it back on the table. 'Do you really believe Hugo's bacteria can make gold?'

The straightforwardness of her question was a wash of relief. She shrugged one of her shoulders, exposing a sheen of sweat on her upper arm, dotted with tiny sprays of soil, like starbursts. 'He trusts you implicitly, that much I can tell,' she added.

'Well, I have certainly seen the bacteria. And what's in them. It's hard to doubt what you can see with your own eyes. I've been into that laundry nearly every day and there's been nothing to make me question this isn't exactly what Hugo says it is. The experiments and the research all sound fitting and proper. He's meticulous about them, and there is nobody else who has access to that forgotten little room. But I hear you, Vivian.' He turned to face her and put his glass on the table. 'It seems so preposterous. Creatures making gold. Who could have imagined?'

Vivian was watching him as he spoke, and he felt himself colour. It was rare for him to talk like this: an unsolicited soliloquy, unbidden by the religious needs of others.

'Alchemy,' she said, taking another sip.

'I have to be honest,' Marick said, 'I am quite uncomfortable using that word. You can imagine why.'

'Well, I may not have much of a background in science, Marick, but I know you can't make gold from nothing.'

He let out a breath he hadn't realised he was holding. 'This is precisely the point where I began this journey. But the more I talk to Hugo about it, the more I realise how little we all understand about the way science works. Your husband has tried to teach me a few things about biology, chemistry, even subatomic physics, and about how so much of our physical universe is built on extravagant guesswork and hypotheses, with theories being repeatedly and definitively proven wrong over the years. Nothing's ever unassailably right. All those disciplines, those ideas, have their limits, he tells me.'

'Does he really say that? That he's committed to proving all possible theories wrong, in order to prove this one right?'

Marick thought back. Had Hugo? Or was this what Marick had wanted him to say. To assure Marick of the robustness of his scientific inquiry. Marick's throat was dry, and he took a sip of his own drink. It was tart, narrow, tasted in the nose more than the mouth, but when he swallowed, its passage down his gullet was cool as a wind change. They sat still for a short while, the afternoon taking no notice of them. 'Strange things like this are happening all the time,' Marick added, 'all over the planet. It's just this one has happened in our backyard.'

Vivian laughed, a glorious tinkle of a sound. 'Not this one, thank God, disaster zone as it is. I'll bring the jug out.'

Vivian floated as she retreated inside. Looking around, he caught sight of the sheep skulls on the back fence and, again, was reminded of death. He thought back to the little bird he had half-buried, wondering how long it would take to become skull and fragile bird bones itself. And the macerated process in between, returning it to soil and worm, to decay and rot. Nausea welled in his stomach, and he took another gulp, chastising himself for mixing the beauty of the afternoon – a gentle chat with his friend's delightful wife – with death. The humidity wasn't helping. When does a body become a corpse? What happens to the molecules, the atoms, the electrons that make up a human? And if all living things are explicable in terms of molecular makeup, then what, in the deepest reaches of the universe, made up God?

'Are you alright, Marick? You look pale.' Vivian had brought out a large perspiring glass decanter, brimful of squash. She filled his glass with deliberation. 'Gold, though,' she said. 'What a thing.'

Marick sipped again. 'I know. Such a fabled substance.'

'Is there a story in the whole of human history that doesn't somehow have gold threaded through it?'

'I don't think so,' he said with a smile. 'At every turn. And not just factual history. It's woven through the myths as well. Is gold an enabler or enslaver of men, you have to wonder?'

'And women,' Vivian said. 'The number of friends I know who would rather have a gift of gold than anything else.'

'Gold is immortal, did you know? It doesn't corrode.'

She cocked her head to the side. 'I do know gold was considered the flesh of the immortals. El Dorado, the gilded one, coated in mud and gold dust to personify the gods. As though he was an underground god himself. But tell me where it fits in your book.'

Marick smiled. 'The Bible? It's everywhere. The Israelites dancing around Aaron's golden calf; the temples built by Solomon with their columns of gold.'

'This is fascinating. I never get to talk like this. Where else?' Vivian leant forward, her chin resting in her free hand.

Marick tipped the rest of his drink down. He'd read so much about gold in recent days, and here was an opportunity to let the knowledge loose. 'Jason's Golden Fleece for a start, retrieved with the help of his Argonauts. And gold is in all the great stories of civilisation – Babylon, Nineveh, Persepolis. Thessaly. Tutankhamun's tomb. The Urals. The Balkans. Marco Polo, the great fabricator, told the court of Kublai Khan he'd seen mountains of gold in what was to become Japan.'

'Marco Polo was a liar?' Vivian asked.

'One of the best,' he said, grinning. 'Nobody ever knew which of his tales were true. His travelogues were embellishment and fact mixed together in glorious accounts of what he'd actually seen, or, in the end, only in dreams. Golden cities draped in exquisite silk, kingdoms where men married ghosts, sirens and sorcerers who could summon sandstorms. Much of what he wrote was done from a prison cell, when he was conveniently thrown into a cell with a writer.'

Vivian laughed again. 'How do you *know* all this. It's fantastic.'

'Too much time inside the covers of history books of a night, I'm afraid.' He continued, 'Gold rushes all over the modern world – the bitten sands and lightning raids of California, the Klondike in the Yukon, Ballarat, Coolgardie.'

Vivian looked into his eyes while he spoke, which caused a sort of electricity to spark in his limbs. He was saying too much. His brain alive with history, but perhaps dulled to everything else that was possibly trying to warn him.

'I've got something to show you,' Vivian said, and she pulled out a folded piece of paper from her pocket. She swept around to his side so they could both see as she unfolded it before him. It was an article, printed onto gleaming white paper, but he didn't focus on the words immediately. A knot tightened in his chest. She stood so close her perfume and her syrupy breath were indistinguishable. The garden tilted.

'Has Hugo seen it?' Marick found it hard to read the words, only knew he must say Vivian's husband's, his friend's name, out loud, like an incantation.

'Not yet. I thought I'd show him tonight. An entire website from the Australian Association of Alchemists. Look at this.'

She rattled off a whole lot of statistics and summaries. While she did so, her bare arm pressed on the back of Marick's own. The pressure of her limb was perceptible and unyielding. Marick was unresisting, perhaps being uprooted like the browning weeds in a heap nearby.

'Actually, I think Hugo has heard of them. Yes, he has.'

Vivian appeared a little disappointed. 'Oh,' she said, and moved back to her seat. His arm, where hers had been, cooled as though it had lost a companion. This was all so wrong, in ways Marick was not able to grasp.

'Your job. Tell me about your job, Vivian.' He looked up at her. A change of subject was all he had.

She gave a wry smile. 'I'm a counsellor for student services at the university where Hugo used to work. That was where we met. I do love the job; I really do. You must know what it feels like, to listen to people's turmoil and see them come through it, with nothing to help them but conversations in private spaces. It's a very intimate thing. I'm sure you understand, with your vocation.' She took another generous sip and fanned her face with her other hand. Turning sideways, she recrossed her legs, then pulled away some of the moist strands of hair that were clinging to her neck. 'Have you always been a priest? What brought a man like you to the church, Marick?'

A man like him.

'I was actually a simple company man for a long time,' he turned to her. 'Hardly even that. I only went to theological college after the divorce.'

'The divorce? You've been married?' She put the back of her hand to her cheek. 'Hugo never told me.'

Marick realised Hugo had never asked.

'Long time ago,' he waved the conversation away, as though it was a fly, lazy in the heat. But there was something odd to her expression.

'I've always thought people of the cloth have some sort of spiritual indemnity from the real-life slings we mortals suffer,' she said with a smile. 'But of course, you don't.'

She reached over and touched his hand. Although her gesture was gentle, it was as if a lightning strike passed through him.

Setting down his glass, he rose in awkward hurry, unsure of his movements.

He made excuses. What they were, he couldn't remember as he went over and over the details of the afternoon while sitting that night taunted by the silence of his unit. The only things that came to mind were the inscrutable expression on Vivian's face and the clouds. Huge, indolent, portentous things that were roiling away in the east, growling up and over the horizon. The air would be trapped soon, with nowhere to let off its steam.

'Looks like a storm,' was all he recalled saying as he left.

FOURTEEN

Diane and Marick noted down each of Claudia's milestones in a baby book, in anxious, uptight words. Smile, roll, sit, sounds. None seemed in the slightest delayed, each of them planted without fail in the middle of the bell-curve. Another paediatrician said similar things to the first.

'The cerebral haemorrhage was significant. It's excellent to see her developing so well but sometimes it takes a while to know whether there are any long-term effects.'

'How long?' Diane asked. 'When will we be in the clear?'

The paediatrician shrugged.

When Claudia was nine months she had her first convulsion, and the world went a little dark. Marick and Diane were watching her when it happened. Claudia had been sitting in a soft fold-up couch, chewing on a rubber toy. She made the quietest of noises – a truncated gasp, more a grunt – and turned pale as though her entire circulatory system was wiped clean. Marick was rooted to the sofa, unsure what was going on. Claudia grew stiff, almost rising out of her little seat. Her eyes rolled, her arms began to thrash.

Diane screamed. 'She's swallowed something. Help her, Marick! Do something.'

Marick careered over to Claudia and picked her up. Her back was arched, her arms and legs ratcheting, and a sea of bubbles oozed from her mouth. His panic blinded him, and he couldn't work out how to hold her tiny writhing form.

'Claudia! Claudia, darling!'

The thrashes slowed into wheeling jerks. Her lips turned from white to a ghoulish purple.

'Call an ambulance, Diane!'

Diane yelled down the phone to the emergency number, while the three of them changed forever in that front room.

Later, Marick would find it hard to remember much else about the evening.

The neurologist reassured them the following day. 'She's made a full recovery. Completely back to normal. It might have been the haemorrhage at birth, or it might just be one of those things.'

They performed an EEG, hooking her up to enough wires to power a city. And in consultation with a team, the paediatricians decided that it was not just one of those things, but she'd be at risk of seizures for an unknown length of time. Possibly only childhood, they said.

They brought Claudia home from the hospital, carrying prescriptions for medications with long names neither of them was comfortable pronouncing, and they began life again, watching her like a hawk. When it became clear the drugs were working, and Claudia remained fit-free, happy and continuing to develop in babbles and crawls and hugs – recovered – Marick turned to wondering when Diane ever would.

The doctors met with him separately and asked how Diane was travelling.

'It seems to be slow,' he had to say a number of times. Mostly she was sluggish and would not shower, or sometimes didn't change her clothes for days, but her hours were often spiked with bouts of intense anxiety. She was fixated on Claudia's hearing and insisted they have it checked over and over again. The audiologist would sigh when she saw the three of them sitting in the waiting room, Marick playing a game with Claudia's fingers and toes.

'We have to be sure,' Diane would say to the receptionist. 'Look at her father.'

Marick had tried to explain to Diane that his own problem had been a cruel combination of mean luck and bad management. A single forgotten vaccination part-deafened him overnight.

'Measles does that, honey. Claudia will be vaccinated on the day, on the minute.'

Diane would not be convinced. 'I'm not having her going through school being laughed at.'

Marick wondered how Diane saw him, how she had perhaps always seen him, but particularly now, smeared in vomit, with Claudia strapped as often as not to his chest in a papoose, getting thicker round the middle. He believed her words were not meant as an insult, but Marick could feel them as corrosive. He said nothing, and continued to accompany Diane to the audiology appointments, each time leaving with a perfect score.

Eventually Marick had to return to work. Diane's father grew tired of bailing them out. Upstate Downtown was sold.

'We'll set up another one when you're ready,' Marick told her.

Diane wailed in her room the day the settlement went through. Most of the money was returned to Diane's father.

'It was all I had,' she sobbed, which struck Marick as a peculiar thing to say, all things considered.

That wasn't all that Diane's father grew tired of, either. A few days after Claudia's first birthday, Diane's mother rang her in distress, to tell her not to look at the local newspaper. Diane bought it anyway. Three girls had come forward, all waitresses at her father's yacht club working weekend jobs while they were studying at university, to make a complaint that held up when they were interviewed by police in separate rooms. Everybody at the club knew it; it was just the way it was.

'Who doesn't like young girls?' Diane's father had been known to spout to his mates in the men's-only clubroom. 'If God hadn't wanted us to have a go, why did he make their boobs and arses so firm and grabbable?' The men had all agreed; it was only a grab. Nothing more than that. The girls wore short skirts anyway. In no way was it right that a man of such standing as Diane's father should have his life ruined by three attention-seeking girls. Fortunately, there were two excellent lawyers who also had their boats in the pens at the club. They managed to slaughter the girls' defence before it even had chance to draw breath.

Nobody read the local rag, Diane's father reassured her mother. Those girls were all gold-digging liars, he maintained, which Diane's mother went to her grave believing. But Diane's parents needed to go away for a bit, to let it blow over. They chose Spain. The firm chose the next in charge to head up the company during the hiatus. Marick hoped he'd get promoted in the reshuffle, but somehow he was overlooked.

Another year went by. Diane struggled at home with Marick back at full-time work. They tried day care, babysitters, au pairs, but every day and every combination seemed to bring almost insurmountable challenges. Diane yelled at Marick, picking out things he didn't realise he had done. He found it difficult to respond.

Claudia had one more brief seizure. Diane was convinced Marick had forgotten her medications. He reassured her, showed her the bottle. She broke down in tears. They went back to the neurologist. Nothing to worry about, he said, but upped the dose anyway.

And then, into Claudia's third year, Diane emerged as if from mist. She looked around and saw the sky of a morning, started brewing coffee for Marick before he went to work, and went for walks with their toddler in the stroller. Claudia began to sleep through the night. Their daughter played; they all began to laugh. Diane's fug dispersed, evaporating like dew. Colours seemed crisper. Diane was weaned off her own combination of anti-depressants, and they both felt like life could start again.

They'd been renting all along, and they thought now was the time, or it never would be: the opportunity to ride into mortgage country.

'A house of our own,' Diane said. 'It'll be a project.'

The place they found was weatherboard and beaten. Beaten iron and beaten plumbing. Uneven floors, a lingering smell of washing powder, and a ragged yard, situated on the outskirts of the city. Even so, it was barely affordable. Diane had been advised by a real estate agent driving a Maserati that buying the worst house in the best suburb was the smartest investment anybody could make. On a single salary but with the security of life employment, this had seemed sage advice. Diane trusted real estate agents.

Within their first year, however, a gleaming new city rail was built right through the suburb's entrails and it was no longer close to being the best.

Undeterred, Diane set about transforming the house.

'White,' she said, and she meant it. Walls, appliances, every link and every fitting. Even the floorboards were painted white, although they would crack and splinter within six months of their makeover, requiring all the furniture to be moved again in order to 'freshen up' the martyred planks.

They hadn't returned to sharing the marital bed. Diane's body was closed to Marick. She could be found in the bathroom, crying, pulling at her fecund rolls that had appeared or pinching her stretchmarks until they turned red.

'Don't look at me,' she yelled at him once.

He tried to reassure her of her vast beauty, multiplied in its maternal grace, but she had proven impossible to persuade. She wore baggy clothes to hide her breasts, track pants to go walking.

'And you wake up at four in the morning on the dot,' she told him. 'Tossing and turning. I can't sleep.'

Marick slept in the spare room, closer to Claudia's. It was he who got up in the night if she cried out, and he kept a baby monitor in there, turned up to full volume, just in case.

When Claudia was two and a half, Marick asked if they could revisit the idea of a christening.

'I know the early times were terrible, darling, and we were right to put it off, but it's very important to me.'

Diane, after several weeks of resistance, agreed.

It was beautiful ceremony, and Diane glowed as she handed Claudia over to the Reverend. Claudia, who knew she was too big to be held by anyone but was so entranced with the pageantry and attention and her cream-coloured dress lined with lace and pomp in which she was allowed to prance up and down the aisles when the main event was over, with her hair wet from the baptism, put up with all sorts of things she usually wouldn't and frolicked the entire day.

Life continued to improve for the trio. Kindergarten, reading, brief family holidays that involved caravans and beaches and rockpools and rain. Song. Proud finger-paintings displayed on the refrigerator. No further seizures. Claudia was normal. Diane had purpose. She cooked again, returned to her friends. Marick pinpointed the instant, and he could not be convinced otherwise, that the joy they were all growing into stemmed from the day of the christening. It was as though something had shifted, and he couldn't help but feel, in his lighter moments, that somehow God had returned to his side. And all for a baptism, he smiled. He invested in encyclopedias.

'God, they are so old-fashioned,' Diane said. 'I can't believe they even print them anymore.'

'It will be a legacy,' Marick said. 'When I die, I will hand them on to Claudia. The history of the world in leather.'

'Don't you dare say that word, Marick,' and Diane looked wide-eyed with terror, and he chastised himself. He could only take things so far. 'You're my rock, Marick. The thing I rely upon most.' She came up behind him and clasped his shoulders, resting her head on his back.

Diane joined a large interior decorating firm that let her do designs from home.

'They love my work,' she said after the first month. 'This is the best thing!'

'Yes it is, my love,' Marick said, and they wrapped themselves together, remaining that way until Claudia free-wheeled in and broke them apart with her fizz.

They grew to love the trains rumbling past their back fence, although the constant vibration had created cracks in several of the window frames.

'Reminds me of Europe,' Diane said. 'That buzz in the air that's left behind after they pass, like anything is possible.'

'Anything is, my darling,' Marick said, and together, they watched the sun go down.

◦∖ii⁊∖◦

Marick let himself into his unit. Whatever was going on with the weather made the whole place oppressive, like a knee on the chest. He couldn't discern, though, what the sensation inside him was; was it heartburn or shame, or the heat absorbed in Vivian's sunlight?

He filled the kettle and switched it on. It was one of the metal types, with a shine so clear he could see his face in it, stretched and distorted like a sideshow. He paced around the unit while the kettle worked itself up to the boil. He had a compulsive desire to recall Bible verses, an old game he hadn't played for years. An activity to shoulder out the other crazed thoughts heckling in his head. L, he thought. Old. Leviticus. One of his least favourites.

Heavy on judgement, light on understanding. The verse that stood out, and he had to turn away from the knife of his reflection, was the one that said, *Let no man with physical defect come to the altar.* Anyone blind, or lame, with disfigured face or deformity, was not welcome. The literal once again, forbidding him a seat at the table. God's word. He looked again into the side of the kettle and turned his head from side to side. His hearing aids – smaller than the monstrous ones of his youth – still marked him. Plus, look at him. Thickset, heavy-faced. He found himself unpleasant to look at and chided himself for the vanity of even wondering. Funny, he hadn't given his appearance a thought in years.

He had planned to pen some sort of sermon that evening. There was a selection of material he'd worked on filed away on his old laptop. Perhaps he could exhume some of those sentiments and cobble them together to create something passable.

The kettle clicked off, and at the same time a text beeped into his phone. His heart gave a round thump. It would be Hugo, asking what the hell is going on? What was Marick doing sneaking around his house with his wife? He took his time making tea, like a last meal: choosing the cup, holding the tag on the teabag and jiggling it every so often, adding the correct amount of milk. Once he was certain it was satisfactory, he took the tea and his phone out to the courtyard, where he sat in his wicker chair, bought second-hand when he moved in and already faded from the sun. The night air was clammy. The stars were faint, lost under smudges of cloud. He sipped his tea and put it down by his side. He couldn't face his phone.

C. Old. The game was to choose a letter at random, and then Old or New Testament. Keeps the brain sharp, he had told himself. Chronicles. *If you seek Him, He will be found by you; but if you forsake Him, He will forsake you.*

Do it quickly. Rip it like plaster, he thought.

The message was from Vivian.

So lovely today. Can't wait for Christmas x

He couldn't drink the tea.

FIFTEEN

It was five o'clock when the crowd moved in. The rumours had caught the wind, scattering through streets and phones and minds long ago made up about such things.

A throng swarmed over the narrow traffic bridge from the city, the paint on their signs barely dry. Emotions that began the afternoon in a light lather were transforming into a roar – the sound of a growing undercurrent. People disgorged from buses and shouted their way past nearby shopfronts and cafes. The headcount was in the hundreds, their footfall ominous and creating a drumbeat.

Christmas Eve and the weather had decided to turn. A God in need of amusement had boiled the clouds up further, souping the place in thick humidity. A wet dust devil battered some of the marchers, making it difficult for them to keep in step. There was static in the air and a marshy green colour to the sky. The weather forecast had been playing it safe, perhaps not wanting to disappoint people before the big day, but it was clear to most that an unusual tempest was about to break.

The mob, however, was not to be deterred.

Marick and Hugo had been drinking coffee together when word of the demonstration ruffled the cafe.

'Let's go look,' said Hugo, and Marick followed close behind. There had been no mention between them of Marick's visit to Vivian yesterday, no flicker of anything amiss in a single word they exchanged. All Hugo had done was confirm the time for Christmas lunch the next day, and promise Vivian was going to produce something edible this time – she'd bought the ham and turkey pre-prepared.

They hurried to the hospital entrance, trying to raise their heads above the sea of staff, all of whom had the same aim. As they passed the volunteers' shop, they heard Dolly hiss.

'Get in here.' She hauled them both over to the welcome booth at the front, where she half-pulled the shutters across, allowing them to watch the proceedings unseen. 'Won't do any good to have the chaplain mixed up in all of this. Not on Christmas Eve.'

'Do you know Hugo, Dolly? Hugo Francis?' Marick asked.

'Mr Francis,' she said, and clapped one hand over her mouth. She gestured towards the looming crowd. 'It's you they're on about.'

It was a hodgepodge out there – men, women, a handful of children hoisted high on shoulders. Several globs of rain hit the ground and the light speckled further.

Somebody had a megaphone and was shouting brassy, unintelligible phrases. Although the words were difficult to distinguish, the crowd responded each time, throwing up cheers in reply. A banner sailed off to one side. Rally cries flared. Several waves of people crossed into the church grounds on their way to the hospital entrance. The crowd thickened. Another small swathe poured in from the west, parting around the fig tree as though it were Moses standing there.

The three of them peered through the slats. Marick's chest tightened like a python had him. There were tribes of people, skeins, clusters. He looked over at Hugo, who stood stiff with disbelief. Marick gripped his arm. I'm with you, he wanted to say.

'They sound like they're baying for blood,' Dolly said.

'What do they want?' Hugo asked.

Dolly pulled her glasses down to her nose to read some of the placards. '*Only God can Create*,' she read out. '*Exodus Still Speaks.*'

On the edges of the crowd there seemed to be shadowy, threatening figures, only a heartbeat away from some terrifying act, but when Marick tried to fixate on the peripheries, nothing was there, perhaps just the result of the sullied light.

Hugo read out another. '*Your government wants your child to have autism. Stop Vaccines Now!*' He looked at Marick. 'What are *they* doing here?'

'What are any of them doing here?' Marick responded.

None of them had an answer.

A refrain erupted from the side. 'Research belongs to the people!' There appeared to be some dissent between the groups. Factions emerged, shouting at each other as much as working on forward movement.

The light dwindled further. Now bystanders were gathering, drawn by the noise from the streets around – a city audience granted a reprieve from eleventh-hour gift purchases. A helicopter thudded overhead, its rotors slow and thumping in the dense, humid air.

A current of priests streamed from the front entrance of the church and stood with their heads tilted in what Marick could only presume was horrified silence. He could see them from where he was hidden, and he recognised a few. How scared they must be, he thought. A few stragglers were traipsing through the church grounds shouting things incomprehensible.

Marick was concerned for Hugo, who was standing rigid next to him, as white as stone.

The noise from the mob moved like a swell, rolling up, then down again. Skirmishes erupted in pockets; perhaps it was the tension between groups. Several people marched straight through the community of homeless people, resulting in a brief war of profanity. Maybe it was simply the air's viscosity, the proximity of muggy bodies that robbed people of their temper. The result was trouble that could be felt from where the trio were concealed.

The drops of rain amassed and the helicopter sloped off, presumably knowing what was coming. A squall, warm and strange, shot between the protestors and swirled around them. People surged forward, an advance party closing in on the hospital entrance. The automatic front doors opened repeatedly like clappers. From inside, Marick could smell bursts of earth. It was more than the gentle odour of new rain; it was a rising minerality from the crevices of the earth, as though the ground itself was exhaling.

With the rabble flowing closer, the shouted slogans grew more unified.

'What are they saying?' Marick asked.

'It sounds like *Show us the gold*,' said Dolly.

'Oh God,' said Hugo. His mouth had fallen open, stuck there like an injury.

They turned at the sound of footsteps coming up behind them. An entourage from the Medical Executive strode by. Marick and Hugo ducked, seeing Fraser in the lead. Several were wearing paper crowns; purple and orange ones, the sort regurgitated by supermarket Christmas crackers, which came wrapped around the jokes.

'That's the Head of Operational Services,' Dolly whispered.

Marick nodded. They knew.

Fraser carried a plastic cup, trying not to spill its mustard-coloured bubbles. The entire train of executives looked insulted, doubtless having had their top-tier Christmas drinks interrupted.

'It's about the gold, sir,' one of Fraser's underlings said as they passed.

'You've got to be fucking kidding me,' Fraser said.

As the hospital doors opened for the procession of executive members, a bolt of lightning fissured the clouds. The sky closed back over, now the colour of granite.

Other curious staff members had fallen in behind the executive caravan. Looking out to the ambulance bay, Marick realised there was a queue of emergency vehicles, unable to make their way through the pack. They were backed up to the road beyond, bottle-necked and frustrated, with one or two of them sounding their horns.

Fraser elbowed his way out of the front door and raised himself to his full height. He yelled something, but his voice was carried away on the wind, lost among the other sounds.

Marick crept out behind the executive group to get a better view. 'Best you stay behind,' he said to Hugo, who was nodding in robotic fashion.

A van with a television crew had managed to creep through the crush where the ambulances had not. Bearded men in black t-shirts jumped out with equipment and set up tripods and cameras. They had a scoop. Nature, however, had other ideas. As the shouts gained clarity – 'Abomination! God will judge you!' 'Fraud!' – the sky unzipped again, and the rain converted to a pelt of hail.

Placards were suddenly held over heads, a few people ducked for cover, but the brief attack seemed to incite the mob further, as though they had something to see to the finish, and not even socks of ice would deter them.

Marick heard Fraser speak. 'This is a farce.' He turned to a colleague. 'Call the police.'

In what seemed like only minutes to Marick, a squad in riot gear howled into the square. Officers poured from their trucks, leaving sirens spraying circular noise and light. This achieved what the weather had not. People began to scatter like animals in panic. The television crew kept filming.

Suddenly the attention swung in a different direction. Calls went out for help.

'Get an ambulance,' somebody hollered.

'They're just there!' from another.

The tide of protestors drained from the front entrance to reveal a puddle of violent movement. Police elbowed their way through, shoving people aside. Two paramedics followed in their wake. The automatic door opened and closed like slow applause.

Dolly came up behind him, and Marick could feel her breath.

'It's Jed,' she said. 'One of the regulars. He's always taking fits out there.'

The man's sodden body was dragged from the scrum like a fish. He was bucking and drooling, seizing in the wet. A thin, watery line of blood trickled from his mouth.

'Don't worry,' Dolly said to Marick. 'He'll stop soon. I've seen this happen a hundred times before.'

The helpers got to work, surrounded by the now-silent onlookers. Jed's body made peculiar angles as he fitted, like an abstract rendition of human. Marick's heart pulled off its leash, watching how the tonic-clonic motion unrigged the poor man, stripped him apart. A familiar terror crawled into him. Dolly's words did not reassure him, and Marick feared the poor man's fit would burn on and on until Jed's brain clogged.

One of the paramedics scrabbled through his bag, while the men with the Perspex shields and facemasks stood, unsure what to do.

At this point, some sense seemed to filter through the remains of the gathering, and people pulled away. This allowed another team from the Emergency Department to get through with a trolley. More wrestling and administering medications followed, and Jed was lifted onto the stretcher. He was packaged up and wheeled away, expended and limp, into the department beyond.

Once the cavalcade of protestors and paramedic staff had left in the shadow of the riot police, with evening having arrived and the hail reverted back to a depressingly warm rain, the remaining mob lost interest and dispersed. A few children threw the last of the hailstones at each other as they departed. There was an air of disappointment. No necromancer had turned up. The evidence of the wicked experiments they'd been assured via messages and chatgroups were going on right under the city's nose had not materialised, and each of them could think of better things to do with their time. It was, after all, Christmas Eve. They were all wet and a little uneasy and needed to be home wrapping and so forth. If somebody was really practising alchemy inside the hospital, they'd find a more suitable day to come back and see it for themselves.

As the welter retreated, Hugo emerged, slowly, to join Marick and Dolly. The square emptied, leaving only the restive homeless group. The Executive Team was long gone, and the priests had slunk back into the church. The plump church lawn, which had been fattened in readiness for Christmas, was now mush, churned to mire, torn up like it had been strafed. Scattered among the piles was litter: cardboard cups, cans, the remnants of the waterlogged signs.

It was shock enough for Marick, but then he looked at Hugo's face, which was pale and shaken.

'Woodstock, but for Satan,' Dolly said.

Marick turned to her in surprise, but he understood what she meant. They all spent a minute or so looking out at the carnage. The automatic doors had come to a rest.

'I'm going home. This is too much.' Dolly added, 'But I'll see you at nine tomorrow, Father. In the amphitheatre.'

Marick nodded. It *was* too much. But his breath was settling. The sermon, though? Tomorrow? He felt even further away from it than before after all this, and he was no closer to deciding what he'd say.

'Of course. But I have been meaning to ask, Dolly. Your results?'

'They'll be in the last mail run today. I have a good feeling about them. And a good thing too after all of this. It will be my

New Year. One kidney lighter.' She waved them away. 'Try and have a good night, both of you. Get this whole business out of your heads. Christmas Eve is supposed to be special.'

No, it's not, Marick wanted to say. The meltwater ache that began at this time for the past five years had already started its seep. He did not want to hear the words. Christmas Eve.

'Nine o'clock, Dolly,' he said softly. 'I'll be there.'

'And after that, with us,' Hugo said after she left. 'With me. I can't do this without your help, Marick. I know I've said it before.' Hugo shrank a little, appeared to battle with a thought. 'Am I asking too much, Marick? Too much of you? You must tell me if I am.' His voice was the quietest Marick had heard.

The question felt like a jolt. 'What? No.' In the last five years, Marick could not recall a single instance where somebody had asked him either of these things, and now here was a confluence of a request for help with how he might feel about it. It was almost a foreign tongue. He wanted to choose the best words in response. 'Hugo. I'm deeply honoured to be here for you, to help. We're in this together, now more than ever.'

Hugo turned quickly away from Marick, and his voice of old returned. Business-like, spare. 'Right. Tomorrow at twelve.' And he walked off down the empty corridor in the direction of the guts of the hospital, its own organs: the treatment plants and the switchboard and the kitchens. It looked to Marick as though Hugo was wiping one eye while he walked.

SIXTEEN

Claudia took to school with a quiet tenacity, and Diane again grew concerned.

'I don't think she should be anywhere on her own, or be out of the teachers' sight. What about the trees in the playground? Disasters waiting to happen. She shouldn't be climbing them, Marick.'

'But she doesn't want to do any of those things,' he said.

'There's that, too. She shouldn't spend so much time indoors. It's not healthy for children. I'm worried she doesn't want to do normal childhood things,'

'Some kids are not designed for the rough and tumble,' Marick replied. He had no idea what normal childhood things were. 'And she hasn't had a seizure in years. We should let her grow into whoever Claudia is meant to be. Let her find her own normal.'

These conversations were difficult, and Marick grew accustomed to his answers landing like tiny mortars.

Claudia was bookish, there was no argument there. A girl alive inside pages.

The heartening thing for Marick during those early years, with their daughter climbing the rungs of her own Claudia-shaped ladder to the world – grade one, a pantomime, the recorder, grade two, grade three, outstanding report cards, with 'very advanced reader' making repeat appearances, grade four – was that Diane and Marick were in its enterprise together.

Diane enjoyed the freedom of working for somebody else.

'What was I thinking, wanting to run my own business?' The company she worked for was winning awards for its designs, and often Diane's ideas were at their core. She earned herself the title of consultant and could exercise her creative whim. She found a posse there, too. Adding to her friends from college, several of whom had stuck around during the lean times, there was a bunch of girls from the office who met every Friday night for drinks.

'We're such a diverse group,' Diane said. 'There's a buyer, one of the girls from accounts, two of us designers, and the part-time book-keeper, who's a whiz at tax time. I love them; I really do.'

Marick found his own job dwindling into background noise. He turned up, met deadlines, gave the company no trouble, and had the sort of reliability that meant he wasn't noticed, the best sort of reliability there is.

The firm had grown into a huge clanking outfit. Diane's father never returned, instead taking early retirement and a deal that danced on the edge of the law – endowing him with the sort of money Marick could barely conceive of, with details of an agreement Marick did not want to hear.

'I thought I'd miss them more,' Diane said one day. 'I'm just glad they're happy in Seville.'

After they left, Diane had tried to set up a video call once a month so they could see their rosy-cheeked, bloomingly healthy granddaughter, but the months stretched, dates were forgotten, and Claudia progressed from not sitting still during the forced encounters, to not being found at all.

Claudia and Marick read books together like fiends. Every one they could find. Library books, hand-me-downs, second-hand-store discoveries, and occasionally shiny-paged ones from shops about magic and myths and monsters. It was a nightly ritual they weren't to break for over a decade.

Another regular appearance during their conversations was a discussion of what Claudia wanted to be when she grew up.

'Ditch-digger,' Marick would make guesses. Hearing her giggle at something he said was the most precious thing in the universe.

'No!' Claudia would say.

'Street-sweeper, with a big broom then.'

'No, Daddy.' Her laughter had the tinkle of sunlight.

She would cycle through the usual when it came to her turn. Doctor. Horse-trainer. Astronaut. Ballerina. A mapmaker. That became another shared fascination. Marick had taken to collecting maps as well as the heavy set of encyclopedias. Claudia was ecstatic when he unrolled the feathery paper of a random map choice and told stories about the places she chose by letting her finger drop.

'Everything that ever happened in history is inside the lines of one of these,' he explained to her.

As the years passed, Claudia's horizon expanded – archaeologist, judge, author, scientist. 'What about what you do, Dad? I could do that.'

'Oh, my darling girl. The last thing in the world you want to be is a payroll officer.'

Marick bought Claudia an illustrated Bible.

'Do you think you should be indoctrinating her so young?' Diane said. 'Really. I believe we should leave it up to her to work out whether she wants to be religious or not.'

I'm not sure it's a choice, Marick wanted to say. He had not forgotten his promise, made in the fearful black of night eight years ago, but figured settling on a quiet life, with God as a possibility, felt as much as he could manage under the circumstances.

Around then he found the courage to tell Diane about that night.

'It was so awful. Terrifying. I thought I was going to lose you both. I made a pact with God, that I'd give him whatever He needed of me if he'd pull Claudia through. And you, of course,' he'd said as he leant over and kissed her.

'You made a Faustian bargain? You promised your soul for our lives?'

'It was with God, honey, not the Devil.'

'But still,' she said, although Marick could see she was pleased. She patted the back of his hand and smiled.

She didn't mention the Bible again, happy for cheerful verses to be woven into the father and daughter night-time regimen: stories of a flood, a sanitised David and Goliath, a humorous whale's maw with a surprised Jonah, and a miracle birth.

Diane stopped accusing herself of body crimes in the mirror. She began to get undressed in front of him again, and they returned to making quiet love on the odd occasion they were sure Claudia was asleep. Marick swam in the warmth of her body. The deflated areas that had nurtured Claudia were sanctuaries for him. Safe havens. Although he would wait for an invitation, he would clamour with love and compliments and desire without fail, every time she offered one.

'We are so lucky,' he said, so many times she would give him a playful slap and tell him she knew.

They adapted to the changing routines of life, the seasons of growth, the roll of time. They made a point of going to Claudia's events together, an unassailable protective force. Whether for a concert, or spelling bee, or athletics event (never enjoyed by their uncoordinated Claudia), both Marick and Diane would turn up together, sitting as close to the front as they could. They waved like maniacs at her, no matter how she performed.

When Claudia turned nine, she found her name on a medley swimming relay for her school house.

'But they know I can't swim.' Claudia wept in her narrow bed with the fairy sheets the night before the carnival.

'Darling, you can swim,' Marick reassured her, 'just not very fast.' But she was not to be placated, and Marick lay with her on her bed, holding her close, calming her wet, sobbing breath, patting her thin white arms, loving her minty smell, until she shuddered to sleep.

Diane and Marick made sure they were there early for the event. They had discussed it over and over again. Claudia had not had a fit in seven years. Her medications remained unchanged, and the neurologists had said that if she went eight of them seizure-free, they could wean her off the drugs altogether. They wanted her to blend in with the conventional, not ever have to stand apart. But still, the water always made the pair nervous.

The races were held at an outdoor pool, in May, too cold for a swimming carnival, Marick thought, as they found seats close to the finish line. The factions were arranged by colour, with children darting about like schools of fish in matching ribbons and war-paint and cries of the valiant filling the open-air stadium. Towards the end of the morning, they watched Claudia lining up, skinny and as pale as bone, shivering in a loose-fitting bathing suit and wrinkled cap. She was shorter than all the other girls – the birthright handed down by her father. The smell of chlorine and unnecessary sunscreen was powerful, and Marick and Diane looked on with their hearts ready to break, seeing Claudia unprotected against the cruelty of the world.

'She'll be so cold,' Marick said.

'They shouldn't have forced her into it,' Diane said, her voice tight.

The race across six lanes was neck and neck, until the third swimmer in Claudia's team tired and fell behind. The other teams were almost finished, about to get out of the pool to cheers from the crowd, when Claudia jumped in. She never faltered. Although her stick arms flopped and folded and barely propelled her, and she regularly bumped into the lane markers more than once, looking up to see where she was, she kept going. Diane and Marick held hands so tight they found red marks on their palms for hours afterwards. The other teams had walked off to celebrate at the podium, while Claudia swam on, arm after limp arm. She did not stop, even though she must have known her teammates were glowering and tapping their feet with their arms

173

crossed. When she made it to the end, to a muted cheer from the teachers who were trying to show an example of sportsmanship to the heedless students, she pulled herself out of the pool, and wouldn't glance up at her parents.

Marick wanted to say something to Diane – perhaps this is what true bravery looks like – but he was so choked up, he couldn't. When he looked over at his wife, he saw she, too, had silent tears glistening on her cheeks.

By night-time Claudia had forgotten the humiliation, and they all went out for hamburgers and chips, a rare treat, topping it off with ice-cream. Claudia, scrunched between her parents in the warm restaurant booth, declared it the best night of her life.

'We should take you to Italy one day,' Diane said. 'You'd love it, sweetheart. Rome. Oh, the stories in that place. And the art. Let's.' She turned to Marick.

Marick stretched over Claudia's head and kissed Diane, which made Claudia giggle again. 'Yes, let's. Let's catch trains and see snow and eat pasta until we get our shirts so dirty with sauce they won't let us in anywhere. Let's chart out a plan. On one of my maps!'

But the practicalities of such a plan were another thing, and Marick had to put it off, year after year. It was a costly endeavour, Marick told Diane, late at night when Claudia couldn't hear. Diane agreed. It was hard for them to line up that sort of leave, anyway. But they'd get there, both of them had no doubt.

And then Claudia turned twelve.

SEVENTEEN

After the protest, Marick could not quite face going home. It would be a storm-stirred sort of evening, with a whole lot of washed-up silt that no Christmas music or walking or throwing himself into sermon preparation would fix.

Having discovered his security card gave him an all-access pass to the hospital – an advantage of being God's representative there – he thought he might slip into the Emergency Department to check on the poor convulsing man, Jed. The frenzied sights of the afternoon had been sickening, and he knew he had to bear some responsibility. Hugo was the scientist, that was true, but Marick was more than detached witness. He wanted to avoid thinking about what his label might be. Enabler? Guardian? Collaborator?

He swiped himself through the department doors. If he stayed a practical route and immersed himself in the simple acts of his role, he might be able to avoid the dilemma rattling away at him. What business did the hospital chaplain have spending his time underground, circling dangerously close to the irreligious?

The Emergency Department looked like a casino inside. Although the sky outdoors was now low and dark, with the swollen clouds still occupying every cubit of sky, inside the lights blazed with no respect for time. Lines of people curled out from waiting areas, and trolleys with their allocated bodies formed queues in the spaces. Security staff muscled among the patients. Noises that sounded as though wild animals were tethered arose from somewhere. The whole riot of life has converged in a single space, Marick thought. It was dazing. Christmas Eve.

True to Dolly's word, and to Marick's complicated relief, Jed was up and about, talking loudly, taking up space, asking the nurses what had happened outside because he'd missed the drama. Getting no response from staff who were busy with others, he walked past Marick, discharging himself from the department, looking gleeful.

The steady, intense motion was a wreath around Marick, leaving him untouched, as though he was the eye of the place. He wondered how anyone could hear anything over the hurricane, this racket of screams and abuse and alarms. The assault was on all the senses, not only his hearing aids. He couldn't place the smell and didn't care to. It was the smell of things underneath, below ground, unwashed, disintegrated. He decided he would leave, brave the evening, but as he turned, a nurse caught sight of him and his giveaway gold cross and bounded up to him.

'Father, I'm so glad you're here. There's a family in the relatives' room, waiting for their son to come in. He's arriving by helicopter. Any minute. The chopper was delayed by the weather, so the parents are waiting here already. They're very distressed, understandably. Their boy has had a bad accident – motorbike, in the wet. He's seventeen. Poor kid, it sounds like he's had a catastrophic brain injury. I asked if they had someone to support them, and they asked for the chaplain. That's you, right?'

Marick nodded. Seventeen. Not tonight. He couldn't do this tonight.

'So we were hoping,' she continued, 'you could be with the family while the resuscitation is going on. I was on my way to page you.'

He inhaled, ready to make an excuse. Marick, he told himself. Shape up. You are better than this.

'Inside,' she added, nodding over her shoulder. 'We'll have a nurse there to answer any questions. It often helps with the grieving process, evidence says. Closure can begin early, if he's going to die.'

'While you're working? In the resuscitation area?' Marick had been wondering when he was going to strike the moment of *Too much, I can't go on*. This was going to be it, surely.

'You won't be in the way, Father. Don't worry about that.'

On Christmas Eve? No. He was not worried about that.

Seventeen. A son. A family.

Before he had anything else to say, more frenetic action broke out. Marick was carried into the resuscitation room on a current. Trussed up in restraints and flanked by flight paramedics and doctors and nurses, the boy was rolled in. Orange foam blocks were walls for his neck, tubes and monitors surrounded him like an audience, and ventilators and pumps were doing the living for him. The team descended onto his body.

The parents? They were handed to Marick. He whispered an introduction and stood beside them. The mother held onto Marick like a life preserver, which he suspected she imagined he was. They stood in a corner while coordinated activity rippled through the team. Bags of blood were hung over the boy, squeezed in by serious-looking nurses. These were chased up by pints of straw-coloured liquid. Infusions were changed, X-rays were taken, somebody sliced into his chest and threaded a tube into the cavity. One of the doctors coordinating the action was the woman he had seen from before. She nodded, a quiet act of recognition and solidarity. It buoyed him. Enough.

Marick kept his focus on the parents. They asked little of the nurse allocated to them, and she offered snippets of information, trying to gauge their need. Their need was for Marick, it seemed.

'He's our boy. Our only. A good boy,' the father said.

The mother gripped Marick, pale and speechless.

'His head. His poor head.'

The nurse told the parents they wouldn't be able to give them any sort of prognosis until they had the CT scans. 'It looks grim, though,' she added, as though she had been taught that giving false hope was unforgivable.

'But there is a chance ...' the boy's father trailed off before asking the question.

The nurse made a gesture, a sort of shrug, as if to say her hands were tied. By what, Marick wondered.

Marick recognised an opportunity. 'Let's pray, while we're here.' What else did he have? He watched the motion of the team, the nurses hooking up wires and lines and moving with grace, the doctors doing the same, and he felt like a child himself.

The parents wept soundless tears of gratitude. 'Yes. Please,' said the mother. 'We need to pray with everything we've got. For a miracle.'

The father dropped his head. And while the landslide went on in front of them, the three murmured words of prayer and supplication.

'Ask God to save him,' the father said. 'Tell him we'll do anything. It'll have more power coming from you.'

'God doesn't need bargains,' Marick said, feeling his hypocrisy as he said the words. 'He makes the promises to you, at times like this. One of those is that He'll be there every step of the way.'

Marick stumbled inside himself. He couldn't trust his own words, to speak whatever truth was supposed to fit here. There was enough truth, however, laid out in front of them, as the boy was wrapped up like a gift himself to be moved on – first to the scanner, then the ICU.

He hugged the mother. She was limp in his arms.

'I'll follow up every day,' Marick said. 'And I won't stop praying.'

'Neither will we,' the parents said, and he sensed them building the fortifications they would need in the days to come.

And in less than a minute, everybody was gone, leaving nothing but an echo in the resuscitation bay.

Marick took deep breaths, drawing in oxygen during the brief reprieve.

In no time, industry sprang back to life around him – a rapid cleaning by a battalion in readiness for the next patient. The doctor who'd nodded walked back into the resuscitation bay. She had a thin line trailing down her forearm. It looked like blood.

'Thank you. And thank you for the other night, too.'

Marick started. There was nothing for which he deserved thanks.

She continued. 'Sometimes there's so little we can do that taking care of those who'll be left in the wake is the most important thing we can offer. So I appreciate you being here.'

'Will he survive?' Marick asked her. Each time he saw this doctor, she looked more tired, as though every encounter was subtracting parts of her, and it wouldn't be long until she was a living ruin, a composite of ghosts.

'Depends on his brain scan,' she said. 'If it shows an unsurvivable injury, he might qualify as an organ donor.' Her phone went off. 'I'm sorry; excuse me.'

⁕

Marick made it home by eight, in time for the late-edition news.

It was all there. The marching, the placards, the chanting. At times the action was obscured by fat drops of rain on the camera lens. Huddles and ambulances and a voiceover all converged to show the protest was about unnatural research going on behind the closed doors of The Public. An interview with one of the hospital executive staff – Fraser it was, Marick could see – reassured the viewers it was some kind of Christmas hoax. The reporter agreed it did all sound far-fetched.

'Our main concern is for the poor trampled gentleman who is currently in critical condition because of this selfish, poorly thought through, disorganised demonstration.'

What? Marick looked up and swallowed. Jed was clearly visible on screen, convulsing as he was dragged from the crush. The camera panned out to a more palatable view of the slogans

180

and a sweep across the spires of the church. Fraser was laying it on thick, Marick thought. He had seen Jed's discharge and expected the man would be back among his compatriots, fierce in their communal survival.

'The whole Executive Team,' Fraser hesitated. His hair was unmoving like plastic. 'All of us, are sending thoughts and prayers for a speedy recovery. Those involved should be ashamed of themselves, disrupting the function of a place dedicated to serving the sick and the vulnerable.' Fraser was pleased to declare this ridiculous little skirmish over. No more would be said about it. After all, what nonsense was the suggestion somebody was creating gold. And then the news moved to reports of Santa taking to the sky on the Royal Flying Doctor Service and the latest rise in house prices.

Marick had no appetite. Nothing tempted him. He would delay going to bed, knowing it would only be a stewing night ocean of neurosis. And memories.

But the sudden memory of having not written his sermon delivered itself first. He retrieved his laptop. Scrolling through previous material he had written, he discovered it all to have come from another life. His missives were so abstract, so diffuse and generic, even he had a hard time working out what he'd been trying to say. He had listened with rapture to the speeches of his contemporaries so many times, knowing they had heard God talking directly to them, guiding them. Now, trying to understand why his words were never that lofty, he recognised what he'd experienced back then. It had been envy.

Perhaps he could mince together some of the homilies, extract *something* good – but there was nothing. This is the sum of my past attempts at a clerical life, he thought. What it's been reduced to. Smoke inside mirrors.

Perhaps I could write a poem, he thought. He picked up a nubbin of pencil and a scrap of paper. How hard could it be, to write poetry? He'd been reading it all his life. But when it came to getting any words down, he found not a musical one materialised. He had no clue where to start, or what to say. The longer he sat with words unwritten, the stronger the pull to torture himself became. There seemed little point fighting it any longer.

He reached inside the ground-level cupboard of his lounge-room cabinet and pulled out the map, unrolling it with delicate fingers. The papery smell of dust got to him every time. He hadn't kept many of his maps after forsaking the white house, but this one could never be thrown away. This was the one he and Claudia had crowded over, planning their Italian trip together, and there were lines and markers and stickers and notes in psychotic patterns all over that distant country. They'd done it on holidays, near the beach. He stared at it until his vision blurred. Five years ago, and it remained too agonising to keep open for long.

He rolled it back up, replacing it with gentle precision.

The hours shifted. Midnight approached. No sermon, still. Get something down, he told himself. He attempted a sentence or two but they had no substance at all. They sounded like bad air.

Marick looked at the useless phrases, crumpled the paper and dropped it into the bin. He googled 'Christmas Sermons' and printed off the first one that flashed up.

EIGHTEEN

Marick was slow to realise Diane was sliding again. He'd thought she was having some type of mid-life pilgrimage into herself, spending more time in the bedroom, unhappy with her work.

'I don't feel I'm getting anywhere with my designs anymore,' she said. She cancelled her weekly get-togethers with the girls, and then she was the one awake through all hours of the night. There were days of tears, when they streamed down her face without noise, discovered when he looked for her of an afternoon wondering why she was so quiet. Meals became a chore. She missed a succession of Claudia's events.

It was only when Diane started ruminating about harm searching out their daughter in bizarre, incomprehensible ways that Marick clicked.

'What if she swallows a whole lot of pills by mistake? Or picks up a knife and slips it onto her wrists?' Marick watched as she turned the same narrative on herself.

A trip to their doctor confirmed it, and Diane was started on new anti-depressants. Much more modern, they were told, very effective, fewer side effects. But they were glacial kicking in and hardly skimmed the edge off her illness.

While the drugs attempted to rearrange whatever brain chemistry mix-up was going on, Diane experienced giddying mood swings. For the first time, she accused Marick of hogging Claudia's emotional allegiance. It stemmed back to when she had been in hospital after the birth. Marick could understand this jealousy – he and Claudia had developed something unbreakable during those months. But when he tried to explain, reassure her he understood, she scoffed at him.

'I'm not bloody jealous,' she said. 'Why would I be jealous of you?'

The pills did not agree with her. 'We'll try something else,' the psychiatrist told them. 'There are plenty of other options.' They whittled down choices, all the while with Diane getting worse. When she wouldn't leave the bedroom at all, the doctor decided on a brief hospital stay.

'I might take Claudia on a holiday while you're in there,' Marick said. 'It's not been easy on her.'

Diane could not have cared one way or the other at that point, and Marick helped to pack a small bag and settle her into a breezily decorated room at the private clinic.

'Up the coast, yes?' Marick thought of a hundred places he wanted to take his daughter.

Claudia squealed, the first joy he'd heard from her in weeks. He took her out of school, ignoring the teacher's protestations that it was mid-term.

'She's only twelve,' Marick said to them on the phone. He could hear Claudia jumping around with excitement.

'Right,' he said to his daughter. 'Let's pack our own bags. Don't forget the important things. Games, books, a torch for night-time treasure hunts.' They didn't need medications. Claudia had been off them these past three years.

'Warm clothes,' she said.

'Whatever,' he replied, grinning.

'A map. Let's continue the Italy one.'

'Let's.' And he hugged her hard.

They drove north. Two hours. An audio book played through the tinny car speakers. Marick had hired a cabin in an unfashionable beach-side resort and had his choice of units since nobody else stayed there that time of year. It was still winter, despite what the calendar proclaimed. The unit was blockish, with mismatched furniture and faded squares on the wallpaper where pictures had hung, but a courageous little bar heater warmed up the place in no time, and they both had their own narrow rooms. Claudia went about arranging hers straight away. She took everything out of her backpack, putting her soft unicorn on the bedspread, and laying her toothbrush next to her dad's in the poky bathroom.

'It's amazing,' she said.

'We should check the beach,' Marick said.

'Make sure it's there.'

'Absolutely. Tell it not to go anywhere because we've got some exploring to do.'

'Make sure it's not scared of the storm that's coming.'

'Are you scared of the storm, my angel?' Marick asked, kissing her head.

'Not with you here.'

185

They pulled on mismatched items: beanies, second-hand jackets, boots – and strode out onto the sand, less than five hundred metres from their door. The storm was a squib, but it still gave the sky a depth of colour that made them marvel and try to find words to describe it.

'Rock.'

'Elephant-coloured,' said Marick. Claudia laughed.

'The colour of water down the bottom of a well.'

'Bravo! Perfect.'

They set off to investigate the deserted expanse of dusky sand. Tight coils of surf turned over mechanically at their feet, necessitating a sprint every time they got too close. There were games to be played. The dunes were foothills, intact shells were money. They found flags for fortresses and washed-up pieces of plastic to decorate a sandcastle. The rush of the ocean expanded both their minds until they were exhausted from it. They bought a soggy pizza from a nearby store and snuggled together on the sofa to eat it. Afterwards they wiped their greasy hands on each other. Marick read a story – there had barely been a night without one, even now when she was beyond the age for them. He tucked Claudia into bed with the deep growl of thunder indistinguishable from the roll of the waves beneath.

'It is perfect, Dad,' she said, and closed her eyes for a kiss on the forehead.

It was too early for Marick to go to bed, so he waited until he was sure Claudia was sleeping and stepped back out onto the vastness of the ocean's edge. In the gaps in the sky a jewelled splendour was visible, the waning crescent of moon with an ivory light. One day they would have a house with an ocean view. Diane would get better; he would save more. He wondered whether part of the attraction of looking over the bottomless sea was the fact it could never be built out. They would never have to look through a neighbour's windows. It was freedom of vision, an unendingness of sight. He looked up to watch the ripples of the cumulonimbus, edged with merciless storm grey-black, and he felt like howling. There was not another soul on the beach, and only distant flashes of lightning to keep him company, so he stripped off all he was wearing, and beat his pale soft chest for the rapture of it, running like a madman into the waves. He bobbed up and down in the thick salty wash of the water, not anywhere near as cold as he'd imagined, and looked up at the sky. In that moment, Marick knew exactly what God was.

When he returned to the bungalow in his wet, sandy clothes, feeling sodden with the joy of being alive, he realised Claudia was awake and had turned her light on.

'Can we do the map? I'm not tired after all.'

'Can we do the map? Of course we can! I'll just get changed because your dad is a soaking fool.'

The storm rolled over the top of them in cells. Thunder built up to sky-splitting crashes, then faded into far-off rumbles before returning again, wild gardens of sound overhead.

Italy. They worked out the craziest route they could. Claudia had brought coloured pencils and stickers and they made up new ways they would zip around the country. As it grew later, the methods of transport became stranger. Camels. Rollerskates. Airships! Eventually the map was covered in circling lines and drawings, and Marick knew he'd have to find another one to plan a more sensible trip.

This time she was asleep before she made it to bed.

He sat down with a mug of hot chocolate and looked again at the map. What was it that made maps so enticing? These flat surfaces having sacrificed a dimension, drawn by men who mistook themselves for gods. How we humans warp and alter our reality to fit a map, he thought. This one and its crazed additions held nothing of the cobblestones and piazzas, the promise of his wife's intimate curves, the smell of cigarette smoke, coffee with the consistency of quicksilver and the scent of the earth. The Italy they would take their daughter to would be very different. But exciting in its own way. It always was, seeing the world through the eyes of a child.

The pair spent five days in their salt-crusted heaven and weren't bored once. They hired fishing rods and caught nothing. They walked and walked until Claudia needed to get a piggy-back ride. The stories and plans got grander. Marick slept like he never had before, his dreams colourful and benign and disappearing quickly on the rhythm of his heartbeat. When they packed to leave, they could smell their clothes, unwashed and heavy, and they realised they'd not eaten a vegetable the whole time. They drove back down the highway singing songs and changing the words, trying to make each other laugh, determined not to let their mood or their plans evaporate.

The hospital stay was extended and took its time, but Diane surfaced. She had gained weight and moved more slowly, but she returned to them whole. Marick resolved to take better care of her. He would look out for the signs of deterioration, be patient

188

with her moods, listen when she needed to rest. The medications should keep going, the psychiatrist said.

'The good thing was,' Diane said, 'I made a new group of friends in there. Some really nice women. It felt great to be understood, for once.'

Marick absorbed the implication. The important thing was that the three of them moved through this life together, as a unit.

Diane cut down her hours at the interior decorating firm, but her enthusiasm for design crept back. Things began their march back to normality, like a homecoming. Claudia graduated primary school, one of the top students in her class. She played the lead role of Alice in Wonderland at the end-of-school concert, and Marick and Diane sat together again in the second-to-front row, clapping until their palms stung.

At the beginning of December, Diane approached Marick. Her voice was tentative.

'The girls I met at the hospital – there's three of them – we've been keeping in touch.'

'Hmm? Yes, honey. I'm really glad, too.'

'Well, it's just that they are all going on a retreat together, you know, a week of wellness, and they've asked if I'd like to come. It's one of those things with yoga, and walks in the bush, meditation sessions and vegetarian meals prepared by a chef.'

'It sounds wonderful. You must go.'

'The only thing is it's on the Christmas week. It finishes on the Friday, which would be Christmas Day. I could catch an early flight home, be back for lunchtime; it would just mean missing Christmas Eve and the morning opening presents. We could delay the festivities, though. What do you think?'

'Isn't there any other time you could go? A different week?'

'That's when the girls have booked. When they could get time off work.'

'I don't know, love. Christmas is so special.' Marick had been thinking about this one for months, looking forward to it after the year they'd had. Pyjamas crumpled from sleep among the mountains of wrapping paper, the parents drinking tea while the child goes bananas over gifts.

'They can't go any other time. I said I'd be back by lunchtime. We'd still have pretty much the whole day. All their families are happy with it. Marick, I don't think you get it. How much I need this.'

Diane's voice was creeping up the register and Marick could feel the tension between them doing the same.

'Are you sure there are no other dates?' He hadn't yet met these women. Didn't know their names. Diane spent hours on the computer, sending messages back and forth to them, but as far as he knew they hadn't been meeting up. It felt like betrayal, for Diane to choose then to be away from him and Claudia.

'You got to have your little jaunt with Claudia. I've not been away anywhere for a year. This would be my thing, Marick. My one thing. I can't believe you're making me feel guilty for one single request.'

She started cleaning the kitchen, picking up plates and cups, banging them down into drawers, slamming cupboards. Corrugated sunlight splayed across the white bench. He had no choice.

'Of course, love.' He kept his sigh quiet. 'As long as we get to have the rest of the day, just with us. I'll tell Claudia, and we can postpone the presents until lunchtime.'

Diane turned and beamed. 'Thank you; thank you. You won't regret it. They've got a weight-loss stream, too. Thank you.' And she walked over and kissed him on the cheek.

The thought of the retreat seemed to spark a cylinder that had been idling, and Diane went through the next week full of energy. She organised for the floorboards of the house to be painted again and spent three days without break 'de-cluttering'. She let the white back in. By the end of her spree, the house gleamed like a car showroom. A new Christmas tree arrived, ordered from an American internet site that specialised in boutique trees. It was white, of course, and came with red, tinny balls scattered over it like flak. Diane put it up without Claudia. No tinsel, no gifts under it this year, she said to them both. Spoils the aesthetic.

Diane bought herself new yoga pants and a mat. Claudia and Marick drove her to the airport at five-thirty the morning of her flight, with the sky pinking up like a newborn baby taking its first breath. The girls were chattering about nothing in particular. Diane was excited, he could tell from her voice. He was content to watch the life-affirming beauty of dawn rising up through his side window.

When they arrived at the airport, Diane realised she had misread the ticket and boarding had already begun. They raced in panic to get her checked in and gone and she had to career through the gates to make the flight. As she was swallowed up by the formalities of the place, she turned for a last wave, blowing a kiss because she'd forgotten to give her only child a proper one goodbye.

NINETEEN

Christmas morning began pulpy. An armada of clouds hung around for Marick's solitary bowl of cereal, then slunk away to the east. The temperature, however, never settled on pleasant, leaving no-one happy: not the traditional beachgoers, nor the full-roast cooks. It will be back to searing tomorrow, the papers said, so enjoy the reprieve, but the soup-like feel to the day meant everybody had something to complain about.

The otherwise empty number two carried Marick from home, over the soft swell of the river and into the inner city with its festive belligerence – the showy glitz readying for its day in the spotlight – depositing him outside the quiet of the church.

He had not slept, had not expected to, lying instead like a board on the bed. Despite his waking nightmares – non-stop visions going at him like vigilantes – he'd managed to hold tight until morning. Now he was ready.

Walking towards the church grounds he sensed them alive, moving. Closer to the gates, he saw a three-person army, with Dolly at the front. She had a roll of garbage bags tucked under one arm and it was clear she was in command. Her support team was moving across the empty space, stamping on any mounds and waves of damp dirt, picking up rubbish left behind by the previous day's wet, enraged protest. Two garbage bags were already full, stacked close by. A number of wooden planks, presumably sourced from a builder's waste bin had been dragged over and placed on the mud as duckboards.

Dolly stretched her back, looked over to him and waved. Her pair of helpers, two of the homeless crew he noted, did the same. He strode towards them, and caught the reflection of the early morning light, the colour of canned peaches, glinting off the stained-glass windows on high.

'You really are something, Dolly,' Marick said, treading down a rogue pile.

She smiled, looked at her watch, and said to the two men trying to one-up each other stomping down the last of the small drifts, 'We'd better be off. You are all welcome at the chaplain's Christmas service, of course.'

Dolly guided Marick through the bends of the hospital, past a large security gate, and back out into the open – his makeshift outdoor church for the morning, the natural auditorium sunk between the psychiatric unit and some of the less popular outpatient clinics. There were grassy rows and knolls and a couple of bench seats if the elderly needed them.

'I'm expecting a lot of people,' Dolly said. 'I've been spruiking like mad.'

But the knolls remained unoccupied. A crow landed on one of the benches, cawed for a bit, then left. The few who did meander in wore wrist bands claiming them as inpatients. Counting

Dolly, there were six splayed out on the lawn, plus a lectern that wobbled and a microphone that shrieked with feedback every time Marick spoke.

It was not a success. As he read through the sermon, an argument broke out between two of the men at the back, and another person departed before Marick could read his short Bible passage, which he only realised halfway through was the wrong one.

Afterwards, Dolly and Marick sat on one of the benches. It had been stripped of most of its paint, and only a few sharp curls of varnish remained. She polished her glasses on her dress and peered into them as though they held some answer. Insects moved through the thick damp grass under their feet. Marick watched the organised determination of an ant colony.

'It might have just been the location,' Dolly said.

The hospital's machinations produced a low-level hum behind them. Marick imagined the service taking place in the pomp of the cavernous chapel across the road: the soothing chants, the parade up the aisle − sombre and reverential − the ritualised anonymity, and with God in plain sight.

A man in stained blue pyjamas and copper-coloured fingers sidled up to Marick. 'That was beautiful,' he said. 'Just what I needed.'

Marick looked up at him. 'Was it?' He was so familiar with his inability to move so much as a blade of grass he was not sure what the man meant and reminded himself the speaker was an inpatient in the unit beyond.

The man lit a cigarette as his reply.

'I take full responsibility, Father,' Dolly said, picking up her purse. 'I wonder if, after that dreadful protest yesterday, people are a bit wary of this place. Tell me, Father. What is Mr Francis up to, down there in the basement? Everybody's talking about it. Should we be worried?'

Marick hauled himself up, then extended a hand to Dolly.

'It just feels like the ground beneath our feet has moved,' she added, executing a regal rise. 'A miracle is a miracle for sure, but then there are things that pretend to be, just to test us.'

'I understand how you feel, Dolly. The truth is I don't know yet. I do believe Hugo can be trusted, and he is doing what he's doing for the best reasons. I honestly cannot answer the question as to what it all means. He needs our support though, because I suspect the road is going to get rockier for him.' Marick packed his notes back into his satchel. 'But what about you, Dolly? Your letter?'

'My acceptance? It's sitting at home under my little tree. I don't get any presents since Mervyn passed away, so I thought I'd make the letter mine this year.'

The pair wished each other the merriest of days, a sentiment Marick found hard to reconcile with reality, and they headed off, she with purpose to the west, he wending back through the warren.

Before Marick headed off to the Francises' house, he would make good on his promise from yesterday. Entering a dedicated set of elevator doors, he rose to the intensive care unit.

The doors pinged open and Marick presented himself to reception, asking for the boy by name. The receptionist looked at Marick's small gold cross and nodded, as if to condone such a spiritual visit. The boy might not be dying today, she could have been indicating, but the difference between life and death here was merely technical.

The inside of the unit was a refrigerated white pod. It did not belong to the rest of the hospital. The walls were straight and ordered, lined with equipment and signs, and with washbasins, suction outlets and glove dispensers arranged as regularly as fenceposts. Its smell was pure clean. Patient after supine patient were laid out in a grid.

Marick approached the bed. The boy was strung up with a caterpillar of pumps and pulleys. A nurse changing some sort of monitor sunk into his half-shaved head looked up at Marick and beckoned him closer. Surrounding the boy was a jungle of plastic, vines of tubes inserted in his neck and a ventilator with its navigational screen doing the loud, rhythmic breathing for him. Another nurse was writing notes on an oversized chart at the foot of the bed.

'Are the parents here?' Marick asked.

'We've sent them home for a bit. They were by his bedside all night,' she said. 'Not a great day for them to be sitting having to think about such horrors, but they wouldn't be the first.'

Not a great day at all. A few hints of Christmas peeked out from odd places – a card next to a bed, a stack of gifts at the nurses' station, but otherwise the unit, and the day, were both sterile.

'Would you like to sit, Father?' the other nurse asked.

'Thank you, just for a moment.' The nurse pulled a white plastic chair over for him. He thanked her again, then spoke to her, not sure how to ask. 'Will he make it?'

The nurse looked doubtful. 'Too early to prognosticate,' she said.

A soft alarm went off and the nurse turned her attention to it.

He watched the boy for a short while, lulled by the cadence of the machinery.

After a minute, and looking around to make sure nobody could hear, Marick leant in and whispered. 'I am so sorry. Sorry for the world's cruelty.' A robotic breath punctuated his speech. 'I hope there's not too much pain in there.' He touched the boy's arm. It felt greasy.

Marick hesitated, checked around again, then lowered his voice further. Although he supposed he should be praying over the boy, it felt more beneficial to converse. 'You should have heard my sermon this morning. It was appalling.'

But what was he doing? Confessing?

He carried on. 'I am appalling. I betrayed Dolly with how bad it was.' He should stop there. 'And now I feel I'm betraying Hugo somehow. Betraying his trust with my doubt. And with ...' He shook his head, not wanting to speak of Vivian out loud, in the presence of this life on a threshold, which might be on a path to some sort of innocence. 'All of it, one great betrayal. I thought those days were done. Of betrayal. You wouldn't have been like that. You won't be, I mean. Keep going, my boy, get better.'

The nurse reappeared by Marick's side and he stood. He pulled his shoulders back and gave a brief nod, only thinking to make the sign of the cross as he left.

TWENTY

Viewed from the sky above, this isolated city with its history of scrap and unease was a collage. The roads and the parks and the houses formed a tessellated pattern, but only as far as a scrubby scarp of hills to the east. This scraggly ridge hemmed the inhabitants in like a wall, reminiscent of its recent penal past. Within the city's bounds the sprawl was flat and spreadeagled, with a great dry nothing beyond three of its sides. The fourth was the coast, which from on high looked the same, only blue.

As the big day progressed to noon and with the clouds jostled off and away, the air seemed hyper-real, as though the sky had been polished to a furious shine. Closer to the ground a few of the city folk were out and engaging in sunny-satisfied and festive activities. The majority, though, were inside their houses, paying homage to their Christmas lunch, the pivot point of the year round these parts.

The parents of the boy could not eat. They crouched in their home, ignoring the phone calls from well-meaning relatives. They had sat with their son through the night, praying until their throats were raw. His CT scan looked like nothing but fuzz to them. One of his physicians explained, however, that a healthy brain should look like defined loops and whirls, not this homogenous greyscale. This was something called diffuse axonal injury – words which sounded light and benign to them. They were not, the doctors said gravely. The likelihood he'll wake up is low, his pressures are through the roof, they were told, but neither of them understood a word, only that nothing was certain. As they sat together, gripping each other's hands, they talked about where his memories would be now. Do they vanish, wiped clean like a children's toy-screen? Would he wake up and remember he had just received his entrance offer to university? Such unprepossessing images, they thought, those scans with their son's brain the colour of lead. How is a whole of a life contained inside?

They cried again, clutching onto each other until the time they could go back to visit.

⋅⋅᪤᪥⋅⋅

On the doorstep of the hospital, the assembly of vagrant people had received a surprise. A few hot meals – turkey, potatoes, gravy, beans! – had been dropped off by an unmarked truck, complete with wooden cutlery and Christmas-themed serviettes. Not enough to feed everybody, but a skeletal woman with a torn, ragged sweatshirt assumed leadership and made sure the food was portioned out equitably. This sort of delivery had happened before, of course, but nobody ever claimed responsibility, so the group, which was peripatetic at the best of times and with little collective memory, never thought to expect it. There were a few squabbles over the meat, but mostly the company accepted what was offered. One of them had a guitar and strummed off-key carols. A rabble of a choir was formed. They entertained anyone who walked by, with a number of coins being thrown into a filthy hat one of them had retrieved from a bin.

Through the doors, the doctor who had looked after the boy the night before was on her final run of shifts. Too many, she thought. *I am too old for this, but perhaps I've always been too old.* This year the hospital executive had stopped the tradition of distributing lunches to people working this least-coveted shift of the year. An issue with health and hygiene they claimed. Instead, a basketful of tuna and cracker combinations was brought into the communal staff dining area. *Help yourself*, a handwritten sign on the basket said, *with compliments from your Executive Team, with our festive wishes.* By the time the doctor got there, all the flavoured selections were gone, and only plain tuna in oil remained. She sighed and heard the bat-phone go off again.

Further out into the suburbs, Lilyana, the Croatian cleaning lady, was sitting outside a small Catholic church, listening to the hymns and the service through the thick wood of a side door. She had settled herself in, with a fold-up chair and a small picnic – only a few items, most of them soft. She had such trouble chewing these days. You should come inside, someone had pleaded with her years ago, but now they were used to her doing this. The regular parishioners returning year after year would wish her a routine Christmas greeting and carry on to the front entrance. They'd stopped asking if anything was wrong. She was under no obligation to tell them, she thought. The music was so beautiful, it brought the prickling of tears to her eyes. She tore off a piece of bread and allowed the service to roll out into her memories.

⁖\ɴ⁊⁛

Dolly unlocked the front door to her bright, neat house. She had a leftover curry in the fridge from the evening before and she reheated it in her microwave, serving it on her best crockery. It was Christmas after all. After tidying the kitchen, wiping the bench clean until it shone and the house was filled with the smell of citrus, she made a cup of chamomile tea and sat down. Underneath her miniature Christmas tree was her acceptance letter, still sealed.

'Merry Christmas, Dolly,' she said to herself.

It was not an acceptance letter.

Dolly was thanked for her offer, but, as had been discussed, her age and biochemical profile had rendered her unsuitable to be a living kidney donor. She was invited to sign up for the tissue donation register – for her bones and corneas once her days were done and those parts no longer had use for her. Dolly inhaled a grain of rice, which sparked a coughing fit lasting minutes. Her eyes watered and she was rendered briefly blind. This was how things were to be now, she thought – without vision, without purpose, and with two lazy kidneys.

She stared at the wall. If God had gone to the trouble of directing her dreams, and indeed also bringing the gift of the miraculous to their very hospital, then why this nonsense with numbers? Serum levels indeed. Electrolytes and filtration rates. Mervyn had believed in the power of numbers, though. He was always quoting something or other from *New Scientist* about the poetry of mathematics, equations which underpinned anything thought to happen in the known universe. More reliable than religion he said, and she had scolded him.

Sitting with her hands clasped, Dolly prayed furiously. And in hardly any time, God answered. Dolly remembered, with a flash of things falling into place, a headline she had read not long ago while tidying up the piles of magazines. God with a sense of humour, she thought, speaking to her through *New Scientist*. It was an article about kidney health: *Myths and Misconceptions*. The title had stuck in her head. She rose and marched to the sitting-room bookshelf. And there it was, close to the top of the nearest bundle. She read the subtitle. *Hydration: the Misunderstood Formula*. Dehydration causes kidneys to underperform, it said. A straightforward truth. An equation in itself. Dolly realised she must have gone to the laboratory without having had enough to drink the day of the tests. The solution might be entirely simple.

Dolly returned to the kitchen, pulled a glass from the high cupboard and filled it with water from the tap. She began to drink. One glass down with ease. She filled it again. As soon as the laboratories were open – Boxing Day, for sure, she thought – she would get on the early bus and march straight back in to sweet talk the staff into retaking her blood and sending the ceremonious results through to the donor coordination office. She drank a third. Unfurl the standards. Sound the horns! Another! There was no amount of water Dolly could not drink if it meant at least one of her kidneys was hearty and warm and sent on its merry way to a grateful new home. Come on, kidney! This is our chance! She wondered which would respond better – her right, or her left?

She'd been up since dawn, what with the clean-up and the poor chaplain's service, and forgave herself the need for an afternoon nap. She settled onto her bed with its crisp sheets and slept for several hours, dreamless, until her bladder woke her, bursting for attention. A little groggy from this unaccustomed drop-out from the world of the conscious, Dolly reoriented herself and collected her glass, walking with a wobble into the kitchen. She drank. Setting a digital alarm as a reminder, she planned to down a glass every hour. She went to the toilet again and watched the bowl fill with urine. It became clearer each time she did. Jubilation. It was working. I can produce a lake, she thought. Then the lake became crystalline, clear as diamond and became the lake where her father took her fly fishing on his days off.

'Why on earth would you go out fishing when that's your job?' her mother asked.

'Because Delores wants to go,' her father replied, and he'd tuck her underneath his huge arm, her and the tackle and the cut sandwiches, and they'd drive out in their jalopy under the brilliant sun until they reached the sparkle of the lake, sapphire, you'd call this, her dad said, and they'd wade out to where the water was waist deep and they'd laugh and make up stories about the little fish they felt nibbling their ankles, or the pink flashing feather fly he cast out which her father said was wiggling its little arse and Dolly laughed more and her father said, 'Don't tell your mother I said that.' More water! Water lapping at the shore, tiny waves bounding into her hands. The hem of her skirt was all wet, her shoes soaked on the banks. Now her dad was laughing louder. The sandwiches were all soggy, right the way through but that's okay, Delores, your mother made them so they might taste better his way and they laughed and more water, Dolly. Another glass. Another hour. Maybe one more.

Her bed was more difficult to locate this time. Perhaps she should line up a few glasses to get her through the night, so she wouldn't need to walk to the kitchen. She dozed off, fully clothed. The alarm beeped again, but it was odd, and sounded like a fire alarm she had heard when she was little, was that somewhere in town? She tried to find the toilet again. It was not where it was supposed to be, where it had been before. She was not in the right house. Her breath was ragged and the gurgling in her throat sounded like the drainpipes behind her school. Air tried to scramble into her lungs, and she clawed at her chest to help it. She crashed into a wall where there was supposed to be a door. Putting out a hand to steady herself, she saw her appendage was a sunken anchor, heavy in the sea. She could smell rust.

Dolly realised she had forgotten to kiss Mervyn. Or was the kiss for her father? Great tuna jumped out of the wall, and she turned quickly. A particularly large fish flew right over the top of her, and she lunged to avoid it. Because a doorway was open in a place it should not be, Dolly fell through it. Quite slowly she fell, and she called out a strangled help in her wet, muted voice.

A corner of the kitchen table stopped her head with a great extinguishing smash. Dolly's descent was completed in silence, ending on the tidy, tiled floor. A pool of molasses-like blood leaked from under her. She could see it from the corner of her eye and she wondered when the lake had got so dark. And then the only noise that came from Dolly's house was the incessant alarm, calling out for her in the dark every hour.

The blood congealed underneath her. Dolly did not notice the cold.

TWENTY-ONE

Marick realised he had no gift for his hosts. Unacceptable at any time, but Christmas? He rustled through his storage cupboard, feeling behind the stacked linen and the folded jackets he never wore – and pulled out a vintage world map. It looked as new, and he was sure they would both – Vivian for certain – appreciate its value. He had no wrapping paper but found an old ribbon to tie around it and a generic blank Christmas card with a line drawing of the nativity on the front. He scribbled a brief message. Mainly of thanks.

He was grateful. The thought of going over to his friends' house, spending the rest of the day in their company, brought on a contained relief. He wanted to be marooned on the island of Hugo and Vivian, to let their friendship and conversation wash over him.

In a rare act of extravagance, Marick called for a taxi. He was fatigued from the recent days, the trains would be infrequent, and he did not want to be a second late.

On the way over, he sunk into the back seat, content to listen to the vacant songs on the radio. He noticed the driver looking at him through his rear-view mirror.

'I must be doing the Lord's work today,' he said. 'Transporting his foot soldiers.'

The taxi smelled of smoke and artificial pine, with a linger of sweat. A residuum of people in hurries. Marick looked at the catch of his reflection in the mirror and could see his gold cross. His announcement to the world. He unpinned it and put in his pocket. There was an unexpected freedom in the act.

'No offence, Father,' the driver said.

'None taken,' Marick replied. 'I'm off-duty.'

The driver stared at him a little longer, then returned his attention to the road.

Hugo met Marick at the door, one hand outstretched and the other patting him on the shoulder, and Vivian came up behind her husband, reaching around to kiss Marick on the cheek. He felt enfolded.

'Come on through,' Hugo said.

'What's this?' asked Vivian on receipt of Marick's rolled up offering. 'A present? Marick, you shouldn't have. We haven't got you anything.'

'It's a map,' he said.

'I adore maps,' Vivian said.

Jazzy Christmas carols were playing on the air, filling their home.

'Not too modern for you?' Vivian asked Marick.

'Not at all.'

They went through to the backyard, to the now-tidy table arranged with a festive red cloth and trinkets, and Marick relayed the story of his Christmas sermon. He realised it could be amusing, cloaked in retrospect.

'A congregation of five, one of whom talked into his wristwatch through the whole thing,' he said. 'I'm sure I could hear him trying to call the FBI.'

Vivian's laughter pealed like a carillon.

'I bet you were brilliant,' she said. She emitted good cheer. Exactly what Marick needed, as though the crises of the last few days could be erased by her poise. She looked the sort of casual that was somehow the opposite – sculpted and stunning. When she stood to move to the kitchen, he saw all of her – the way she wore her swaying, slow-motion skirt, her loose, light top, her ballet flats. She could have been floating. Her beauty was kinetic.

Vivian brought out waves of food and Marick watched Hugo, knowing how much their lives must be engulfed by her aura. It caught in his throat. Diane had possessed a similar energy. Once. He tried to grab at the sensation, bring it to the table to ground him, but it disappeared. Diane had come in a memory last night, of course, but then it had been ferocious. All the wrong type of energy.

'Great job, Viv,' Hugo said as he took a plate from her.

There were no experimental dishes this time, Hugo announced. They were not venturing outside the cuisine of the Christmas tradition, artificial and concocted as it was, which led to a discussion as to why Christmas was so hung up on customs. They all had a different opinion – nostalgia, the devotional, the benefit of the ritual. Marick tried to get up and help, but Vivian put a hand on his arm and said, 'It's alright; Hugo will do it.'

'I hope you're hungry, Marick,' Hugo said. 'We were supposed to have Vivian's side over as well, but Paul's been under the weather these last few days so they and the boys can't make it. Now we have a severe case of over-catering. A gross surplus of ham.'

Vivian completed the line-up of dishes. 'To be honest, it's not such a bad thing. I'd rather we didn't have them around right now. Paul's been ringing us all week. Desperate to get in on the ground floor of Hugo's discovery.'

Did she articulate that last word with distaste, or was Marick being over-sensitive?

They sat, Hugo carving off thick slices of turkey that sweated with juice as he lay them on plates. Vivian poured gravy over the mounds of vegetables. Hugo called a halt.

'Did you want to say grace, Marick? I'm sorry we didn't think of that.'

'It's fine, Hugo.' He wanted them reassured, as comfortable in his company as he was in theirs. 'You may have noticed I'm not your traditional servant of the Lord.' There he was, observing himself, open for the first time in years. It was a surprising solace, admitting one's own vulnerabilities out loud. 'I'm still trying to work out what one of those is, truth be told.'

Vivian said, 'This is going to sound odd, but I've never truly spoken to a priest before. Never got to know one. Admittedly, I've not had much call for it. You're not what I thought a priest would be, Marick.'

Marick did not want to know what Vivian might have thought he was, so he settled on smiling at her, to convey that he understood. He turned the question to Hugo.

'What about you, Hugo? You've come from a rich line of faith.'

'Do you mean my Indian heritage?'

'Do you know,' Vivian interrupted, 'that for many years, while we were dating, I didn't know Hugo was Indian? I thought he was Greek.'

Marick looked at Hugo. His friend's complexion was certainly pale, his features as Grecian as they were subcontinental. It would not have occurred to him. But how surprising for Vivian not to have known who she was committing to.

Hugo shrugged. 'We didn't talk about it, but I never *hid* it from you.'

A second of silence sat, strained between them.

'May I pass you the cranberry sauce, Marick? It's delicious,' Vivian said. Her voice was drum-tight. 'Locally sourced.'

'In answer to your question, Marick, we didn't really settle on a faith when I was young. And as I got older, I've preferred to take a bird's-eye view of religion. See it all, so to speak.'

'And now you consult your star signs.'

Marick thought Vivian was trying to make an amusing comment, but her eyes narrowed, suggesting the opposite.

'Still hasn't prepared me for any of this though,' Hugo said.

And it was the *this* that occupied them as they ate. In a way, Marick was glad to be discussing the gold again. The topic was so consuming, with so many alleys unexplored, and yet they had to move forward, shift from the current stalemate.

It emerged that they'd all been doing their own research.

'I wrote a few things down,' Hugo said. 'Let me get my notes.'

As he went inside, Vivian ran her fingers through her hair. She appeared to want to say something to Marick but didn't know how.

'Is the food alright?' was what she settled on.

'Vivian. It's magnificent. More than I deserve.'

Her smile relaxed again into something he found wide and fathomless.

Hugo returned. 'Here it is.' He read from a notebook. 'Alchemy is an exploration of harmonics. All substances, breathing and inert, have a spectral resonance. A unique vibratory nature. Even Einstein said *Everything is energy. Beyond that is divine.* Take the second law of hermetics, where everything has its opposite: day – night, hot – cold, wet – dry. You can even extend this into a sine wave – two opposite energies but one single wave.'

'Hugo,' Vivian said. 'Do you believe any of that? Because it sounds perilously close to mumbo-jumbo.'

'I didn't say I believed it.' Hugo looked hurt. 'But if we don't have our minds open to all possibilities, we risk being blinkered. Take medicine, for example.' He directed his next postulation to Marick. 'I think if you asked most doctors, they would say there is much to healing beyond the biological principles they understand. Why do you think all the alternative medical fields flourish? Closing yourself off to certain realities because you can't reduce them to graphs and diagrams is a dangerous thing.'

'I want a glass of wine,' Vivian said, standing. 'Can't I have a glass of wine?'

'Sciencism,' Hugo said, ignoring her.

'That makes no sense, Hugo,' Vivian said. She walked to the outdoor fridge and pulled a bottle from what appeared to be boundless supply of alcohol. She poured them all a drink in their water tumblers without further word.

'Sciencism?' Marick asked. 'That's an odd word.' He wanted to support Vivian as well.

'It's a scientific fallacy. A type of logical fallacy really,' Hugo said, taking a swig, not pausing to thank Vivian. 'A trap, where people believe scientific hypothesis and fact are unassailable truths. They disregard the contribution of the humanities, you see, just because those human qualities can't be defined numerically. You should understand this of all people, Marick. The influence of humans, of spirituality, of the ineffable.'

Vivian made a groaning noise.

It occurred to Marick how odd it was to have to defend scientific methods to a scientist. 'But Hugo, there's a flipside to this, isn't there? I hear you, that there's a frailty to science when faced with a universe of immense complexity, but hasn't this sort of thinking opened the door to the plague of conspiracy theories? By downgrading rigorous truths to ideas that can be trumped by opinion?'

'People need something to believe in, Marick,' Hugo said. 'It's a harsh world out there.'

More turkey slices were distributed, perhaps in an attempt to let Hugo's statements settle. Marick wanted to say he thought the point of the scientific method was having the courage to prove your theories wrong, but the last thing he wanted to entertain was the concept of Hugo arguing for the opposite.

'Well, I've been doing my own research,' Vivian said in the pause. 'What if you're looking at this all wrong? Have you considered whether what's going on in the bacteria might simply be accelerated evolution? I mean, don't you get the feeling many other things are now spiralling out of control? The climate unregulated, antibiotic resistance that you keep reading about, things unknown released from permafrost. What if these bacteria have evolved mechanisms and processes we are simply behind the eight-ball in recognising?'

Hugo stared at his wife. Marick could sense his incomprehension, as though he had never heard her come out with such things.

'That's not possible,' Hugo said slowly. 'Evolution has its own timescale. Could not care less for us puny humans and our sense of time.' He made formless doodles in his notebook. 'Although,' and he looked at Marick when he spoke, which Marick found odd, because he should have given credit to his wife, 'there are other examples that look a lot like that. The malaria parasite, tuberculosis, staph, other bacteria that have developed resistance at frightening rates, sometimes in front of our eyes, on the very culture media we have under the microscope. But that is adaptation, not true evolution.'

'Is it?' she asked. There was an unmistakable undertone of contempt in her voice. Marick was unsure where it was directed. At Hugo? Humanity? Biology itself? 'What else are we modern humans doing except altering the course of evolution? What is medicine achieving, except saving those who might in a more natural system die? Because doesn't preventing the premature death of people with suboptimal genetic material mean passing on their defective genes, essentially stopping evolution in its tracks? Man as God.'

Marick busied himself with the last of his turkey.

'Not very Christmassy, Viv,' Hugo said.

Vivian opened her mouth to speak, pursed her lips, started again. 'Neither is voodoo.'

Hugo replied quietly, as though only for himself. 'I'm the one with bacteria changing history.'

Again, a painful silence followed. Marick's knife squeaked across the ceramic of his plate.

Vivian looked to Marick. Her words softened a little. 'Does it make you uncomfortable, Marick, talking of evolution?'

Marick shook his head. 'There are some things that require faith, that leap into the unknown. But evolution, true evolution and the palaeontological records of our planet, these are truths not up for debate.'

He didn't want to admit they had been. At theological college, they'd had an exchange program. An international delegation, primarily from America but also a smattering of other countries, had come to stay at their dorms of residence for six months. Creationism was a hot topic. The teaching of Charles Darwin's theory heretical. Fossil records were entirely misinterpreted, the visitors argued. The marks of Noah's flood were clear upon them. And that was not the only controversial topic – the literality of the miracles, the historical facts and verifiable occurrences in the Bible were frequent subjects for their heated deliberations. Marick developed a small obsession with these ones, cross-referencing the good book with historical records. There were arguments late into the night. He bought more maps – blown-up, expanded charts of the malleable Middle East. Many of the philosophical shots being fired by the group he recognised as bluster and bias, little more than a charisma-based reality, true only to those within the adoring circle. They'd kept him company for a little while, these intellectual skirmishes, at a time when not much else did.

Hugo, Vivian and Marick's plates emptied, leaving only turkey bones and carcass, congealing gravy and crusted knives and forks placed in cruciate fashion over the top. Hugo picked at the remains of bird flesh.

'I admit,' Vivian said, directing her words at Marick, 'I feel less knowledgeable about the machinations of the world than ever. I have a student who's studying acupuncture. Needles into mapped meridians of the body, a disruption of energy forces. Where a pinpoint in the foot can change the dynamics of the ear. He did it to me during one of our sessions – put pressure on the ball of my foot for a headache. Worked brilliantly.'

'You let your students touch you during your sessions?' Hugo's tone migrated into something rawer.

Vivian fired a look at him. 'Don't go there, Hugo.'

The moment hung.

Hugo changed the subject. 'I'm parched. It's Christmas. We need another drink.'

'Oh, please do,' said Marick. The atmosphere had grown sharp edges and this was the least he could think to do to smooth it.

Vivian watched her husband as he refilled her glass, then his. Her arms were folded and stiff.

'Yes. It is Christmas,' Marick added, referring to the wine, but he meant all of it, hoping to rekindle the joy that had flamed out in the dead-end they had argued their way into. He realised how much he needed to see the two of them harmonious. Just one day, just this day. As though a hint of discord might fracture the thin defences he had in place.

Hugo collected the plates and took them into the kitchen. A magpie warbled a song beyond the back fence.

As soon as Hugo had gone inside, Vivian leant over to Marick's glass, and touched it gently with her own. She raised hers to her lips without breaking eye contact with him and sipped. Sweat prickled on the base of his neck. Her eyes were fierce, he thought. As much yellow as green in this light. Drops of amber. Extraordinary. The magpie's music continued, notes dancing into the yard, among the branches.

'Sounds like a serenade,' she said.

Marick had no response.

Hugo returned, pulled out his chair and sat, and, as though they had all agreed to circle back to the start to the medieval beginnings, opened his notebook again.

'I've got more,' he said, and picked out several other entries. 'How about this, from a primer. *Alchemy is simply the ability to bring things to a greater state of perfection.* So, in a way, isn't this exactly what we're doing?'

'I think we've heard enough, Hugo,' Vivian said.

Hugo looked down at his notebook. Stared at it. Took a great slug of his wine.

'We haven't. We've hardly started. Unless you've got something else to add, Vivian?'

Marick clutched his thighs. He did not want to be part of any conflict. Not today.

'I can tell you I looked into gold for rheumatoid arthritis.' She pulled her shoulders back. 'Hasn't been used in years. Used to be given for all sorts of things, including tuberculosis. Didn't work much for that either. Just a blunderbuss anti–inflammatory. So you've got to wonder what this company is up to, sniffing around, wanting to invest.'

'But that's just it, Viv. They *do* want to invest. If they want to sink money into us, imagine the heights we can take this to. What does it matter about their original intent? I've been giving this a lot of thought. If we made the contract watertight, retained every bit of intellectual control ...' Hugo's cheeks had flushed in the sun. 'Viv, you just have to trust—'

'Do not call me Viv. I've always hated it.'

The magpie had ceased its song. The air had also stopped whatever movement it had.

'You're one for hate,' Hugo said.

Hugo and Vivian stared at each other, communicating in ways Marick had no access to.

His familiar nausea swam somewhere deep. No, no. Not today.

The shape of his friends grew clouded, indistinct. He stood and excused himself. Said something useless. They didn't stop him. The bonhomie, now dissipated and gone, had been nothing more than disguise. Camouflage, hiding the memories of the same day five years ago.

He had to get home. It was the place he least wanted to be, but it was where the memories could bleed out. He'd needed distraction; he got focus. Because it would come now. Of course it would come. It always came.

TWENTY-TWO

Their Christmas week together was a carnival, with Claudia on school holidays and Marick on leave as the firm wound down for the break. Their days were play and colour. Diane rang every second day – she sounded buoyant.

'It's indescribable here. I wake at six a.m. without an alarm, just to the birds singing, and honestly, I jump out of bed. I've never had so much energy. Pretty sore from the yoga, but that will pass. Can I speak to Claudia?'

That morning Marick had taken Claudia to her friend's house. He had decided they would do two Christmases. He could not entertain the thought of Claudia waking up without at least the pretence of a visit having been made down the chimney with gifts stuffed into overstretched stockings. Claudia had stopped believing in Father Christmas years ago, but they had made a wordless pact they would carry on regardless. With Claudia in the care of another family that morning, he could spend some time at the shops, choosing a medley of surprises.

'Sorry, love, she's at Annabelle's. It's wonderful to hear you so happy, though. It sounds beautiful.'

Diane went on to regale Marick with the details: the lightness of the meals, the sunrises, the wellness sessions, the rambling bushwalks.

'I reckon I'll be throwing away my pills for good after this,' she said.

Marick wanted to tell her not to be too hasty, but he thought he'd wait until she came back. He didn't want to put a dent in her joy.

He raced from store to store, buying pointless but amusing things. He wanted to hear his daughter laugh as she unwrapped each one. Never had he enjoyed shopping so much.

When he collected Claudia from her friend's, she was flush-faced with delight.

'We made gingerbread men,' she told him. 'Sorry, we ate them all.'

On one of their evenings together, Claudia and Marick constructed Christmas crackers, writing their own jokes to put inside.

'They have to be bad, remember, Dad.'

Claudia was making Diane a little birdhouse out of clay and matchsticks for her gift. She and Marick had begun following a blueprint but they'd tired of its ordinariness and were now crafting something elaborate.

'It's the Taj Mahal of birdhouses!' Marick said.

'Yes! The Queen will come to live there.'

'I don't know what to get your mother yet. What do you think she'll want this year?'

'Dad, you ask me every time. I never know. When I ask her what she wants, she says, nothing. All I want is you, she says. Every year.'

'I can't get her nothing.'

'Why not get her some swimming things? We could all go on a beach holiday, like the one we did together?'

'Great idea, my darling,' and he kissed her on the head. 'You feel hot,' he said.

She shrugged.

'Best have an early night, just in case.'

The next morning was Christmas Eve, the annual day of anticipation. Claudia had come down with a cold.

'What a shame,' Marick said. 'Just in time for Christmas.'

Diane rang early to say hello, and to give them her good news.

'I've managed to get on an earlier flight. It means I'll be back as you're both waking up. I'll catch a taxi straight home so we can still do our presents together.'

'You wonderful thing, Diane, this means so much. Thank you. We are so thrilled you've had a brilliant time. Can't wait till tomorrow.'

He motioned to Claudia as he passed her the phone; *don't tell your Mum about the cold, she'll only worry.* Claudia understood.

'Fine, fine, yes,' Claudia said. 'Yes, I'll look after him. See you tomorrow.'

Claudia was listless. Her temperature hovered high the whole day.

'It hurts to swallow,' she said.

'You poor chicken.'

He made several trips to the chemist, returning with Panadol and jellybeans and throat lozenges. It felt like overkill, but he rang a GP hotline. He got the practice nurse.

'What symptoms does she have?' the nurse asked.

Marick described them all, and they sounded inconsequential.

The nurse agreed and reassured him. 'Just a cold,' she said. 'But does she have any underlying conditions?'

Marick started to say no, but then remembered the seizures of old, those distant dark days.

'Hmm,' the nurse said. 'In those circumstances we'd recommend you go to your local Emergency Department to get checked out, just to be sure. Routine, really. It's just that I can't make any assessment over the phone. I'm obliged to warn you, though, the wait times are pretty horrific at the moment, and they will be even worse tonight. Christmas Eve is always so busy.'

Marick thanked her, and went back to check on Claudia. She lay on the couch, limp and wan.

'I'll finish the birdhouse if you like,' he said.

She shrugged.

'And it might be best if you go back to bed.'

Marick tucked her in. Her breath smelled like wheat gone mouldy. With the cocktail of things he'd spooned into her, she had defervesced. She had a flash sweat and told him she felt better.

He was relieved. He did not want to spend the entire night in the Emergency Department only to be told she had a cold. If she was still sick in the morning, he'd take her in after Diane got home. They could go in together. Let his baby sleep tonight.

'Still, rest up, sweetie. Tomorrow's a big day. Double the day, really. You want to be as well as you can. Do you want a story?'

She shook her head and drifted off to sleep. Her slumber looked calm and untroubled. He watched over her for a little while and thought he would take advantage of the time to do some flamboyant wrapping of her gifts, which he placed quite artfully, it he didn't mind saying so, around the living room, creating a violence of colour among the white.

He would have an early night himself. But first he would have a glass of wine. Celebrate all the wonders in his tiny world. He pulled a two-thirds drunk bottle from the fridge and poured its stale remains into a glass. What did it matter that it tasted terrible?

After a single glass, tiredness overtook him, and he promised himself he'd rise early to tidy up. He only half-undressed, then collapsed on the bed. Dreams came to him through the night. At one stage Italy flew by as he watched with his face pressed against the window of a train carriage. He spotted tumbling farmhouses, tiered vineyards, rustic churches with spires on hilltops, groves of trees all plump with fruit, lakes and light and clouds lying over mountains like lovers. He felt the noise of the tracks while he slept.

When he woke the next morning, Marick was surprised he'd slept so long. Any other Christmas morning, Claudia would have come into his room, waking him with shouts of delight at the discovery of gifts delivered in the night. He rolled out of bed and pulled on the long pants he'd left scrunched on the end of the bed. At that precise moment, he heard a car pull up out the front. He looked at his watch. It would be Diane. Perfect. They could wake up their daughter, both of them, a surprise for her.

They walked into Claudia's room together. And there was their daughter, on the floor, blue and sock-eyed and contorted, the burnt-out contractions of a seizure still hanging on, jerking her with its slow, rhythmic, final dominion.

There were screams, shaking, presents spilled from Diane's airport-branded plastic bag.

Ambulance. Sirens. Questions. IV lines. Drugs. Oxygen. Tubes. Heads shaking.

A blind journey. More questions. Where were you, he remembered being asked.

CT scans. Induced coma. Lights shone in eyes. More EEGs. Words he didn't understand – non-convulsive status, prolonged. Fever-induced seizure. Complications. Coagulopathy. Clots. Venous sinus thrombosis. Like a stroke in a way. Terrible.

Marick was sure somebody said, *It's just one of those things*, but that had to be wrong. There was fault to be had. This seemed clearer with every conversation.

'She went to bed with a sore throat.' He would say it over and over and over during the next few days.

Little else remained in his memory from that day, from the next or from those that followed, except that hell had entered their lives and would never leave, would never take a break. And Diane's words, which she repeated so many times he lost count.

'She would have been crying out for you. Crying out for your help. You didn't even hear her? Or were you just too drunk?'

The empty bottle was a crime scene as far as Diane was concerned. It was still there when he was prohibited from setting foot through the white front door ever again.

Claudia's intensive care unit stay was long, but the details of it Marick never knew. Within a few days, he was barred from visiting, banned from even making phone calls to enquire. Diane had called on her father's lawyer friend to help with the initial salvos, and then her parents returned from Europe. Her father went to war.

Laid out in a dizzying array of legal documents and threatening letters was a litany of reasons why Marick was unfit to see Claudia in ICU. *Drunk, did not seek medical attention, and other* grievances dragged up from the past Marick barely remembered. His excision from both Diane and Claudia's lives was swift. He did not understand the legalities of the documents, but they were intimidating enough to strike fear within him. He did not know what Diane had been telling them for the correspondence to be so ferocious, and he had no idea how to respond.

'It'd be better if you went away quietly,' one of her legal team told him on the phone, coating threats in the pretence of care. 'That way you won't be dragged through court and have all of this come out in public.' In the brief conveyance he could hear Diane. She was making the final delivery of his own worth.

It occurred to him that he didn't know what *all of this* meant, but he couldn't ask because he was mute. Muted and fragmented. Torn apart and anguished – the kind of anguish that took charge of any logical sequencing he may have had access to. His fault. Of course.

That night played on a reel. The ignored telephone advice. The glass of wine. The deep sleep. *You are responsible, you are responsible, you are responsible.* The chant did not let up. He tried to remember what he'd heard in his dreams. Had she been calling for him?

He was permitted to speak only to the lawyer. *Claudia will be severely disabled,* Marick was told a week into the ICU stay. *Yes, she's out of the coma but she doesn't even recognise Diane, so why would she recognise you? You want to help, the lawyer asked? I'll tell you this. Disappear. Let Claudia and Diane try and repair their life without you making it worse. Diane does not want to see you.*

At this point he liquefied into grief. A grief not for death, but for this fathomless chasm of consequences of a single night. It was a black ocean. A yawning pit. Nothing mattered to him. All he understood was that he'd destroyed his Claudia. He had. He must have. The weight and knowledge of his guilt grew by the day. His sweet, golden-lit Claudia. He was swampland, other times scorched sand, and he was reduced further every nightfall. He was spleen and mid-brain, blood and lymph. Sluggish living, fluids barely pumping round his body; his taste buds gone, his diurnal rhythms disintegrated. His days became simultaneously larger and smaller than life itself.

The sun continued to rise each day though, even if Marick expected it might not. After perhaps ten days of dark monotony, a thought pierced his night. What if Diane was testing him? She was no doubt distraught, in need of support, perhaps waiting for him to live up to some ultimate challenge. He just needed to be brave enough. At one lucid point he wondered whether Diane's extreme reaction stemmed from a feeling of guilt that she'd been away when Claudia fell ill.

They could share the incalculable weight of responsibility and learn to forgive themselves together. He would ignore the orders – how legally binding could they be? – and front up to the white house. For days he tried to summon the courage. One afternoon he went to the pub close by and threw down a steadying glass of wine. He clenched his fists and marched up the front path. She opened the door to him and he went to hug her, but she hissed like a cat, snarling that she would call the police if he didn't leave. 'You're drunk again.' She did not look like the same Diane.

The threatening letters transformed into a restraining order.

His emotions petrified to stone. Desiccated. Deadened. The nerve endings shrivelled away. Guts slit open. The irrational stain spreading. Depth charges. Vultures picking out his eyeballs. A smashed slate of everything that had gone before.

Nothing, nothing, nothing.

It was not just Claudia he had lost forever – and the realisation grew like cancer – but his wife too. The sight of Diane hissing, closing the door to the white house, the only place of love he'd ever known. Every life-rope cut with a single murderous knife.

Marick never returned to the firm. Never handed in his notice. That job, that life, was gone. Her lawyers told him Diane would have the white house, and that Diane's father would support them financially, so there would be no need to ever contact them again. He could take a few items from the house. After that he would not be permitted to set foot in it for ever more. In that moment he realised he would become his own father, and leave without sound, because that's what was required to liberate others. All he took was the photograph of Claudia in its delicate black frame and his maps. Let them make a life without him. He was dangerous, a risk, better for them gone. Thoughts of suicide came knocking – what did it matter if he were never to see them again? – but he couldn't even make a plan. He rented a room in a stench-filled boarding house for men, where he progressed, like rotting meat, to fall apart.

TWENTY-THREE

Marick dragged himself through his front door. The inevitability of his future, he realised, was hitched with blind fidelity to his past. What had he expected from Christmas lunch? What had he wanted from an invitation into the home of others? A leave pass from the bloody-mindedness of time?

He wandered his rooms without aim. The light was dull, the dust on the furniture settled over surfaces like cement. The Caravaggio looked faked and the electric organ ridiculous. He could go out, stroll the limbs of the river, but that idea felt too much like pleasure. The dim confines of the walls were appropriate.

The front window was planked with a safety grille and the latches were rusted shut. His front room was always dark. This had been the cheapest of the three units of the triplex to rent. It was the smallest and had been built with all the windows missing out on the choicest cuts of sunlight. He would rent until the day he died, he knew – never again would he buy a house. Mortgages were for families, ownership papers for folk with a future.

Marick opened cupboards. Closed them again. Picked up a book, couldn't concentrate. Unrolled a fusty map, could see nothing on it. He sat in his living room, watching images of the girl who'd stopped for him at twelve as after-shadows playing in the lightless recesses of his brain. Her life flipped like a series of photographic negatives that he knew were readying to come screaming out in colour to torment him.

He knew Claudia and Diane were in Spain. The lawyers' letters came sporadically in the first year, one to every ten of his beseeching ones. How did Claudia look? He asked again and again. *She's had some recovery. The rehabilitation services are excellent in Spain.* No, he could not get their address. The answers were always short, and near identical. He was reminded each time that the best thing he could do for Claudia and Diane was to stay away. They sounded like they could be Deirdre's words, echoing down a generation. He wondered if Diane ever saw those letters. The ferocity of the some of the responses made him guess she might have. He sent his new address to the lawyer whenever he moved, but still he heard nothing.

His head dropped into his hands and he slowly bent, as though he was being compressed. He imagined Claudia wheelchair-bound, and Diane blazing with an eternal fire of rage and blame, hovering over their daughter, spooning liquified food into her mouth.

You fool, he said to himself. It's been five years. Five years you've had to move on.

How much he had wanted to turn to Hugo, to Vivian, to ignore the lunchtime meltdown, to beg for their patience, their understanding. 'I may be a useless friend, failing to facilitate peace, but here lie my reasons,' he would have said, or something like that. How he'd wanted nothing more than to bathe in their acceptance and love. But now here he was with grievous thoughts of Claudia bulldozing everything else away, howling as they came. Today, yes, the memories were going to gnaw at his bones as savagely as ever. The same as last year and the year before, back to the day the recollections were born.

He stood and stepped to the ugly corner cabinet, unlocking it with the miniature filigree key stuck on an angle in the lock. After peering into its recesses, he pulled out an old bottle. It had a decaying label on it, and Marick had to wipe the dust off to check it was sherry. He poured a glass of the thick, autumnal liquid and downed the syrup in a few gulps. It stung his nose. He poured another, hoping it might be able to anaesthetise the tumult in his head.

The year after Claudia's stroke existed only in scraps. Marick could barely remember a single concrete thing he'd done. Their separation had emerged from its black chrysalis as divorce, achieved incisively with signatures sent through the mail. It was mourning without the punctuation of death, and he guessed he'd withered inside it. Perhaps it was this that had scoured away all his recollections. Grief tended to turn most people either hard or soft, he realised. Marick had simply become extinct. But what he did remember, with a blade-like clarity, was it finally sinking in that the greatest gift he could give Diane and Claudia was to cease to exist for them. It was the first glimmer of hope he had, that he might be able to do the decent thing, to prise some integrity from the wastelands. He had remained faithful to this commitment from that point.

Another glass, sticky as treacle, he swamped down his throat. He could feel its thickness spread from his pharynx, into his blood vessels and up into his brain, lifting some of the weight off his bleakness.

He would walk to the river after all, and he tipped the rest of the bottle into a thermos.

It had turned into a type of madness, that first year of desolation. Delusional. Occasionally hallucinatory, with Claudia's voice singing out from other rooms and corners. The theft of sense, of time, of plans. Only once had he seriously considered trying to find them. He looked up private detectives, searched for schools in Seville, but it made him feel so traitorous, so dirty, that he abandoned the effort before any action took root. The white house had been sold. There was no shadow left behind. After that, true to his word, he retreated for good. Disappeared to them all, the only thing he had left to give.

A faint breeze shifted the air as Marick walked. Near the banks of the river the long grass blew in italics, with insects weaving through the rippling greenery.

The river. The river. Hardly a soul was about. Perhaps everybody else was inside, bloated with lunch, drunk with the intimacy of family. He had the path to himself. The river was so much: storied, route-changing over epochs, fertile with life and sediment and silt. All rivers were the basis for civilisations – spiritual, coursing, thrumming, musical.

Marick sat on a mounded bank and closed his eyes, listening to the rush of the water. Minutes passed before he opened up again to the world, taking another slug. His head was suitably light now, his nightmares parading as daytime visions dulled enough to manage.

In an area near him, the river had been peeled back, a result of earthworks nearby, man-made attempts to tame its tidal nature and protect the puny path, to hold back its inexorable progress. The excavation had left a murky, weedy seabed and the smell of decay – the exposed flesh of earth. Not all beauty here, Marick thought, not when humans become involved. Again, the dead only inches from the surface of the living.

The few clouds remaining as a hangover from the previous day clung to the western sky, unwilling to leave, and the sun began its descent for the evening through their bellies. Marick watched, drank more of the sherry and let his disgust for himself play around unhindered until it slowly dissolved, leaving behind the scum that would never fade.

The colours of the sky commenced their morph to gold, and in a strange, tipsy burst of insight, he saw beyond their layered tones. For years he had hoped in desperation God would sweep in and reveal some meaning to what had happened on that Christmas morning and in its aftermath. Now, in the course of a few weeks he had entered a new world where the unthinkable could happen, may have happened. Morph and change and transformation. Without any God at all. A nowhere God. Here he was, a part of it, of life, meaning something, providing worth to another human not seated in a confessional, and all centring around something more golden than the sky.

Marick finished the thermos but remained still and watched until the sun had sunk. His distress was easing, the blast of memory waning. He was a little drunk, and glad enough to be so. The world had adopted a serene spin. He lay back and saw the first star appear and wondered whether he ought to acknowledge to himself that for those years, moribund as they were, the church had been more a place to hide than to find meaning. All he'd done was postpone his real search.

The future. The future was where he needed to direct his gaze. As if in semaphore he saw signalled out in his head, *Hugo, the Alchemist. The Accidental Alchemist.* He found himself accepting the title for the first time.

He was thinking he could sleep there in the warmth of the evening, when his phone blurted out an alert. A text message.

It was from Vivian.

I need to see you x

TWENTY-FOUR

Boxing Day arrived, heedless. Most people woke late, planning to honour the Australian traditions of the day: blistering sunburn, swimming pools, barbecues and beer. Others ignored the morning kookaburras, collating combinations of cricket, playlists, TV and sloth, wondering how to recycle their Christmas lunches into sandwiches.

Marick did neither. He had risen early with a carping headache, determined to make recompense for the night before. He dressed in sober clothes and planned to drop into the hospital. His promise to visit the boy daily was ballast at a time he needed a mooring.

Shaking out cereal from a box into a bowl, he remembered the text conversation he'd had with Vivian, which he sensed had continued far longer than it should have. He pulled out his phone to re-read the messages.

With relief, he saw they were innocuous, apart from the quantity of them, the final one being sent, by her, at midnight. She explained she needed his shoulder. Hugo didn't understand her right now. She felt uneasy about what was going on with the bacteria. *It feels as much a philosophical issue as a physical one, don't you agree?* she had written. *I need to talk to you*, she had texted again. *Tomorrow? Where?*

His replies were a little looser than he would have liked, and he saw the *x* he'd put on the finale, promising to find time. At least he'd suggested somewhere neutral. The central city gardens. Noon. He'd be able to walk there from the hospital. The weather had unclenched, so it should be pleasant among the walkways and rotundas.

In the intensive care unit, the boy's parents were sitting either side of his ruined body: his east and his west. New machinery corkscrewed from his head, and as Marick came closer he could see a small lid of skull had been lifted off. More monitors were stacked up next to him, one on top of another, with a loose synchrony of wave forms and colours and patterns connecting them all.

The father scrambled to his feet as Marick approached. The mother looked beyond him with glazed and glassy eyes.

'It's a last attempt apparently.' The father gestured to the equipment intimately spiralling into his son's brain. 'If the pressures won't come down, they may go on to declare him brain—'

'Don't say it,' his wife spoke, her gaze now in focus, her tone sharp.

The father took Marick a small distance away so his wife could not hear them.

'They're talking about him being an organ donor at this point. But she's,' and he looked over at his wife, 'well, she's not ready to have the conversation.'

'How long can they wait?' Marick asked.

'It'll only be days. Too much longer and the rest of his body will start to pack it in. The process itself takes a few days, so it would be better if we could enter into it soon. Maybe you could talk to her. Give her something to hold on to, believe in, even if it isn't God.'

Marick stepped back to the bed and walked around to the other side. What could he give her? He had no desire to hand her aphorisms and churchful platitudes. He understood the cliff face in her sights, her view a plunge into a bleak and bottomless purgatory.

He pulled up a chair, and to the regular exhalations of the machines, offered what he did best.

'Tell me all the things you are worried about.'

She looked into his eyes and began to cry, slowly at first, a quiver. But as she spoke emotion surged and she did not stop, as though this was the one thing nobody had done so far – ask.

She told Marick about her son. She described him as a child; fair-haired, excellent at maths. Great at kicking a football, not always so good at catching. Constantly hungry. She relayed in detail the sight of him riding his bike down the hill near their house, his hair blown back like a flag of freedom. Marick's own tears threatened to come as she filled in the layers. Too close he thought, but he didn't move to wipe his eyes.

She held Marick's hands. Loved by his teachers, she went on. Always wanted a dog, but we never got him one. Tidied up without being asked. There were more, memories, vignettes, a life. From the corner of his eye, Marick could see the father shuddering in silence, also lost in what she was saying. High school, the place at university. An on-again off-again girlfriend who couldn't bring herself to come and visit. The cousins driving up from the country. His favourite one, a little girl, she's twelve. Bella. The two had such a special bond. It will kill her, when she sees.

'No, it won't, darling,' the father walked round to her side, and the three of them knotted together, hanging on to one another with energy that came from elsewhere, not their wearied bodies. They all surrendered to the moment, and once they were spent, Marick understood a corner had been turned.

'You'll make the right choice,' Marick said to both of them. 'And it will be a decision made out of love. It will always be yours and you will never need to doubt it.'

The mother hugged him again, and Marick nodded to the nurses on the way out.

The silver elevators floated him down to the ground floor. There were few people around. The father had been right, Marick reflected, about the gravity and significance of believing in something. Something to hold on to, he had said.

As Marick walked out to the front, he reflected on his allegiance to Hugo. That wild strange man, with the stranger things under his care. They'd each chosen the other. Somebody to hold on to, too. Faith as choice. Friendship as precious intention.

The other thing that sparked his thoughts was the mention of organ donation. He would check on Dolly, see how she was getting on, she and her admirable dream of passing on a kidney. Crossing over to the volunteer shop, he saw it was open, the lights inside buzzing, but there was no Dolly, simply a wizened woman he had not seen before.

'No, Father, she's not here. She was supposed to be in at nine. I've tried phoning but it just rings out. I'm a little worried to be honest. She never misses a shift,' she said. 'Here are her details.' She scrawled down a number and address. 'Perhaps you could look in on her.'

Marick peered at his watch. It would be tight, but if the bus timetable looked favourably upon him, he could be at Dolly's and back to the park with a little time to spare. The sensation he had, picturing Vivian sitting on the park bench in the sun, was too complex to name. Whatever it was, it was accompanied by a low heave in his stomach. What did he know of her, and what she wanted? Or himself in this circumstance? And wasn't this the core of it? He hurried to the bus stop to make sure he could pull off his complicated arrangement of visits.

Trying Dolly's number as he slipped through the suburbs, he also had no answer. The bus passed into an older section of town where many of the houses were wilted, their paint bleached in the sun. The driveways were decorated with ageing cars, fences and awning trimmings sunk, becoming too heavy for their years.

Dolly's house, and he was not surprised, was an exception. Charming and low, it was fronted by an archway embroidered with brown vines. He ducked through. A jacaranda with an explosion of purple blooms owned half the front yard. The path leading to the front door was lined by an honour guard of roses. On the verandah, a matching pair of wicker chairs sat at a conversational distance from each other across a varnished outdoor table, and running along the fringe of decking was a precise line of herbs in pots.

Marick rapped on the door and peered through the frosted strip down the side. Lights were on inside, and when he rang her number again, he could hear its pert response just beyond. He called out her name to nothing. Something was not right.

Creeping around the side, he saw a high window, perched open. Marick looked up at it and sighed. There was no alternative but to drag one of the chairs from the front and stack it against the wall. He hoisted himself up and poked at the old flywire. It gave in, detaching with a puff of dust. He managed to wriggle up and through the aperture between pane and window. His shirt hooked on a nail and tore a small rent in his pocket, but he could haul his clump of a body through and he dropped onto the floor below.

'Dolly,' he called out. 'It's the chaplain.'

The house had high ceilings and wallpapered walls, that now he was in there had the odd look of nightmares. 'Dolly?'

As he skulked down the hallway, past cabinets of curios, Marick thought he heard a noise – a filtered groan. He saw her legs first, with their bare, unslippered feet poking through a door, one rotated at the ankle.

Clambering down next to her, he discovered her delirious, moaning.

'My leg,' she said.

A puddle of congealed blood had seeped into her queenly hair, turning its silver tips the colour of cherries.

'Oh God,' he said, and crouched down beside her. 'It's Marick,' he added. 'Dolly, you're hurt.'

Her breath sounded full of liquid, but she nodded, understanding him. He called for an ambulance, and sat back beside her, patting her shoulder. Her skin was cold, her lips mottled and prattling of nothing, but she grew quiet in the lull of his reassurance.

Paramedics arrived before he thought of what more he could do for her, taking over in slick movements and practised efficiency, shooing Marick out of the way.

'Fractured neck of femur,' one of them said. 'For sure.'

'Hypothermia and pulmonary oedema,' said the other. 'As well as the head injury.'

'Watch her neck,' the first said, although the words seemed redundant as they taped and collared and sandbagged her into place.

'Who's her next of kin?' Marick was asked, as they slid her up and onto a stretcher, tied her legs, and strapped an oxygen mask to her face.

'I'm sorry. I don't know her that well.'

'Well enough to break in though?'

Marick worried the paramedics might be going to call the police. Perhaps they were looking for something out of the usual to do on a public holiday

'I'm the hospital's chaplain,' he said, which seemed to appease them. 'Can I come in with her?'

'No room, I'm afraid.'

Dolly grimaced as the stretcher was lifted up and onto the trolley for transport. He did not know if she could hear him, or understand what was going on in the hallucinatory, painful movements of shifting her around.

'It will be alright, Dolly. You're going to be looked after. It's your turn now.'

'Her turn for what,' the paramedic said as they exited the front door.

'To be cared for,' he said. 'She's one of the good ones,' he added, but they were gone.

By the time he returned to the city, finding his way to the bench seat in the gardens where he had pictured himself and Vivian talking in the botanical shade, his heart was beating like a beast and it was almost two o'clock. He had not called her, and she had sent no message to ask where he was. Of course, he thought, she will not be there, and she wasn't. He was too late.

It helped confirm that he'd imagined it all. Made it up. He was wrong and foolish and lost in a belief she really did need him somehow. Who was he to need anyway? The stone of the bench had been warmed by the sun, and he sat for a while, watching birds gathering and ducks waddling among picnickers dressed in the uniform of holidays: shorts and thongs and hats. A hot-air balloon sailed overhead and the air was so calm he could hear the burner being opened. It sounded like an expedition, of escape. This was for the best, he persuaded himself, that they hadn't met. There could be none of this betrayal now, whatever innocent intentions he had. Letting Vivian down was perhaps the easiest way to reset the balance between the three of them. The upset with Dolly was the intervention of Fate.

He would have liked to stay sitting there until autumn. Two became three o'clock, and Marick stood from the seat, stretched and took the return bus home. He wanted time to shift on, Christmas and its partner holiday to be done with, packed up and put away for another year. He sent a non-committal apology to Vivian by text as the bus bumped along. *So sorry about today. Something came up. Emergency.* That would do it, and he put the phone away. It did not ping in reply.

But as he walked through the gate to his triplex, there she sat, as blithesome as the sun in his poky little courtyard, smiling at him.

'I know you won't mind,' she said, and she stood up and embraced him, leaving the softness of her cheek next to his, so much more than a kiss.

TWENTY-FIVE

The Theological College Marick signed up to after months of wretched solitude was one of the less prestigious institutions in town. It had an eagerness for full-fee-paying students and a loose affiliation with his old university where Marick held an unblemished academic record, and the faculty were prepared to overlook his deficient history of church involvement.

'Always happy to sign on new recruits,' the ruddy-faced registrar bellowed. 'You'll love it here.'

It was also one of the only residential monastic schools around – precisely what Marick had wanted. Immersion. Not so much hope but resignation. When questioned about his motives for signing up – for a basic diploma with a plan to progress to a Master of Theological Studies – he would always struggle to reply. After a while he designed a dependable answer: *I have been deaf to the call of God my whole life.* It seemed to please his advisers. If they looked as if they were going to push him further, he would point to his hearing aids as though having a little joke. They'd all titter in half-smiles and leave it there.

The grounds were on a few hectares of scrubby bushland on the shady side of a mount. Not quite on top, which was unfortunate they all knew, since the highest ground was always preferable, but that real estate had been earmarked first by a small shopping centre.

The college was peaceful and had a monastery feel to it, with birdsong the only sound of a morning and a clear view to the distant escarpment over which the sun would rise like a promise every morning. Men only, so any fleshly temptation was removed. They were encouraged to stay on campus as much as possible. That suited Marick down to the ground and for the first year he had an austere and monkish room to himself with a flinty bunk, a bedside table and a shelf for books, which did for everything he now possessed. He had put a few things in storage, his maps and array of reference books. His photograph of Claudia had been too much to bear, and he had tucked it away with the rest under lock in some outer suburb.

Marick took subjects in systematic theology, religion in Australian society, church history and biblical studies. Once a week they had small group sessions, held in a cold hall where they sat on fold-up chairs in a tight circle. Part of dedicating your life to God, they were taught, was to open your heart and that was not only something to be done in private – the trick was knowing how to do it in front of your fellow man. Be vulnerable. Trust. Marick never managed. They were asked to share the most difficult point in their lives, a time at which their faith was at its lowest. A young man next to Marick described an opiate addiction and the day he stole from his parents. Another talked of the feeling of having failed God, alluding to his attraction to men. The group applauded gently and sincerely.

When it came to Marick's turn, he had already decided which diversion he would use.

'I asked God to cure my hearing. He didn't answer.'

They all nodded and embraced each other when it came time for coffee and biscuits.

The study units were compelling; Marick was drawn to the historical subjects like a man thirsting. He became expert in avoiding the question of what, exactly, he was doing there. The fraudulence of his presence at the seminary was a quiet demon inside, whispering that he was only looking for meaning, not God, but whenever his doubts about his intentions threatened to surface, he would bury himself back in his studies, proving at least to his supervisors that he was one of the most capable students they'd had. Anyway, he thought, what's the difference? Isn't this part of a holy life? Unravelling the enigma of meaning? Perhaps what he was searching for was a way to transform grief into grace, and the existence of a robed and biblical God was not essential to the process. Or, as time progressed, perhaps he simply wanted reassurance on a single fact, that although he had been responsible for the destruction of his family, he would eventually be forgiven, with some greater purpose to such devastation revealed.

But God was woven through the fabric of the course, and His existence was the one thing not up for debate. Marick had no choice but to accept that, although he never made his uncertainty known. His foothold at the college became strong. He was well liked by his peers, although made no close friends. Few of them did; this was a time for forging bonds with the Lord, not other men.

Marick threw himself into communal chores, happy to peel potatoes or spend hours with his hands in soapy water, scrubbing dishes. At night, on his thin mattress and scratchy sheets, he would wonder how Diane was getting on. The loss of Claudia was a scythe through him, never absent, but he also missed his ex-wife. He missed the familiar, round warmth of her. When he managed to lock Claudia, and what he'd done, away in some oubliette of his brain, he afforded himself memories of their years of happiness. Perhaps this was all he'd ever get. Brief, beautiful images, powered by pretence.

He didn't blame Diane for reacting the way she had. Night after night he lay in half-sleep until the nightmares clocked on, allowing into his head the knowledge she must have suffered too, and how little he'd been permitted to give her in support. But too late. Too late. He knew he would never love another woman. Would never want the kiss or the smell or the taste of another.

By the end of the first year the Americans had moved in and the cloistered silence was over. He only endured a few months of them before he packed his few belongings on a flat, brooding morning, and found himself a cheap rental – the wedge of triplex that was suitably austere itself. He brought his meagre belongings out of storage and set himself up for the long haul.

⁂

'Of course. Vivian. You must come in.'

Panic rose inside Marick again, wild hooves rearing behind his breastbone. What was she doing here? He would give her tea. Ask about Hugo. Send her back to him. He fretted about

245

the state of his kitchen, and he babbled on the way in, disguising his worry with whether the milk was in date. He strode to the fridge. It was.

When he relayed the story of Dolly, he was swathed in compassion and understanding.

'You poor man,' Vivian said, and put a hand on his arm. 'How awful. No wonder you couldn't make it.'

She offered neither excuse nor explanation as to how she had found herself in his courtyard. Today her lips were coral pink, her hair pulled back, her nose sun-kissed, her dress almost translucent in the light.

While Marick returned to fussing in the kitchen, she wandered round the cramped innards of the rest of the place.

'What a magnificent picture,' she called out. He presumed she meant the Caravaggio – the only other image was his daughter, framed into eternity in the privacy of his bedroom.

He poked his head round the door.

'Oh yes, the *Death of the Virgin*. I'm not sure why I liked this one so much. I think it might be the rebellion of it. The original painting was torn down by the anti-Reformation movement in Rome. It was considered a disgrace, blasphemous because he depicted Mary as being real – and it was removed. The great man was lambasted as a crank. Caravaggio as failure, for celebrating truth.' He tried to smile. 'Tea?' he asked, although he'd already made it.

'Lovely,' she said. 'Come sit down. We need to talk.'

They perched across from each other. Vivian leant in, their knees close to touching.

The room was too warm. 'Maybe I should open a window?' He stood again. 'Are you comfortable?'

'Perfectly,' she said.

'What can I help you with?' Marick asked on his feet, awkward standing above her. He wanted to couch the conversation in the generic. Remove whatever the sweat behind his neck was telling him.

'Hugo trusts you. I trust you,' she said. 'Please sit down. I need to come out with it. This whole thing of Hugo's. It's too preposterous. Frankly unbelievable. The more I think about it, the more difficulty I have with the concept. Bacteria making gold. Marick, do you know how it sounds?' Her lips sealed in on themselves and she held a hand over the steam of the tea, as if daring herself to flinch.

Marick sensed the tension in her movements, the irritation.

'Come on,' Vivian continued looking directly at him. 'I can't face being humiliated again.' She picked up the tea and sipped it, holding the mug with two hands. 'I simply wanted to ask you without him around, whether you're taking this seriously.'

There was something unpleasantly victorious in how this made Marick feel. She had come to him, to ask him, holding him to a higher standard than her own husband. But that thought led to nowhere good. Reset, Marick, he tried to tell himself.

'Vivian, I completely understand your concern,' he said. He was going to add that trying to wrap your head around something that had never before existed, and theoretically should not at all, was a huge leap – but Vivian had sprung up from her seat, and she charged to the window.

'Do you, Marick? Do you?'

Her voice was angry. She was angry.

Lifting a shutter, she looked outside. 'That's all real. Daylight. Concrete. Trees growing from dirt and water and carbon dioxide. That, I get. Although you don't have any trees here, do you?' She turned to him and smiled again, her hostility evaporating.

'No, I'm afraid. Pretty awful, isn't it?' He smiled in return.

'What I want to know, is do you believe him?'

'Hugo?'

'Yes. My husband. Are his bacteria producing gold?'

Marick hesitated. 'In a way this leap is easy for me. I don't understand any of the processes in the first place. But there is something I do know, and it's that I believe Hugo is telling the truth. And whatever is going on in his lab, Hugo is committed to uncovering that truth, layer by layer.'

Vivian narrowed her eyes, and for a moment he saw her pupils were as small as entry wounds. She looked away and sighed, saying nothing in response.

'I believe in you too, Vivian. I can see how this must be difficult.'

A minute must have ticked by before she spoke again. She looked around. 'Did your wife live here?'

Marick winced. 'No. I only started renting it ...' – he swallowed – 'after.'

Taking slow steps, Vivian walked over and sat down next to him. The chair was only meant for one. Horrible thing it was, Marick was aware, with an embarrassment of metal skeleton extruding from the fabric of its arm. He could feel the entirety of her warm side pressed against his. Her perfume was subtle, the smell of fields of flowers.

He pulled at his collar.

'Why do you love maps so? What do you see in them?'

Her question gave him the opportunity to remove himself from the chair.

'Let me show you.'

Marick crouched to open one of the cabinet drawers and he reached inside. He wanted to tell her they were his company when the Bible became too claustrophobic. That they offered possibilities. But Vivian spoke, her words staccato.

'It's just he makes me feel so small.'

'What?' Marick said, standing.

'Hugo. Like he considers me lesser. As though I'm not part of his great new life. While you are, Marick.'

Marick stood, artless with a rolled map of the Middle East in his hands. What can I say? he thought. That there is no competition here? 'No, no. That is not the case at all. He adores you. I can tell.'

'Can you, Marick? Really?'

Vivian was sending up flares, Marick sensed, and he did not know where to walk, how to position himself near her. Her beauty was a monstrous pull. He hadn't dwelled on female beauty in years, not since he had been lost in his own wife's. It was such a difficult thing for him to understand. Easy to react to, difficult to rationalise. Beauty was both unimpeachable privilege and prison. Foreign. A box. Both surface-thin and something that could overpower the heart of the bearer. A construct designed to hide as much as it revealed. This was all wrong.

'The Middle East,' he said, his mouth dry, rolling out the map.

They sat on the floor. They were giants towering over the topography, looking down over the journey of the lines and the symbols. Easy distraction.

'Every event in the Bible can be traced to somewhere in here,' Marick said and pointed without giving Vivian time to respond. 'With enough reading between the lines, that is. All those occurrences. Everything ever written.' He pointed out Jordan, Syria, Palestine, Jerusalem. 'But the thing is, little archaeological evidence has been found. So much of what we know comes from story. Story and interpretation. But once in a while something turns up. Something concrete.'

He was going to continue to babble. Let these old dead stories fill the clumsy space. 'Take King David,' Marick continued. 'He's the pivot point for all the religions: Jewish, Christian and Islamic. There's a fragment of basalt in a museum somewhere, carbon-dated back to the ninth century before the birth of Christ, inscribed in Aramaic, claiming it to be from the House of David. At some point, isn't that what all leaps into the unknown are? A balance between evidence and faith?'

Vivian sighed, looking from the map to Marick's intense frown and back to the floor. He was talking irrelevance, he thought. Or being too opaque in imagery. Addressing her as though she was a parishioner. He needed to frame it better.

Vivian shuffled around so she could look at the map from the same angle as Marick.

'Such a fascinating part of the world,' she said. Her mood had swung again, and was now contemplative, with her head cocked to one side. 'Hugo and I once took a Middle Eastern cooking class. I can't recall why, now, since he hates cooking. I think we were trying to find a hobby we could enjoy together and it seemed very multicultural and hip at the time. I bought a whole lot of spices and a tagine. I'm not sure I've ever used them.'

'It does sound very stylish,' he said. He could feel her knee pressing into his. His throat threatened to close in, having her so near, so fragrant. Her voice filled the room.

'Do you truly think all those stories were real? That they were literal?'

He realised her hand had come to rest on his thigh.

'In the Bible, you mean?' He could not work out whether the heat he felt was coming from within, or the room itself, but his discomfort was making it hard to get his answers out right.

'Exactly. What about the miracles? Curing the crippled and resurrecting the dead? Commanding the weather? Water to wine? Nothing to fishes?'

Marick looked at Vivian. He didn't have the ability or the energy to lay out what he knew was a very complicated answer, somewhere between actuality, allegory, need and teaching, or possibility and promise, or the challenge of interpreting words written by men who knew they were guided by the hand of something greater, which for these stories was their God. It was all too complex, and by the time he thought of how to move the conversation on, Vivian had leant over, and kissed him.

All the thoughts that should have come to him, chose not to. He ought to have permitted alarms to sound, to wonder whether the questions she had come to ask were mere excuse, to rail against her finding him attractive and what could she possibly be thinking, or simply to recoil from what amounted to a final rank betrayal, but none of those things arrived to quench the fire in his head, the burning heat in his mouth.

She kissed him with lips as soft as dreams, a kiss as slow as a season, deeper than belief. It was overwhelming and he couldn't remember ever feeling that sensation before, although he must have, some distant bell was telling him. The moment drew out into two, three. Vivian explored his mouth. They were connected, and it had happened. He could sense himself pulling away, but somehow this did not translate into motion. Her kisses were a declaration he could not understand. Something monumental. He couldn't open his eyes. He could hear nothing. But out of the nothing came the intrusion of his phone ringing, shrill and insensitive.

'Don't get it,' she somehow mouthed into his.

But the reality of the noise opened up his mind to those absent concepts that hadn't had a chance in this first round and he stood up and half-staggered back.

'Vivian, I'm so sorry ...'

He grabbed his phone from his pocket. It was Hugo calling. He held up the phone to show her.

'Shit,' she said.

He answered.

'Marick, I need you,' Hugo said.

Marick walked away from Vivian to talk. His lips stung.

'What is it?' Marick asked.

'We need to get them out. Tonight.'

Marick wiped the back of his hand across his mouth. 'What do you mean?'

'I mean I've been fielding phone calls all afternoon. On Boxing Day. I'm pretty sure the executive of the hospital and the drug company are somehow in league with each other. They know where the bacteria are, I guarantee it. We have to rescue them, Marick. I'd ask Vivian but she's out with her girlfriends this afternoon. They'll be having drinks and I won't see her all evening. There's too much equipment to carry on my own. And anyway, I reckon you'd be a better accomplice, my friend.'

Marick found responding difficult. 'Where are you going to take them?'

'Back to our house, I think. Viv won't mind. She's come around to the whole thing.'

Marick looked over at Vivian, who was sitting on his couch, curled up with her feline legs beneath her, looking disillusioned. She made the words without sound – *What does he want?*

The situation felt dire, the reality of it made him queasy.

'Of course, Hugo. Of course I'll help.'

'Great. I'll drive by your place and get you. Twenty minutes? Have you got any heavy-duty bags? And it's a heist, my friend. Wear something inconspicuous.'

Marick began to give Hugo his address, but realised Hugo already knew it. Putting his phone away, he looked over at Vivian.

'I heard,' she said. 'Looks like I'm going home then.'

'Vivian, I am so sorry. About all of it. I shouldn't ... We shouldn't.'

She shrugged and waved him off, to indicate, *leave it.* Collecting her handbag, she walked over to him and kissed him again briefly on the lips.

'Vivian, we can't,' was all Marick said.

'Can I come again?' she asked, as though she hadn't heard him.

'Vivian ...' he repeated.

'I've got to go,' she said, and she did.

TWENTY-SIX

In twenty minutes precisely, Hugo roared into Marick's driveway in a battered old Honda.

'Sorry about the ride,' he said to Marick. 'Salary of a scientist, I'm afraid.'

'Are you sure we should be doing this?' Marick asked as he slid into the front seat. He had found several bags, none suitable for this sort of thing. What sort of thing, he asked himself? A late-night biological burglary? It was bordering on the absurd. All of it.

'Which bit?' Hugo turned the key, and the motor chugged over several times before starting back up. 'Stealing back that which is rightfully ours? Or the alchemy in the first place?'

Marick did not want to look at Hugo. He thought his guilt would be a beacon, his insides still raging. 'We shouldn't use that word, Hugo.'

'Fair enough. But regarding the bacteria? The whole setup? It's all my property anyway. My equipment. My future. Nobody else has a right to it.'

They cruised through the quiet streets under the pulse of streetlamps and their sodium-vapour glow. Vines of coloured lights were strung through trees, and icicles and reindeers flashed in windows with a kind of sad glory, clutching to the remnants of Christmas.

Marick's mind was racing, trying to keep abeam of this discussion. Should I bring Vivian into the conversation? Mention her in passing? he wondered. In the end he decided to let the conversation find its own way there if it were meant to be.

'Where will you put them?' he asked. 'It's a big undertaking.'

'I know,' Hugo said. 'But I've done it before. Re-homed them. They've survived a few emigrations. I had a bad feeling about the conversations today, Marick. If I don't willingly give the bacteria up, they'll be taken anyway. There was talk of all sorts of deals being made – huge donations to the hospital by this company. It sounded threatening.' Hugo gripped onto the wheel, shaking his head. 'So, my friend, it's now or never. And then we can negotiate, on our own terms, on our own turf.'

Marick went there. 'And are you sure Vivian won't mind? Having a laboratory in the house?'

'Why should she?' Hugo glanced at Marick as they swung around a corner. They broached the hard edge of the city with its ordered lights and tree-like decorations.

'No particular reason,' A compromise, Marick thought. 'It's just such a lot of equipment.'

'She's a funny girl alright. I do wish she'd be more supportive of all this. She's treating it as though this is a burden rather than the opportunity of a lifetime. She has so little respect for it all, and in a way then, for me. She's been happy enough to enjoy the extra money I've been able to bring in from the bacteria so far, without so much as a thank you, or any interest in where it came from – until now. Marriages are like that though, aren't they? They fade with complacency. You drift along. You lose the spark. You have less and less in common.'

'But you seem happier than most couples I know.' Marick was scrambling, wanting to make them happy simply by saying so. And it was not a falsehood, because he knew no other couples these days. 'And you have done things together. Like your Middle Eastern cooking classes.'

Hugo looked hard at Marick as he pulled into the front of the hospital. 'We've never done any cooking classes together. Are you thinking of someone else?'

Before Marick could digest this, Hugo switched off the engine and jumped out of the car. 'Let's do this, Marick.'

Inside the gills of the hospital there was little except humming background noise, the entryway dim and mostly empty, the public holiday having temporarily cleared the place of its industry. They walked past the blackness of Dolly's shop, and he wanted to tell Hugo about the incidents of the morning but was nervous his summary might bleed into the rest of the day's occurrences. Hugo was striding off anyway.

'We should hurry,' Hugo said. 'And look discreet.'

Slipping down to basement level three, they avoided the obstacles, and clambered through the narrow entrance to the laundry. They stood for a few seconds, reverent among the life.

'We could be superheroes coming in here,' Hugo said. 'Gods ourselves. Masters of the impossible.'

'Let's just get these things out,' Marick said. 'You direct me.'

They heaved the voltaic cradles into the bags. Marick carried a centrifuge. 'We'll need to make several trips,' Hugo said.

Ferrying out the pots and plates and the microscopes, they wove back and forth through the threads of the corridors, leaving the incubator until last. On that final trip they carried the hulking thing out of the laundry between them like a litter. When they reached the elevators to take them up for the last run, they waited for it to return to them, but according to the panel it appeared to be forever more stuck at basement level one. They eased the incubator to the ground and Hugo repeatedly jabbed at the button. No success.

'Bugger,' said Hugo. 'We'll have to find an alternative way.'

They hoisted the incubator into the crooks of their elbows again and hobbled back past the laundry to the other end of the corridor. There were the fire-escape stairs that would take them up past Marick's office, but both of them agreed that three flights of stairs with this thing would be impossible. Marick peered into the stairwell and saw with surprise there were more steps heading downwards. He'd never noticed these. But any steps were out of the question, so they lumbered back the way they had come and passed through a set of sliding doors that grated as they closed behind the pair. The light was frail, and occasionally a globe clunked on while they passed, activated by an ancient motion-sensor hidden somewhere. They huffed along, following the curve of the corridor.

Halfway round the bend was a wide door, labelled with some sort of hieroglyphic font. Ancient runes, Marick thought, but he was not going to risk voicing *that* out loud. Hugo put out a hand to open it, and they both pushed it wide. Inside was some sort of chamber consisting entirely of valves – grey, white, black, some corroded, some gleaming – which were making a churning, pulsing sound as though it were the heart of the hospital.

'This is not right,' Hugo said, and they set their load down again. They looked ahead, recognising nothing, and hauled the incubator again into position.

As they struggled and panted, another set of lifts came into view, the doors painted a washed-out blue. Neither of them cared where it took them – their primary need was to be relieved of the incubator, which had seemed to gain weight with each step. Inside, they lowered the thing to the elevator floor. They calculated three floors up, but on stepping out of the lift not a thing was recognisable.

Hugo indicated forward. 'We've got no choice. We'll find a directory.'

When they thought they should be close to the main exit, they realised they weren't. They turned a corner into a huge, elongated room of puzzling height. It had a low-slung ceiling and a dusty parquetry floor. It was neither crawlspace nor normal room. Cramped and low, it suggested the architects had only been half-hearted about the ceiling's apogee. In a corner were rusted sinks and cupboards and a long serviceable desk. A small area at one end of the desk looked tidied, as though it had been recently used, and there was a newish cushion on the nearby chair, but apart from that the room had the smell of abandonment. A place long ago forgotten. Hugo's hair almost touched the roof, but Marick's had plenty of clearance.

'I wonder what this is for?' Marick asked Hugo.

Hugo shrugged, as Marick peeked around. He wanted to know, and had a spidery idea come to him.

Hugo was impatient. 'Come on, Marick. We're here for me, not a hospital safari.'

The incubator was again heaved up and the two men exited out the other side, discovering a working set of lifts and a lustreless directory board which indicated that one further floor below would disgorge them directly out of the hospital.

With aching arms and an exhalation of relief, they settled the incubator into the cramped car. The boot and the backseat were full and Marick balanced the bacteria on his lap. Hugo drove slowly so as not to risk a drop spilt. Neither had much to say on the way back to Hugo's house while the comet streetlights flashed their slow tails into the car. Marick's mind wandered to food – he had not eaten all day – and he imagined lamb, Moroccan spices, dolma, mezze, falafel. His mouth watered like treachery. As they approached the house, he reviewed the day's earlier events – his mind's eye blinking on repeat. What would he say to Vivian?

Hugo called her on the way. 'You're home? Good,' he said on the phone as he drove. 'Could you come out and help us unload?'

Vivian greeted them at the front. She had changed into a demure dress with lace on the collar and sleeves to her elbows. She said a non-committal hello to Marick and proved strong in hauling pieces of equipment inside. Marick wondered if he might have imagined it all. A kiss that could never be repeated.

Marick started to offer help in setting up the equipment, but watching Hugo and Vivian together, working as a team, he decided he should leave them to it. Hugo offered to drive him home, but Marick sensed he did not entirely mean it, so he mumbled something about the train and headed off.

259

That night Marick didn't stand the photo of his daughter next to his bed. He drifted in and out of sleep, hoping to invite in anything but the kiss. Rome would work. He begged Diane to return to his dreams; he conjured palazzos, a marble torso they had both found in a museum basement, gelato, daylight and iron doors and bakeries. But no. On the dot of four, he woke in the netherworld, the purgatorial in-between, and he tried to speak but couldn't form the words. He looked at his arms and tried to move them but discovered the connection between brain and limbs severed and useless. His hands remained slumped on his chest. He was a sitting duck, prey that could not move, and he could sense fiends in the shadows awaiting their chance to attack, doubly enraged at his sell-out. Eventually he gave in to them, let the demons have their fill. Marick then slept, dreamless and lost, until morning.

TWENTY-SEVEN

On the bus heading into work, Marick's thoughts returned to the strange room he and Hugo had come across. He pulled a banana from his bag as he bumped through the suburbs, sliding a fingernail into the curve of its skin. It released its mushed, pale smell and a man in a suit in front turned and frowned at him.

The idea nudging him since his conversation with the staff by the church fence joined forces with that room. What if he could use that place to establish some sort of sanctuary, a centre for companionship and talk? Branch out from death and disease. Create a place for people to have fellowship, find support? He could make use of his one skill – listening. Dear God, he thought, with the bus's suspension jolting through him, he wanted to do *something* useful.

Maybe though, he thought, this was a search for something to occupy his mind rather than Hugo, Vivian, and the gold. And more so, that kiss, which loomed like an asteroid on collision course.

Down in his office, he pulled out his hospital map, now creased and folded into the softness of cloth. With his index finger, he traced where he thought the room should be, but found no hint of it. Turning the map sideways did not help. He admonished himself, You're good at maps, Marick. But there was no evidence of a half-floor, a tucked-in long room, a potential space. He sat back, thinking; he would have to recreate their sneak around from last night.

Marick failed. He tried to locate the route from the outside in, reverse what they'd done, but he could not find any powder-blue elevators. He wondered whether they'd been repainted a different colour overnight, not entirely unexpected for this place. He must be close, he thought, but as it became clear he would have to return to Hugo's now-empty laundry and work his way up, he glimpsed the same emergency physician ducking through a side door and out of sight. He followed her and spied her turning a corner and walking into the low space he had not been able to find himself. She sat down at the small cleared area of table and pulled a notebook from her scrubs pocket. He waited at the door and watched, unsure whether he should interrupt.

He was an intruder in this space. She was in a reverie, in communion with what she was writing – he should let her be, he thought. But remembering how misplaced she had looked only a few nights ago, a castaway in the night, he told himself to be bold.

He cleared his throat. She looked up.

'Oh, hello,' she said, and she returned to what she was writing.

'I am sorry to interrupt,' he said, and she faced him again, 'but I was wondering if you know what this room is?'

She looked around. 'This place?' she said, shaking her head. 'It is quite odd, I grant you that.'

'May I?' he asked, gesturing to a chair.

'Of course.' She laid down her pen. 'A better answer might be, I don't know. I found it months ago. I haven't seen anybody else come through here. It's one of my joys, you see, finding the hidden places in the hospital. I've a long way to go yet. This hospital is a labyrinth of epic proportion. It's almost mythical. I wouldn't be surprised to hear of a minotaur in its depths.' She gave a brief laugh. 'Which I don't really mean, of course.' Her serious expression returned.

Marick understood that in a way she did mean it.

'Or Rumpelstiltskin, spinning gold,' he responded, 'if we're talking fables.'

'Exactly,' she said, and they both fell quiet.

He let the moment have its due, allowing the fanciful to sit without challenge for a bit.

'But why I'm here, and why I ask about this place,' Marick said, 'is because I have been hoping to find somewhere unused.' He pulled his chair in a little closer. 'To be honest, it was the conversation I had with you the other night. Do you remember?'

'I do. We were talking about the random horrors of the hours. The march of the broken and the injured we were seeing. It felt overwhelming.'

'Yes, and I wondered whether you had anyone to talk to about it. Maybe someone at home? At work? Where do you let it all out?'

'Let it out?' she asked slowly.

'Yes. Debrief. Ventilate. Be heard.'

She shook her head again. 'I don't do that. Ever. All the things in here, all the decisions, all the violence, the death, the pleading, my own inadequacy in the face of it, all of it gets shoved down deep, the residue from one patient crushed on top of another. It won't ever come out.' Her expression was distant. 'I'd be a volcano, a pressure cooker with the valve finally unscrewed.'

'Maybe that's what I could be here for,' said Marick, raising an arm to gesture taking in the muffled space.

She shook her head and returned to her notebook, doodling on the page. Marick saw she had a few sentences written down.

'You're writing something?'

She flipped her notebook to its first page and pushed it towards him.

When I realised I had become a stranger to myself, she had scrawled as some type of beginning, *I went underground to write the story of my hospital, not knowing it would take the opportunity to write the story of me.*

'Intriguing,' he said. 'What's it for?'

'It is supposed to be the start of a book I want to write. About this place. But I've been coming here for weeks, trying to get things down, and I can't move any further than this. The stories in this hospital defy translation into words. Maybe that's my point.'

She looked dejected – tired and scraped out. Her eyes were sunk in bruise-coloured pools.

'That I do understand. Would it help to talk to me? About any of it?'

She shook her head.

'Why not?' he pushed, past any point he ordinarily would.

'Because you cannot understand. So what's the point?'

'Perhaps the point is that changing your experiences, putting into words those things that have become heavy, damaging weights ... maybe they can sublimate, float away.'

Closing her eyes and rubbing at her temples, she almost whispered, 'Nobody wants these words out in the world. Nobody wants to know what it's really like in here.'

Marick said nothing. He waited.

'How can you describe life raining destruction down on life?' She offered. 'What are the words for poverty, inequality, racism, every indicator of poor health you can imagine? How can anyone put into words alcoholism, domestic violence, drug deals gone wrong, money set aside for billionaires but not for preventative health. When it's real. Not fiction. When it looks like throats slit in the middle of the night, spinal cords severed by high-speed accidents, babies born blue to mothers imprisoned by addiction, detained refugees opening up their wrists. The homeless.' Her voice was jittery in her rush to spit her words out.

Marick did not move.

'I thought Emergency Medicine would be noble,' she said, slowing down and looking off to the wall, 'but it's just trying to patch up the broken things at the final stop.'

They spent a brief period in silence. The doctor looked down at her words on the page.

'Talking about it doesn't do any good. You can talk all you want but it's the deeds that matter.'

And that was true, Marick realised. A message of defeat once again. Because who was he without words? What on earth else did he have to offer?

'But may I ask you something?' she added.

'Of course,' Marick said. 'Anything.'

She hesitated for a beat. 'What is God? You must be to be the best one to ask. The rest of us, every person and everything that has ever existed, is some combination of atoms. So what then is it, or He? It's always bothered me, and since we are doing this – I don't know – being honest, perhaps this is my chance.' She picked up her pen and chewed the end of it.

'I will admit to being the worst man of God to ask. I have no answer for you.'

Marick did have a number of lines he could use, but none were good enough for this moment. God as concept. God as being above any physical components. God the ethereal manifestation of faith. God as our combined human spirituality. God as whatever's inside that we need. God as excuse. None, though, made enough sense to him, so he was not going to offer them up to her.

'I understand,' she said. She placed her pen down again.

Such silence in this room, Marick thought. He was a connoisseur of auditory conditions. The acoustics were exceptional, perhaps the result of the proximity of the ceiling and the room's hidden-away nature. It was also warm and spacious and smelled of both dust and cleanliness at the same time, and thus of history, of time, of a future.

'It was a great idea, though, this place you were proposing,' she said. 'But we don't need a drop-in centre. We don't need wellness and yoga and chat. We need society fixed. I'm sorry.'

'Please, do not be sorry,' he said. 'I'd like to thank you, most deeply, for confiding in me.'

'Before you go, you talked about Rumpelstiltskin, spinning gold,' she added. 'You weren't talking metaphorically, were you?

They say history has been made down in our basements. I've heard people talking of miracles. What do you think?'

'In a way I wish it were a miracle,' he said, standing to leave. 'But I don't believe there are true miracles. Only the inexplicable. But maybe that's even better. There is gold down there, but I have a feeling it will come and go, like anything too good to be true.' He smiled and held out his hand. 'Good luck with your writing. Let's talk again.'

'Thank you,' she said, and Marick could see she meant it.

✧

Marick made rounds of the wards. Not many patients had dying on their agenda for the day, and he was able to slip in and out of rooms without getting involved in larger questions. He had planned to visit Dolly, but the nurse in charge of her ward told him she had not long before been wheeled off for surgery.

'She'll be glad to see you afterwards though. She's still a little confused.'

He ignored a text message from Hugo: *Ring me when you can.* His emotions were still too complex, too brittle to be able to chat about *E. coli* and pharmaceutical company deals and alchemists called Brian.

Brian, it appeared, had other ideas. When Marick returned to his office to deal with his paperwork, there the man was, in a clipped brown suit, short and bespectacled and eager.

'I know this is irregular, and traditionally our groups have not always got on well …'

It took some time for Marick to decode what the man was saying, and by the time he did it was too late, and they were both seated at his desk.

'Alchemists and priests is what I meant,' Brian said.

'Ah.'

'Hugo will not return any of our calls, and we believe this is important.'

'I don't think … what Hugo is doing … has anything to do with … your society.' Marick could not work out how to phrase any of it.

'We've got a list of questions,' Brian said. 'Starting with which base metals he's using. I appreciate it's unusual, asking a priest, but these are unusual times. I know he's a good friend of yours.'

'I'm not a priest,' Marick said.

'That's alright then.' Brian brightened, and he leant forward.

'Are you really an alchemist?' Marick asked.

'Well, I'm more on the admin side, but it's an exclusive society. Hence the questions. Which guidelines is he employing?'

'Brian, is it?' Marick was not one to criticise anybody else's beliefs, knowing it would be unfettered hypocrisy, but this was a step too far. 'I really think you're barking up the wrong tree. Hugo – my friend – is not employing any guidelines. He has a unique biological process going on, which he is currently trying to get to the bottom of.'

Marick observed Brian take this as some sort of insult.

'You may not be aware, *Father,* but alchemy is both a venerated science and an art and has been around for countless centuries. And although it may have great tradition around it, custom and the like, there are certain standards. Accepted, global standards.

Alchemy's a privilege, shared by the fortunate few, in order to benefit the many. That's why it's important for us to identify anybody operating outside those standards—'

Marick stood. 'I am sorry, Brian, but this is not a conversation I can have. If you'll excuse me.'

'Then would you be so kind as to ask Mr Francis to contact us. Here's my card.' Brian handed over a rectangle of symbols and numbers.

Marick nodded and tried to demonstrate in the way he took the card and put it to the side of his desk that he was intending to ignore it. 'Good day, Brian.'

The man left, and Marick tipped the card into the bin. His involvement may be involute, but there was no question that his allegiance was to Hugo.

He responded to his friend's text. *The alchemists have been here sniffing around. Good idea to stay at home. How are the bacteria settling in?*

A reply beeped back. *Nothing yet. Worrying. Vivian wants you for dinner tonight. I could do with your eyes too. Come?*

Marick sighed. He answered. *Of course.*

What are you doing, Marick? he asked himself. What in God's name are you doing?

᛫ᛁᚾᛁ᛫

It had been both easier and more difficult for Marick to study the intricacies of theology when he was in his own place, away from the dorms of residence. The triplex was quieter, except for the occasional party next door. He missed the silent fraternity of the college, the meditation of doing dishes next to another wordless man, the hot cocoa at night, the conversation of birds outside his window of a morning. It did, however, allow him to skip the group confessional sessions, and he took comfort in knowing he would get away with graduating from the college without ever admitting what had got him there in the first place.

But Marick's problem was, he didn't graduate. Before he fronted up to the registrar to beg for a deferral, he had decided to take on some extra-curricular units from the university. He thought they would give him a more rounded view on things. Greek mythology had been one. It became a minor obsession for him, plotting out the timelines and family trees of the Greek Gods. Cronus, he wrote down in neat script, the son of the sky and the earth, eating his own babies while they were pink and mewling because it had been prophesied one of his children would destroy him. Zeus naturally did, returning from his hiding spot to free his siblings from his father's guts. The uncle, Prometheus, slung up in chains on a mountain to have his liver pecked out at the sweep of every day, the children around the table of Olympus, the brothers of the ocean and of hell, the song of Achilles and his fleet-foot, the rapes and love affairs and incest, and the dawns, rosy-fingered as they were. Marick read Homer and cross-referenced the psalms of the gods with the epics of man. Then there was Orpheus and the underworld and the silver lips of the River Styx, and in everything he read and wrote down in notes he found himself less able to distinguish between those myths and the stories he studied in his own Bible classes.

He needed to see for himself – a deferral for the sake of his own education. Like Dante, who'd also made an appearance on his reading lists, awoken in mid-life in a savage forest, choked with leaves, unsure if he was on the wrong path. He would go to Greece, easy enough to afford when he'd had the spending habits of a pauper that year. Spain, of course, was not far, but every day he fulfilled the promise made through Diane's lawyers was another day adhering to whatever dregs of integrity he had left.

He planned an itinerary and, knowing how close Italy was, organised a stop-off on the way. A brief trip, and to Rome only.

The city undid him. Although he promised himself he wouldn't, he retraced every step he'd taken with Diane. He visited the places they had planned to take Claudia. He fell to his knees on the cobbles in front of the Pantheon. He wept in front of the mossy boulder remnants of the ancient layers of the city. He could not even bear to enter the Vatican. Every night he spent in his budget pensione, crying. The black floods of his nights were exhausting, like the daily evisceration of Prometheus himself. Marick became obsessed with stone: stone everywhere, under his feet, beneath his fingers, the stone swallowed by Cronus in the misunderstanding it was Zeus, then the smooth stones chosen by David to fill his slingshot when taking aim at the colossus Goliath. Stones as small skulls, stones heaved at the innocent in the Bible for the crime of being female. He began to imagine tying stones to his own feet and dragging them behind him as he walked into the Tiber. When he went looking for the perfect ones, he knew it was time to leave.

Marick hobbled into Greece. He had hoped going further back in time might save him, but things were no better there. His itinerary turned to dust. He visited the wonders with sightless eyes. A walk around the Parthenon, a tour of the Acropolis.

271

Hauling himself up the rocky path behind a millipede of tourists all chattering in marvelment, he hoped for a vision, a lightning connection with the past, but when he came face to face with the ancient Athenian stone – was told by an eager guide that he was standing on the birthplace of democracy, philosophy, theatre, freedom of expression and speech – Marick felt nothing, as though he were dead. He stayed two nights in a hotel overlooking the sea, but all he could see was hot haze, any beauty swallowed by blurred lines and great freighters making mindless trips back and forth. A trip on a dusty bus to Mount Olympus left him feeling queasy and migrainous, and he couldn't get out of the vehicle. Neither the place, nor he, made sense to him anymore. The clarity of realising he had destroyed the two things he had loved was too sharp a contrast. He was the unforgivable.

Marick packed up at the end of the fortnight, salvation no longer on his schedule, and flew home.

He sat inside his house for a month, missing several meetings with his course advisers. Failing several of the units, he was fortunate they kept him on, but they were short of students completing their master's programs, and were prepared, one last time, to make an exception for him.

Things returned to a type of normal. Marick's normal, which consisted of showing up for the basic coursework at theological college, sitting at home, eking out the rest of his existence with tasteless meals and uninteresting books. When it had become clear he had whittled his financial nest egg down to straw, and anyway, he couldn't imagine this way of life continuing, he decided he would find paid employment again. Pointed towards job opportunities posted on the college noticeboard, he looked behind the advertisements and communiques to discover an expression of interest by the central city church, looking for an administrative assistant to the Deacon. Good enough, he thought, and applied.

TWENTY-EIGHT

He had accepted the invitation. He would do it for Hugo.

Before making his way out to the suburbs for dinner, Marick dropped into the ICU. The father of the boy strode over to meet him.

'Thank you for coming, Father. The process has begun.'

They found a seat in the relative's room. The boy's mother sat mute while the father described what was happening in the pod behind them.

'It's all about keeping his organs as optimally functioning as possible. Not just blood flow and oxygen. When a brain is so badly injured, it sends out a firestorm of chemicals, I've learnt. It's a delicate process, protecting the parts of him that will go on to save others from a soup of harmful molecules. I trust the doctors here. They've done an incredible job. They say, all things going well, he'll be good for a heart, his lungs, and more – almost everything, really.'

'It's certain then, that it will go ahead?' Marick leant forward and held both the mother's hands while the father spoke.

'Yes, they've done all the testing. There's no blood supply to his brain anymore. He's no longer him.'

The mother began her soundless crying again, and Marick tightened his grasp on her bony hands. The relatives' room remained clinical despite a valiant attempt at warmth. Abstract paintings that were nothing but coloured daubs were hung on the walls, and vases with plastic flowers were dotted around. The antiseptic smell of the unit beyond had not been kept out. The room had the silence of a vacuum about it, which amplified the choking sound in the mother's throat.

'They're scheduling the operation – the harvesting procedure – tomorrow, Father. Would you be able to be here when the end comes?'

The mother nodded. 'Please,' she murmured.

He agreed and noted down the time.

They sat for a while without need for conversation.

The mother eventually spoke. 'His brain is dead, Father. Does that mean he is?'

'Such a question,' Marick responded, pitching his voice as low as hers.

He had wrestled with this over and over. Whether the body was mere skin for a life, to be discarded once the living was done. 'One thing is for certain, your boy is, has always been, and always will be much more than his brain. Will he continue to live in you, once the sun sets tomorrow?' Marick watched the mother hold her breath while he continued. 'He will. In addition, the parts that equally made him *him*, will be beating and breathing inside somebody else, each of them with loving parents, and university offers and cousins.'

The mother squeezed Marick's hands, then withdrew hers, bringing them clutched to her lips. A movement of prayer without the words.

'He saved us, too,' she said after a while.

The father nodded. 'He granted us a vision of a future we didn't know we could have. We were such selfish people before he was born. Couldn't imagine a life given over to others. But children do that, don't they.' He reached over and joined his hands with his wife's. 'As if you, yourself, are allowed to live for the first time when you bring a child forth into the world. I think it's something about dedicating yourself to the service of another. There's possibly no greater privilege. Loving a child is the best way to discover it.'

'Although I'm sure you'd disagree, Father,' the mother said. 'I've no doubt you would say service to God is the highest aim we can have.'

Marick would not correct them. Let them believe of him whatever they needed. He felt conspicuous there, a man representing falsehood. Because he agreed, utterly.

'Tomorrow,' he said rising. 'I will be here.'

The scenery from the window of the train was yellow, the light thick, the last part of the day opaque with heat-saturated fatigue. Suburbs again slid by.

The repetitive clack of the train gave Marick strength. Whatever had happened between him and Vivian needed to be crushed. Everything in this triangle of friendship was entering a dimension undefined, he thought, with its horizon murky and unknowable. He had crossed a threshold – he was Judas – and this evening was an opportunity to step back to safety.

Walking up the path to their house, he was lured by unfamiliar smells. Smoky spice. Meat. Enticed in, perhaps. For a moment he thought they must be cooking Middle Eastern food together, and within those seconds he wondered if he was in the grip of madness and misunderstanding. He was right about neither of those things, though, he was to discover.

Vivian opened the door to him. She stared at him with an inscrutable, flat expression. Nowhere was her radiant smile. She took him by the arm and led him to the kitchen. The smells were Indian. Stirring a pot, enwombed in a caul of steam was Hugo, and he called a greeting to Marick.

'We've not done this before,' Hugo said, slinging a tea towel over his shoulder. 'Cooked Indian together.'

'I'm trying, if that's possible, to cheer him up,' Vivian said. She raised her eyebrows with a brief motion, but still no smile came. 'He's been so morose today.'

'I've got good reason,' Hugo said, looking at Marick for support. 'The bacteria won't even divide. I have no idea why. I'm hoping it's just a settling-in phase.'

'Did they do this last time?' Marick asked.

'Can we leave this till after dinner?' Vivian asked. 'It's bad enough having them in our house, let alone them taking over the conversation. Marick, come help.'

Vivian gave him responsibility for a wooden spoon and the pot next to Hugo.

'I can smell memory, doing this,' Hugo said. 'The kitchen of my childhood.'

Vivian fixed on her husband. He didn't return the look.

The combination of aromas was piquant: cumin, cardamom, garam masala. Vivian unwrapped ingredients from waxed paper, slowly, methodically.

'Lamb biryani,' she said. 'For him.' And she tossed her chin towards Hugo.

Despite the congenial enough sentiments, the air between the pair felt painful. Marick was tasked with turning the rice over as it cooked in stock, folding it like a ceremony. It was the least he could do – take this small responsibility seriously.

Vivian chopped the coriander, then raked it up along with the other ingredients she'd already attacked, and dropped them into Marick's saucepan. As she leant over to scrape the herbs into the rice, Marick was sure he could feel her breasts pressed into his back. He inched forward, towards the steam. Hugo's glasses were fogged. Marick looked down at the gas cooktop into the swirl of the grains and the turgid spice-laden liquid as the flame burned blue.

'Taste this,' she said to both of them, and held out a spoon, which she put first into Marick's mouth then Hugo's. The act, the sensation, was so earthy, so rich and fragrant and close, that Marick was torn from within, riven down his insides, unsure how much was deep human connection and how much was the frighteningly indecipherable.

'Delicious,' Hugo said, but Vivian seemed to want an answer only from Marick.

'It's very good,' was his best reply, but still Vivian did not appear satisfied. Marick could feel his heart beating hard with confusion.

The gastronomic performance continued. Lamb and onion frying. More spices sizzling. It was overwhelming. The air itself was an oven.

'Vivian.' Hugo's voice had a whine to it. 'Let me go back to them for a bit. You've got Marick here to help now.' Hugo turned to Marick. 'My friend. After dinner I'll show you what's going on in there. In the meantime, you can help my wife with this feast.'

Hugo wiped his hands on his tea towel, did the same for his glasses, and pecked his wife on the cheek. Vivian made the slightest recoil. 'I'll be thirty minutes. I want to set up the gel plates for the night.'

'Make sure you wash your hands,' Vivian said.

'Of course. I'm a scientist, Vivian.'

There were deep bruises in both of their voices, Marick observed from the way they framed their words. Marick wanted the cooking to be done, for them to sit and eat, to talk of insignificances together, and for him to take his leave, early and free, a line drawn in the sand. His mind tried to catch up before Hugo left. How easy it should have been to say no, why don't we all do this together? What fun it is, or something of that nature. Vivian rustled a pile of sultanas together. Hugo left, the door swinging shut behind him.

The smell in the kitchen grew stronger and muggier, as if the insides of the seeds and spices were being released like fireworks while they sautéed. Marick looked around to see if there was a kitchen fan to suck up some of the aromas and fug. It was becoming unbearable. Vivian breathed it all in deeply. 'It will be another half-hour until it's ready anyway. Come.' She took Marick's hand. 'I want to show you something.'

Vivian escorted him from the kitchen. He could feel pounding in his head. This is not sensible, he heard himself saying to some distant place in his thoughts, but he spoke nothing out loud. Coward, Marick thought. She walked in front of him and he could almost taste the sweat and humidity of her. For a devastating moment he did want to taste her, see if she herself had been infused with Indian spices. So wrong. So wrong.

She took him right through the door of their bedroom; a mess of a space, with laundry piles in one corner, books fanned out beneath the bed, glasses of water on the bedside tables, papers and notes everywhere. She closed the door behind her and clicked the lock.

'Vivian, I don't think ...'

'I've been dying to see you again. Have you missed seeing me?'

'Hugo,' Marick blurted out. 'He's my friend. Your husband.'

She pulled him in and began to kiss him. As imagined, he could smell spice, taste the salt and the sweetness at the same time. He could devour her tongue; he could lick her teeth. The heat could melt them together. What a sequence of events to even imagine. She took his hand slowly and guided it, down her shirt, underneath her bra – he could feel its delicate lace edges – and over her breast. Under his hand it felt ethereal itself, cool and perfectly soft.

She made the quietest moaning sound.

'But Hugo,' he tried to say into her mouth as they kissed.

'Hugo,' and she pulled back the tiniest amount, pushing his hand further into her breast, 'is having an affair.'

Marick jolted. 'What?'

'You heard me,' she said, 'a full-on fucking affair.'

Marick pulled away. 'Vivian. This is madness. We can't. But how?' Marick was confused, his mind so dazed he wasn't sure which question applied to which.

'Melanie. I can't believe he hasn't told you. That little piece of work from the university labs. They've been seeing each other all this time.'

'But.' Marick tried to recall what Hugo had said. Yes, *he had turned his head*, Marick remembered. 'That's not right, Vivian.'

'It is, Marick. You don't have to defend him, you know.' She pulled him back towards her, kissing him – harder, determined.

'No, Vivian, this is …'

Marick stepped backwards from Vivian.

'So it's my turn,' she said. 'Marick. Come on. Don't you think I deserve a chance?'

'This is not how any of this works, Vivian.' God only knew what that meant, though, he thought. So much was populating his head he wasn't sure how anything would come out right.

She grasped onto his shirt. 'You find me attractive, don't you?' Her eyes caught the light and he saw they had tears in them.

'Of course I do, Vivian. Who wouldn't? You are beautiful, but …' He wanted to be able to say it: *I am not here to facilitate your revenge.* But he realised how ridiculous it sounded. 'Are you sure that's the truth?'

Vivian slumped down on the bed with her head in her hands. A few seconds later there was a knock at the door. 'Vivian? Marick? Are you in there?'

Vivian shook her head and walked over, unlocking the door and letting him in.

'What are you two up to in here?'

'Vivian was just …' Marick feared his guilt would sound like a clarion from his flushed face and wide-eyed presence in his friend's bedroom.

Vivian offered nothing. A few tears were rolling down her cheeks.

'I know about Melanie,' she said. 'You bastard.'

Marick watched Hugo's face drain of its colour, as though a plug had been pulled.

'For Christ's sake, don't bring Marick into this. He's our friend.' Hugo turned to Marick. 'I'm sorry, chum.'

'You told me nothing happened that night,' Marick said to Hugo. 'When the results were exposed at the lab.'

'Not then. That was true.' Hugo looked directly at Marick, an imploring expression on his face. 'I didn't want you to think I was—'

'You're not very good at covering it up, Hugo,' Vivian interrupted.

'Neither were you,' Hugo said to Vivian. 'Three affairs, Vivian. Three.'

Marick walked the few steps to an armchair covered in laundry and thumped into it.

Hugo and Vivian slung accusations at each other, most of which Marick could not follow. Dates. Credit card bills. Hotel stays. Hurts. Payback and reprisals. The things they already knew about each other. Recapitulations of times past. It became obvious though this was not the first time during their marriage they'd had this confrontation.

Hugo turned to Marick. 'I'm sorry, you had to hear all this.'

'Is it true, Hugo?' Marick asked.

'Is what true?'

Marick could feel the inklings of affrontery inside him, a growing awareness that treachery had come for them all. It felt dangerously close to anger.

'The affair. Melanie. That it's been going on all this time.'

'You would have judged me. See? Going all religious on me, Marick. That whole adultery and sin thing.'

'It's got nothing to do with religion, Hugo. I'm asking you if this thing, about which you told me the opposite, is a fact.'

Hugo looked from Marick to Vivian. 'I hardly ever see her. But she understands me. Gets what I'm trying to do. I am sorry, Vivian. And Marick, I know it's abominable. I'm sorry for the pretence. But Vivian, you've got to admit, with you having all those—'

'That was over a year ago!' she retorted. 'You know that.'

'What difference does it make?'

'None, by the sounds.'

Marick watched them trade their arrows and he wondered how many were landing in old, unhealed wounds. His own hurt and betrayal rose like bile, though. He was a pawn in a game he did not understand, but he was now seeing he was on the losing side.

As though he knew what Marick was thinking, Hugo turned to him.

'Marick, this has nothing to do with the gold. The bacteria. Our bacteria. I consider them ours. I need you on my side. We're in this together. I can promise …'

'I have a daughter.' Marick announced. 'Had. Have.' He knew he sounded nonsensical.

Hugo and Vivian, as if both fiercely aware that what was being said was profound, stopped speaking themselves. There was no sound apart from a faint whistle from the kitchen.

'Do you know my ex-wife's name?' Marick added.

Hugo's face signalled that he understood Marick's question – not her name, but that Hugo had never found time to enquire.

Vivian rose from the bed, walked across to Marick and sat on the arm of the chair. She went to hold his hand, but he saw she thought the better of it, and clutched hers together.

'What is her name? Not your wife. Your daughter.' Vivian asked.

'Claudia. Her name is Claudia.'

Hugo spoke quietly, 'and she …?'

'She was twelve when she had a stroke. In her sleep.'

Neither of them was able to speak. Vivian's tears returned.

Hugo walked over to Marick too, and placed his hand on his shoulder.

'I have never, ever, lied to you about the gold.'

What does it matter now? thought Marick. He did not look up at Hugo.

And, as they sat in the overheated bedroom, the sudden piercing sound of a smoke alarm rang out from the kitchen.

The three of them jumped in unison, as though such an intrusion must be a joke in poor taste. It was the biryani, whose scorch was wafting down the passageway into the bedroom, Hugo and Vivian both strode off to the kitchen.

Marick followed them.

'I'm going,' he said.

'Don't,' they both replied.

But he shook his head, patted Hugo on the shoulder, and left.

On the train home, Marick sat motionless. He couldn't focus. The distress had press-ganged his thoughts. He wondered if he could have lived another life, made other choices. Almost five decades of it and here things were. This. A pain that would never be soothed, and no great God there to help. Surely there could have been an eyeblink in his days, early on, when the sequence of things might have changed; one little alteration in the slip and roll of time, allowing him to live as a different man. What would that man say to him now, to this feeble figure with a hunk of radioactive sorrow sitting in his guts and slowly decaying, eating him away as the years tick over while he begs a mirage in the sky for help?

The suburbs passed in reverse, but to Marick they looked like a lost world.

Strangely, though, that night he slept through four o'clock.

TWENTY-NINE

It was not despair Marick woke with, but a feeling of something having been discarded. Not lightness, more desertion. The emptiness of loss.

He stood in the silence of morning, with tea, in his courtyard. For close to an hour, he barely moved. The sounds of the morning rose: the resurrection of birds and their song, a rubbish truck rumbling through its gears, cicadas tuning up their hum. The hour he was to visit the ICU was foremost in his plans for the day. Hugo would not figure in them.

The number two took him in with few stops. It would be another hot day, and the shimmer of heat had begun its business on the bitumened roads as the bus passed. He adjusted the small gold cross on his collar.

The hospital had resumed its itinerary, the holidays done. And so would Marick. But before he did, he found himself taking the extra set of stairs, down past his own basement level to the bunkered floor below. He didn't know what he wanted to see, wasn't sure what might still be there. The lights seemed smoggy.

A racing thud sounded through the ceiling as canisters were delivered by the pneumatic system. No other living being could be seen in the bends of the corridor. It all felt like a whisper, a tremble, hollow. And as it had done each time before, the corridor looked different – angles replaced, equipment exchanged with reserves.

Marick edged over to Hugo's laundry. Or ex-laundry as it now appeared. The door was swinging – the lock had been broken. The doorjamb had splintered, spikes of wood poking out where the door had been jemmied open at some point since he and Hugo had locked it. He looked up and down the gloom of the corridor to ensure nobody was close and peered in. It was vacant – not a memory left. The benches had been wiped clean, the old dryer door creaking open on its hinge. Another thud overhead. Hugo's laboratory was now a white, lifeless square, reminding Marick, with a sucker punch, of his old house. As though physical spaces got the benefit of reinvention, where people did not, he thought.

Creeping out, he almost ran into the squat cleaning lady he had seen down here before.

'Hello, Father,' she said, again speaking to the floor, her lips barely moving.

'Lilyana,' he said. He sensed her pleasure at his recollection of her name. 'Do you know what happened here?' He pointed at the smashed lock.

She shook her head. 'Always strange things going on down here. Best never ask, I say.'

Marick paused. 'I've been thinking about what you said before. About wanting to confess your sins. Is there any way I can help you?'

'If you a Catholic, Father, then you could.'

Marick gave this its due. He had feigned it before without reprisal. It would not be hard to pretend and give this woman what she needed. But he was done with charades.

'I'm so sorry, Lilyana. But there's a cathedral close by. I could take you there.'

'I no go inside one of them.'

'Are you able to tell me why?' he asked, trying to look her in the eye, but failing. Her stare was not to be enticed from the floor.

Lilyana shook her head. 'It's no matter.' She reached down to pick up a piece of rubbish from the floor, a scrap of paper she shoved into a pocket of her dress. 'What are you doing down here, Father?'

'What am I doing?' he said. 'I'm starting again, Lilyana. I'm going to try to start over.'

'Ha,' she made a muffled sound. 'That like me, every day. How you planning it, Father?'

'I wish I knew. None of my ideas amount to much. I had a thought, to provide a space for a drop-in area for those who worked inside these walls, the people hurting. But it might be that the hurt is too great for that. I even had a room in mind.'

'Hmm,' she appeared to have to give this some thought. 'Up, or down?'

'What do you mean?' Marick asked.

'The room is above ground, or here in basement?'

'Does it matter?'

'Yes, it does, Father.'

'Above, although it's kind of hard to find. You understand the hospital well, Lilyana. Perhaps you know of it.' And he tried to describe where it was, and what he saw it could be.

'I could find it, yes. It's not bad idea, Father. It's just, well, words only do so much. But you'll find a use for your room. I give it good clean, if you like. It's what I'm best at.'

'Oh, Lilyana. That's a very kind offer, but I don't think ...'

'Father, you need my help, or not?'

He looked at her, this woman with her buckets and brushes.

'I do, Lilyana.'

It was as though he had unlocked something himself by saying it. Lilyana lifted her head and smiled for the briefest of moments, but it was broad and thankful and with something more intense than joy. And something so peculiar, after all that had happened, to be dazzled by it, only because so much of his recent weeks had revolved around the metal. He saw Lilyana had a mouthful of gold teeth. And then the shadows of severity pulled across her just as quickly.

'Then of course I help you, Father. I do it today.'

THIRTY

The job had been intended as his new start: personal assistant to the Deacon. The theological college had frowned on it – he had not long returned from his jaunt across Europe, and now he was requesting to break up his study again. But some of the lecturers were secretly pleased. Marick had not lived up to the blazing promise with which he entered his degree, plus it was prestigious to get someone into such proximity to the top men in the top church in the city. It always came in useful, they argued among themselves when his application for further deferral came to senate.

So once again Marick became a company man. The Deacon had a gruff respect for him, and Marick knew it. Marick worked hard, taking over all the accounts and bookwork not only for the top men, but all the men beneath.

'A whizz with numbers,' he knew they said about him.

That part had been easy. What Marick was looking for, though, was not found in the church spreadsheets. He was still wounded from his Mediterranean trip. Every night and every day he grappled with visions of the two women who defined his life, and the hole they had left behind.

Marick attended every service, he prepared notes and briefings for the Deacon so they were there before the great man needed them, he sat in the back of the outreach Bible classes, and he typed up agendas and minutes without missing a beat. But despite his churchly compliance, the road to forgiveness was closed to him.

After a year of skirting around the peripheries – the reliable man with the ledgers and requisition forms and pocket full of pens – Marick was invited into the church's program for clerical training. It was rumoured he was the man favoured by the Deacon to ascend the hierarchy. Things began to make sense for Marick. This was where his professional life could come together if he could only focus.

Marick was tasked with leading some of the smaller break-out groups. Bible studies for teens. Choral planning. Days of celebration. Community linkages. He would talk, in small sessions in cosy offshoot rooms behind the chapel, to people with open hearts – youths and adults and even children – of God's own absolution, extracted from carefully chosen passages dotted through the great book. 'God is love. God is forgiveness,' he repeated. If he didn't examine the words too closely, they were easy enough to declare.

The thing missing was for the same sentiments to be extended to himself. He reassured himself – it just needed time.

Time, though, began to mock Marick. Months passed, then a year, and with every opportunity the words coming from his mouth, spilled over in pastoral care for others, rang increasingly untrue. He began to recognise these proclamations first as doubt, then finally as outright lies.

Each night he began losing Claudia again. Every single night, with sweat and fear and waking up to his heart pounding as though it belonged in battle. Whereas God's love was blinding for others, golden and divine, for him the blindness was dark and menacing. He wanted to tell someone, anyone in the church, about Claudia. Ask where he could find forgiveness, and why God had chosen to ignore him, but all he experienced over and over was himself in a bell jar, pounding on the glass, his mouth opened and distorted and screaming, surrounded by people going about their lives, nobody able to hear.

Marick limped on alone. Alone and unheard. He sat at the back of the Sunday sermons, looking down the aisle to the front where God's son was slung up on the cross, the wooden blood dripping from his nailed hands. In Marick's head, was a silent piercing yowl. The music became dissonant, the chants intrusive. He convinced himself he was hiding it, though, this schism. His superiors would never suspect.

But the cracks opened. He wouldn't sign up for eulogy training and became argumentative in meetings. The senior members began to talk about him again in corridors, this time unfavourably.

'I'm not sure he's suitable, Deacon,' one of the visiting curates said. 'Bit of a wild card.'

Complaints trickled in. He had paced around the room during one study group for troubled teens, arguing in a fevered voice that God's ways were not so much mysterious as confusing, and they'd be forgiven for having difficulty believing at all.

'You'd think He has favourites, the way He comes across,' he said to a group of women who were setting up a women-only Bible class.

'Does He even exist?' Marick scrawled on a whiteboard in one of the meeting rooms late one evening.

One of the senior mentors scheduled a meeting with him to 'talk'. It was a wash of relief. Somebody wanted to ask what was eating him up inside. Someone cared enough to hear about what was bullying him into the anteroom of hell.

Instead, he received a formal second warning.

'I didn't know I had a first,' Marick said.

'It's all documented,' the man said, 'if you want to check.'

He would do better, he resolved. He liked this job. He wanted this job. Marick wanted to be useful beyond the practicalities of paper, but he could feel every day was hazardous. Doubt was pouring from him with every encounter now, and no matter how much he told himself to stay within the pious lines, somehow the questions kept coming out, finding their way into the light. He became entangled in argument, causing one of the junior staff to leave a meeting in tears.

In the end the Deacon called for him, summoning him into the empty vestibule. His voice boomed. Marick's hearing aid squealed.

'It's not working out, is it?' The Deacon had his back turned. 'I had high hopes for you, Marick. But I cannot keep somebody on who does not believe in God.' There were other things he said, but they were lost to Marick in the echo of the place.

Marick had wanted to argue back, that in ways almost impossible for him to explain he did believe in some type of God, just not the one at the top of the religious ladder here. Belief was a two-way street, he had wanted to say. Anyway, they couldn't fault the paperwork, he wished he had retorted.

But he'd said none of it. He had simply trudged down the stone steps to the small administrative enclave, cleared his desk and its contents into a single cardboard box, and departed.

THIRTY-ONE

Early afternoon was the appointed time the father of the boy in ICU had given Marick to come share the threshold of his son's life, that precious transition, so he had the opportunity during his morning to drop in on Dolly.

The orthopaedic ward was another he had not yet visited, and he had to wade through more of the hospital's foreign climes to find it. The route led him down a rampway with a window that looked out over a rubbish and recycling plant. There were chutes and pallets and rusted machinery with pistons pumping away like a steam engine. He leant his head to the window and watched a narrow conveyor belt transporting what appeared to be packaged meals, on square-set trays, in regular succession down the churning incline until they were dropped tidily into a gaping bin below, smashing into their constituent pieces – broccoli, curled brown meat, potato, peas – which were mulched all together, making stew in their death throes.

'What a waste,' he said out loud.

'Pardon?' a well-upholstered woman with a clipboard said as she passed.

'I'm sorry,' he said. 'Nothing.' He continued.

Dolly was setting a cracking pace with a physiotherapist down the middle of the ward when he found her.

'Marick!' she called out.

'Watch yourself, Dolly. Slow down,' the physio said, holding on to one of her arms as Dolly manhandled the walking frame.

'I can't believe you're up and walking already,' he said.

'First day post-op,' the smooth-cut man supporting her said. 'Best way to recover.'

Dolly had returned to her sharp-headedness, and Marick wondered if her injuries had done her some good. She listed off her pathologies: 'Intertrochanteric neck of femur fracture, fixed with three screws and a plate; nasty concussion; pulmonary oedema; hyponatremia. I'm a walking medical syllabus,' she said.

'And too fast,' the physio said. 'Take it easy, Dolly.'

'And I have you to thank, Father. You saved me.'

'I did not,' Marick said. 'I did break into your house, though.'

She reached one dressing-gowned arm across from her walker and gave his wrist a squeeze.

'Well, thank you. Walk back with me.' She waved the physiotherapist away. 'You can go,' she said, and the young man obliged, presumably used to the vagaries of post-operative old ladies.

Marick escorted Dolly and her walking frame, as well as several tubes of fluid running either into or out of her. When they reached her bed, Dolly sat down in a series of ginger movements.

'Have you heard?' she whispered.

He wasn't sure he wanted to hear anything new.

'The gold. It was all a hoax. That's what the girls are all saying. Your friend, Mr Francis, has taken all the evidence and disappeared, and the executive have put out a memorandum saying it is not to be mentioned in public again. A hoax. Can you imagine that? I never believed it of course. Alchemy. What nonsense.'

Marick busied himself with clearing a space on the chair next to her bed as an alternative to answering.

'I think society would do better to read *New Scientist*, don't you think?' she continued. 'Rather than believing crazy theories. I hope those people who protested are embarrassed.'

Dolly looked around as though expecting the other women on the ward to agree, but most of them were asleep or consumed by the glare from screens hung at the foot of their beds. The woman next to Dolly was snoring with a rumble, and one of her truncated legs with a fresh bandage on its stump was elevated on several pillows.

'I can't wait to get out of here,' Dolly said. 'Would you mind helping me back in?'

Marick swung her legs with care onto the bed while she hung on to a strap situated over her, like the bed was a bus. Nurses tiptoed among the patients. One congratulated Marick on his patient-care abilities.

To prevent her talking about Hugo's gold, Marick told Dolly what he had seen on his walk to her, the anti-production line of food, meals being deconstructed after travelling in the wrong direction.

'I know,' Dolly said. 'It's a dreadful squander.'

He thought for a moment. 'Wouldn't it be excellent to intercept them somehow. I bet the homeless folks out the front would be willing recipients.'

'Do you know, I've thought of that before. It's about finding somewhere to serve them though. The Executive Team was approached about this years ago, but they clamped down on any discussion about it, saying it would be in breach of some hygiene and safety laws.'

'But they're perfectly good meals, surely.'

'Good, not gourmet, let me tell you from experience. It's madness though, I agree. The kitchens produce so much food, three meals a day for every patient in here, then half the people don't want them – they're sick or fasting or just plain finicky.'

'What if,' said Marick, 'we had somewhere to channel them? A place where nobody went, inside the hospital, that could be reached without the administration knowing.' Marick was a systems man, always had been. And this needed one. 'Maybe we could set up a process to save the unwanted meals from the conveyor belt. Off the belt and into the mouths of those needing a decent feed. We'd need an army to do it, though.'

'I have an army,' Dolly smiled. 'But we'd need a room.'

'I have a room,' Marick said, and they had a plan.

'It will be a little like the loaves and the fishes. I can't wait to leave here to get started.'

Better than a kidney, Marick thought, and he patted her hand goodbye.

Outside, a few sparse streaks of cloud were spread across the silk-blue sky, visible through the gaps in the fig tree's canopy. Marick strode through its shade and sat down on one of the benches, next to a surprised-looking woman with a rusted shopping trolley loaded with her belongings. Over her knees was a lumpy sleeping bag.

'My name is Marick,' he said. 'The chaplain.'

'We know,' she said. She had several teeth missing and excoriated skin around her mouth, hair like a wire brush and a heady smell somewhere between bushfire and something long buried – but she spoke with a clipped English accent. Another fellow came and plopped down next to them. Several others looked up from what they were doing.

'And I don't know yours. And for that I apologise.'

'Megsie,' the woman said and stuck out her paw of a hand, filthy with life.

'Megsie,' Marick repeated. 'I'm glad to meet you.'

Within no time, Marick had drawn a small crowd, and he went about learning as many names as he could. Two men shared a cigarette, another cuddled a bottle in a scrunched paper bag. A boy flew past on a skateboard. Pigeons pecked at spilled crumbs. The hum of the inner city created their backdrop, and they chatted about nothing of consequence.

'Come back any time,' they called out to Marick as he excused himself after a time.

'I will,' he assured them. 'I have an idea.' It was something.

THIRTY-TWO

When Marick returned to his office, a familiar shape was waiting for him.

'I know you won't want to see me,' Hugo said. 'But can we talk?'

They stood in the corridor, awkward as a blind date. Hugo put his hand out to lean on a super-sized oxygen cylinder left near the door, which let forth a hiss of complaint. Hugo jerked his hand back.

'Come in,' Marick said.

The pair sat across from each other, deliberate and stiff.

Marick spoke first. 'I see they've cleared out your laundry.'

'Tell me about Claudia,' Hugo said.

'You don't have to do this.' The light in Marick's office was like candles flickering, the globes exhausted, like him, from pretence.

'I want to know, Marick. I want to hear about her. Out of all of this, whatever I will lose, one of the things that will deeply hurt is the loss of this,' Hugo put his palms out to indicate the two of them. 'I've been a brute of a friend. I've never asked. Tell me. Let me in.'

'I already have,' Marick said, although he could see Hugo knew this was not the case. He wasn't sure if he had the energy. 'But if we are going to do this, then you first.'

'You know it all, Marick.'

'I don't know anything. Start with Melanie.'

Hugo sighed and slumped into his chair. 'It wasn't supposed to be anything. I did send her off that night I told you about, but I was so amazed she could have done that, reached for me the way she did, that the next week I rang her – just to make sure she was okay. I wanted her to know I supported her, that I didn't blame her for what happened with the *Nature* paper. We started meeting. Vivian was pretty shaken up by the whole fraud accusation. Blamed me for brainwashing my staff like a cult leader. Said it risked her own reputation at the university. She didn't understand what the bacteria meant to me, how intense they were as creatures, their sentience, their abilities. Whereas Melanie, she would look at me with those huge eyes, listening, and we'd talk for hours about the future of protein production, the possibilities, how these bacteria could go on to make even greater things. She believed in me, Marick.' Hugo leant forward and raked both hands through his hair.

'Around that time, Vivian had her first affair. The first I ever knew about, anyway. She didn't even try to hide it. With another counsellor from the university. She'd come home late from work, smelling of wine and somebody else's aftershave. It all got so complicated. I needed Melanie but told myself every time I saw her that I wouldn't touch her. But she was like a drug. Who knows what Vivian needed? I think my wife just enjoyed the charade. It was a game to her. And I could never confront her, because that would mean losing Melanie, the only person who listened to me. Vivian eventually confessed, as though she grew bored of waiting for me to find out. We had months of blazing rows, of course, but then I wondered whether that's what she wanted in the first place – the melodrama, the posturing. It was crazy. A game for which I could never figure out the rules.'

Hugo looked broken. They both sat in the pause, spent. The overhead light sparked and went dim, dragging shadows in from outside. Marick stood to try the main switch, but jiggling it made no difference.

'Mood lighting,' Hugo said with a wan smile. 'I haven't seen her for months, though. Melanie. She doesn't know about the gold.'

'Here we are then. At the gold.'

'At the end could be more accurate.' Hugo said. 'Nothing I can do is bringing it back. They're dying, Marick. My *E. coli*. I haven't slept a wink. I watch them, trying to figure it out. But the culture is slowing to a trickle. Only a small proportion of them are dividing, and then they're like slugs. More than half are lysed, their membranes dissolving under my eyes. I thought I had the milieu perfect, but it seems I'm wrong. They're done.'

Hugo blinked several times, as though to rid his eyes of the glisten that kept appearing. 'So not just no gold,' Hugo lifted his glasses and put a heel of his hand to one eye, 'but no *E. coli*. I'll be left with nothing. And the hospital executive is furious. I don't think I'll be continuing to work here. They mentioned a non-renewal of contract, a huge embarrassment with that drug company.'

Marick realised this was always how the story of the gold was going to end. That it would remain simultaneously possible and not. That there would be no answers. That he would never know how much of this journey held fact.

'But one of my old colleagues from the university rang,' Hugo continued. 'Very smart and dedicated woman. She'd heard about the gold. Asked all sorts of questions, pushing me to explain it, which, of course, I couldn't. I never could, Marick. Sandya has always been in my head, you see, telling me I didn't have to. But this is where it got strange. Last month a paper came out from Germany. A group were playing around with a bacterium named *Cupriavidus*, a little rod-shaped bacterium, not all that different from *E. coli*. Turns out it can manifest a special enzyme, which, under certain conditions can produce gold in an element-rich environment. Minuscule gold nuggets, Marick. But you'd need gold contaminants to start the process off, she said, so that must be happening with yours. I told her it wasn't possible, and she was wrong about that, Marick. Mine were creating from nowhere. From nothing more than their own ability. But she was excited by the prospect of trying again. She's setting up a new biological start-up and wondered if I might be interested. Told me I am one of the most talented bio-evolutionary technologists she knows and wants me in on the ground floor. Cell-free protein production, using only the cell machinery, not the whole bacteria. Huge capacity for a much broader spectrum of enzymes and proteins. Not just gold, but other things new, exciting, *worthy*. It seems like a miracle itself, that she would say this, after all that's happened. It's a second chance, Marick, don't you see?'

Marick wondered for a moment what would happen if he simply stopped listening. Would Hugo realise? If Marick nodded his head, in vacancy. A squatter in his own body. What was he to anyone, after all?

'Which is why, I'm here, Marick. Second chances.'

'For whom,' Marick focused again.

'For us, Marick. You and me. As friends. I want to hear about Claudia. I'm a selfish dolt, and I apologise.'

Marick shook his head.

'Please,' said Hugo.

Marick inhaled, but in that strange little room, a bead of a place underground, strung as though on some demented wire, he let something go and began to speak. Hugo remained quiet, sat forward, took it all in.

Marick told Hugo the story, the one that began in Rome, under the flutter of Italian sunshine and smells and paint, in trattorias, in galleries. Where the lights were like diamantes, and the prosecco free-flowing and there was Diane. He traced for Hugo the way they met, came back to Australia, through the ups and the downs, the fear that inhabited his body like a stone every single day Claudia was alive, the worry that something bad would happen to her. And then he got to Christmas Eve.

'It was a cold. Nothing more. A sore throat.'

He could feel his own throat ache at the memory, heavy like it wanted to close over itself in solidarity.

'And that night, in the early hours, I remembered dreaming. Of Claudia singing. It was loud and joyous, like she wanted me to join in the song. I could hear it like crystal in the fluid of the dream. I woke thinking she must have been awake, singing out to the night, but I heard nothing. I was happy I'd ignored the advice of the nurse. I remember being happy, Hugo. I got up to go to the toilet and considered looking in on her, but' – he wasn't sure he was going to be able to say it – 'but I didn't. I didn't go in there, Hugo. I have no idea why not. Maybe I didn't want to wake her on such a special night, or disturb her if she was awaiting some crazed visit from a non-existent man bearing gifts. I wanted her to sleep. I wanted to sleep myself. And that was it. That is the story of Claudia. And you, Hugo, are the first person I have ever told it to.'

Hugo looked somehow replaced. He walked around the desk to Marick, and, difficult as it was with Marick sitting, enfolded him in a hug that was anything but soft. Marick was being held.

'Brother,' Hugo said.

Marick nodded.

Hugo returned to his chair, and they sat in the silence for a short while.

Hugo spoke again. 'So how is Claudia now?'

'What?'

'I mean, has she recovered?'

Marick could hear his own responses and shaped into words they sounded senseless.

'What do you mean you've never enquired?' Hugo asked.

'It was my promise to them. I thought that if I was utterly excised from their lives, they might have some hope.'

'Hope for what?'

'To heal, I guess. To move on. In both an emotional and physical sense. You know I've never researched the type of stroke she had. I remember being told it was a clot, a result of sludgy blood after the prolonged seizure, but I honestly thought it best if I left it all alone. I knew it was best. For them.'

'Oh, my friend. I don't know a lot about neurology, but I do know children's brains are intensely resilient. Neuroplasticity, they call it. Rewiring and rebuilding.' Hugo sat back down, shaking his head as though barely believing. 'And they've never contacted you?'

Marick shook his head too. 'Never needed to. All the financials had been sorted out by Diane's father.'

'Well, now is the time to change. Look her up, Marick. It's been five years. Claudia will be eighteen soon – of age, an adult. If you won't do it for yourself, do it for her.'

Marick's thoughts sped. Such a thing to say. Such a truth.

Marick glanced at his watch. The morning had disappeared. Hugo stood to leave. They planned to keep catching up, no matter where Hugo was or what he was doing or whatever he was producing. Just the two of them, they agreed. Without Vivian.

'Vivian and I aren't going to last,' Hugo said. Marick nodded.

The pair shook hands, an iron bridge between them.

THIRTY-THREE

When the doctor and chaplain had met in the half-room she thought nobody else would discover, they had recognised in each other the desire for revelation, for knowledge that might put an ocean of pain to rights.

She had wanted to tell him, though, the quest was pointless. Come and see what I see, she should have said to him, where there is no rhyme to the allocation of suffering. Unjust was not the word for it, neither was random. It was simply the way it was. No meaning in any of it at all.

When she had first heard about the gold, she had been, with a scepticism appropriate to her training, dismissive. But then, in the context of the things she'd heard at the bedside of patients, stories told to her which were impossible to believe but the more unimaginable they were, the more likely they were to be true, she became, for the first time in many years, hungry. As though she needed that gold – swum into existence inside the cellular engines of bacteria – to be as factual as day, a counterweight to the pull of reality. That there was *something else*, besides what roared in, ambulance after ambulance, day after day. So she let the magic of the story take root and grow within her. She let the implausible in. It was like freedom, swaying, cutting her free.

She would continue to walk, one foot ahead of the other through the cement warren, starting now, in the diversion of breaktime, a foray of hope in the ambient dark.

As she descended, leaving behind that desk and her department, drawn back underground, she accepted she would relinquish her room to the strange chaplain and his dreams and find somewhere new for herself. A place that would be hers alone.

She turned into a submarine of a tunnel she hadn't come across before, decorated with rusted pipes like plaid. It smelled oily and she hoped it wasn't at risk of cracking, letting in whatever subterranean ooze might be beyond its walls. Next a staircase, heading down. Even further underground there were hints of tree roots appearing in the floor like small coppery tentacles, calcified ridges on walls as though it were an ossuary, disarticulated stairs, dead-ends.

Years and years in the hospital, and she still hadn't come close to covering all its territory. Here, down below, the myths felt possible again. There was always something unanticipated below the surface. Edgar Allan Poe had instilled in her the black thrill of all that was leaden and terrifying about places subterrestrial: *the stifling fumes of the damp earth, the silence like a sea that overwhelms, the unseen but palpable presence of the Conqueror Worm*, as though any descent beneath the observable outer rim was to invite being buried alive. She had found the tunnels here had a dim endlessness to them. They were not suffocating, but had all turns and corners of possibility. Whispers and scurries. Secrets. She did not want to admit she might be hunting for the gold.

On this break, timed between waves, between brinks and edges, the doctor's discovery was something unique. She rounded a cavernous bend to find an old, worn cleaning lady sitting on an upended bucket, talking to herself. The doctor had seen her around; she was short, quilted, wearing a bright-yellow nylon dress which was now hitched up over her knees.

'May I?' the doctor asked, gesturing to the area beside her. 'What are you doing down here?'

'Cleaning,' the woman said. 'Lilyana.' She stuck out a hard-worked hand.

'Oh.' She looked around. There was a smoothness, a sense of occupation, a sheen undeserved by this unlived space.

They sat for a bit, silent, almost companionable.

'Where is your accent from?' the doctor asked. She thought it might be Russian. It was difficult to tell, the way the woman spoke.

'Around,' Lilyana said.

The doctor picked up a coin, half-buried in dust near their feet. She rubbed it to see the date.

'Nineteen ninety-one,' she said.

'History,' Lilyana replied.

'Isn't it wonderful here,' the doctor said. 'I sometimes come down just to hide.'

Lilyana broke into a grin. 'Me too.'

The doctor was astonished to see Lilyana's mouth was full of gold teeth. Not one here or there, a filling or a cap, but gums lined with them.

'Goodness. Your teeth. I'm sorry to stare, but they are very impressive.'

Lilyana dropped her head. 'No. I'm sorry.'

'It's just I've never seen that before. Forgive me. I shouldn't have reacted. I was just surprised.' She felt reassured to know she still could be.

'Do you want to be surprised?'

'I always do.'

'Then I tell you about these teeth.'

Once Lilyana looked up and began speaking with her lips moving normally, she was easier to understand. The insides of her mouth shone, brazen in the light. 'You a doctor, yes? That means you can't tell nobody what I say here? Maybe saying things to a doctor better than in the priest's box.'

'Of course. If you tell me something in confidence, I would never break that faith.'

'Faith,' Lilyana said, 'faith get me in this trouble from the start.'

'Why do you say this is trouble?'

'It's all trouble. It start with trouble, and now I got no way of fixing. No way to say sorry.'

'Sorry for what, Lilyana?' The doctor could see something smouldering inside the cleaning lady, who until that moment had just been another unseen part of the hospital machinery. She knew when to stay quiet and let the story come.

'For what I took.'

The doctor cocked her head, slightly to the side, awaiting whatever strangeness she was about to hear.

'These teeth are old. They not mine. Well they are, but I shouldn't have them here, in this city, down here underground.'

Lilyana rubbed a forefinger over a few of her upper teeth as though checking they were still there. The doctor noticed they were ill-fitting dentures, which Lilyana would suck back onto her upper gum, or alternately crunch at them while she spoke. The doctor could hear the noise they made – a tiny thunder. It was clear Lilyana wasn't sure where to enter her story, how far back to go.

'Thirty years ago I leave Croatia. Maybe longer. War was coming to us again.'

The doctor made herself as comfortable as she could, leaning back onto the concrete of the wall behind.

'Actually, I don't know when this story start,' Lilyana said. She leant forward and clutched her knees. The backs of her hands were fissured and rough. 'Before I was born. That's when. Maybe even further back. Yes, further back. It starts with the terrible war. But that war start because of war before that – maybe all the wars. All of them firing first shots because of greed and power, one bad step after another back and back and back … and so maybe my teeth story go all the way back to the original sin. Maybe all stories do.'

Lilyana looked swamped, fearful of the tale inside her.

'Which was the terrible war?' the doctor asked. She folded one leg beneath her and bent the other knee up to her chin. A faint shower of pollen-like dust fell from the ceiling above them.

'Nineteen forties,' Lilyana said. 'My parents had farmhouse, in smallest village in Croatia. Was said the war would never reach them. Too far. Too quiet. They only hear little bits. We all safe, everyone say to each other. But no. The war come for them like it come for all Europe. Such a tiny place, but people from everywhere lived there. A happy place – Jews and Serbs and Romanians. All sorts it was. People live there because that's where the happiness was.

'My father, he was the dentist. He look after all the villages – people came from miles. They love him. When the war came knocking, well everyone had heard what they were doing to people like them, and they knew they could trust the dentist. They give him all their gold for keep safe. They think they be back after the war passed them over. "I'll make them into teeth for you," my father told them. "I engrave your initials on them, so you know which ones are yours. I can forge you dentures. Your gold will stay in safest place, your mouth," he said. There was a little Catholic church in town. When the army rolled through, most of the people took to hiding in its corners. But somebody didn't like the Jews being in there, made sure the soldiers knew where they were. They all found.'

Lilyana stopped. She had to breathe, and she sucked up and down on her dentures for a bit. With the back of her hand, she wiped her lips. When she brought her hand down to clutch it with the other, the doctor thought she saw a faint glitter on Lilyana's knuckles, but it might well have been the coyness of the light, playing.

'The people of that happy little town not come back. My parents not taken. Never searched. Scraped though the war, only misery and a cellar full of gold teeth my father spent the following years making into dentures. Nobody came to claim them. And then nobody remembered. My sisters and me, we born in that cellar. My father take his dentistry on the road but he never let those dentures out of coal pit. I was nineteen when Croatian Spring came, tanks on the street again. Both of my sisters already dead. One of scarlet fever, one of infection in her bones that never let up. Death comes for us all, sometime,' Lilyana glanced over at the doctor. 'But still. We all want to live. My father, he want me to live, which I never understand how much, till now I guess. I was student by then, my friends all revolutionaries, and my father, his heart froze when he hear what's coming. He packed me off, across borders, across seas. "Go," he tell me, and he wrapped up all those teeth on wire to take with me, give me a life.'

The doctor had not moved while she listened and had to wriggle out her foot which had grown numb. 'So they're yours.'

Lilyana shook her head. 'I promise my father I would look for the people who owned the gold, maybe their children. Give it back. Papa said, "Of course you will, my Lilyana. That is right. But look after yourself first."'

Lilyana's old hands were now trembling. She pressed them harder into her knees.

'I do what Papa said. I look after myself first. I sell the first set and promise to pass on the rest, but then I never went looking, never find anybody to give them to. I didn't do anything for anybody. Okay when you young, but when you my age ...'

She wiped one hand across her watery eyes. 'Then, and it must be God's doing, I lost all my own teeth. They half-rotted to stumps anyway. So I put in one set. Just one, I think to myself. But they fit so bad, somehow I just grind them away, day after day. I ground them down, the gold just gone. I don't even know where.'

Lilyana pulled out the top denture and showed it to the doctor. There were scattered teeth remaining. The wiring was brown and twisted, the golden teeth half worn away.

'Why don't you want anyone to know, Lilyana? You did nothing wrong.'

Lilyana made a guttural, disparaging sound. 'The people of my village trust my father, he trust me, and look, here I am, in the holes of a hospital, cleaning up after everybody. These teeth will be dust by the time I in my grave. They won't even come with me. I steal from the people and their children. Big sin. Biggest sin of all, maybe.'

The doctor had little to say in response. She made the appropriate noises: reassurances that anybody would have done the same, that looking after yourself in those circumstances was no crime, trying to dispel the notion that survival was a felony, but she could see they were glancing off Lilyana, lost without even an echo.

'You no tell anyone,' Lilyana said. 'Promise me.'

The doctor was halfway back out to the surface, to the tedium of the well-lit throughways above ground, when disappointment rippled through her mind – the realisation that perhaps Lilyana's story was the answer to the alchemical bacteria. Gold dust, floating about the place, settling on benches, incorporated into the bellies of the bacteria. That would mean there had been no alchemical miracle, no physical anomaly in the universe with its epicentre in the catacombs under her feet – merely an old woman crunching out unhappy breath as she swung her mop, talking to herself, no-one left to listen.

That night, the doctor spent her time alone with what felt like embers, reality again a let-down. She researched the capability of *Escherichia coli* to concentrate environmental contaminants, but found little evidence to either support or refute it. A few bacteria were capable of gathering elements together and surviving – a little blip out of a laboratory in Germany – but none did so with the vitality the ones here had apparently been showing. Later she turned her search to the village Lilyana had talked about, but found no evidence of it. Perhaps the doctor had remembered it wrong and tried all sorts of different spellings. Reflecting on them, Lilyana's timelines did not make sense either. As the doctor scrambled to recall other parts of her tale, more of it seemed wild. It was difficult to picture the cellar in the village in the hills, furnished with a crucible and white, licking flames and moulds and the blazing eyes of a dentist fixed on doing right somehow.

And at that point the good doctor, who, after all, was going to need to work above ground for many more years, among the flat actuality of society, decided she would not seek out Lilyana again to winnow her words into clarity or truth. She would let a remnant of hope remain, and whatever magic that had happened survive. Lilyana's story, just as it had been told, was better left alone.

THIRTY-FOUR

Marick was not sure he could face the ICU. Telling Hugo about Claudia had doused a deep flame within. The hope Claudia might have had some recovery was beyond anything his head could hold, and it had left him drenched and done. And angry with himself that he'd never considered its possibility. In his exhaustion, he wondered whether he could bear looking into the eyes of the boy's parents during the moments of their son's exit, watching their final gaze over his hollow body. Marick entertained thoughts of Lazarus and his dusty revival, wondering if it was possible every doctor had been wrong, and the boy would sit up, groggy, and ask what all the fuss was about.

As the hour ticked near, Marick began to conjure excuses, elaborate ones, but none in the end believable, and certainly none that would hold weight over the sincere request the parents had made – that he stand beside them while their son was transported out of the ICU to the operating theatre. A terrible word – theatre – the mother had said, as though it was all routine entertainment to remove all the organs which had grown along with him.

They had all been told the timing was critical. At a single coordinated moment, at a signal, a chain of events would occur all over Australia. Other people who had been living at the mercy of a pager would be unzipped, their own devastated organs bound for a bucket. Teams were synchronised in multiple cities, planes on standby, a battalion of trained workers doing their part to get the blood of strangers pumping through the boy's parts.

When Marick entered the ICU, he was expected. A clerk directed him to a different bed in a side room with the door closed. He walked – or felt he plunged – into a scene of calm, a sea rocking with gentle waves of mechanical noise.

The mother walked across and embraced him. 'Thank you for coming,' she said with reverence, as though he had brought God.

The family had set up the room with relics: family photographs, papers, mementoes of a brief life. A scatter of electric candles had been placed around, adding a flicker, ethereal and strange, to the fluorescence and the blue pulse of the monitors.

The nurses moved back so Marick could stand close to the parents over their son, and pray. He'd thought hard about what he would say. And although his voice shook and the smell of medicine gone stale made his head heavy, he spoke. Of loss. Of support. Of love.

'And will God commend you to heaven,' he finished with, 'will He ensure your soul lives on forever, not just in those who love you, but in those who will live on because of you.' The words came out with ease, and while Marick touched the son's forehead to anoint his passage, he felt light.

The door was opened and they could see a grey gathering of people, an assembled team ready to wheel him off. One was looking at his watch.

The mother spoke to the nurse. 'Just a few more minutes, please? His cousin Bella wants to say her own farewell. Please?'

The request was relayed to the leader of the team. He nodded and motioned *five*.

The mother squeezed Marick's hand, and the three of them again bowed their heads. The moment was coming.

Through the door a nurse escorted in a young girl.

'This is Bella,' the father said to Marick. 'She's twelve.'

A twelve-year-old, girl, and Marick could barely look at her.

The machines surrounding the boy, all their steel and plastic, their inanimate beeps and sing-song loops, their swinging and beating and breathing, down to their molecular and lifeless parts, although temporarily all the life the boy had, were still just insensible metal, Marick knew. Unrusting. Immortal. This room, too, was bland and without sentience, its walls and doors, the lights and the steel of the trolley. But there was Bella, standing at the foot of the bed, with her white, soft skin, her alive, shining eyes, her lithe posture and smooth muscle, taking a deep breath, readying herself. A breath which let out a single note. A song she'd prepared for her older, beloved cousin.

The nurses stopped. All the workers throughout the ICU did, as though that single note travelled out from the room, through the door, through the ducts, coming out of the vents in its purity. The machines all quietened as the note became the airwaves itself. A note that was everything alive. Marick could feel it flow into where the steam had been inside him. The note continued until it was replaced by others, no less beautiful, no less pure. The notes became a song became a psalm became a requiem. And as the brief aria of Bella's voice concluded, it returned to that one single perfect note, and Marick sensed the machines hold their breath. The living among all that was not.

All was still when Bella was done. Marick could hear nothing. Not so much as an echo, for seconds. And it was a greater peace than death, that moment. The boy was to be scattered better than ash all over the country, and it was as though everyone realised it at the same time. It occurred to Marick this could well be deemed a miracle. True and tiny in here, but spreading as ripples throughout the country. So that others could live. Something from nothing.

It was then time, sweet time, and the anaesthetic team came in, working in quiet, orchestrated efficiency, one with a solitary tear on his cheek. The lines were changed over. The cylinders swapped and transport machines hooked up. The mother leant over the boy and kissed his forehead. The father did the same. Each movement, every last moment, carried a lifetime of meaning – every shape and every sound and every occurrence did, because they were the humans and they brought the occurrences to life. Finding meaning and connection, that's what they did, and the world was inside that little room, until the door opened for the last time, letting the entire light of the universe in, and Marick prayed to God and to the universe, which at that point, he realised, might be entirely the same thing.

THIRTY-FIVE

Encouraged by Hugo, Marick looked Diane up.

In the suburbs of Seville, along with a local woman, Diane had established a small shopfront. *The Essence of Australia. Bringing the outdoors of Down Under to your own indoors*, the website said. She was still using her married name, and seeing it there, pixelated among the kangaroos and beachy themes made him feel feathery. The shop had a green and gold awning and looked to be sandwiched between a bakery and a low-rent fashion label in a concrete-heavy mall. It could have been anywhere.

He stared at the website. Could not bring himself to click on the *About* tab.

❦

Dolly had taken to her new role with gusto. Marick came in every day to the low room to help. She'd thought of everything. Her army had a roster. A combination of volunteers from the shop and staff she had recruited through an elaborate messaging

320

system with its central node her shop window telegraph, including senior doctors, had signed up to help.

'I'm not surprised so many have come on board,' Dolly said to Marick. 'One of the nurses said it felt like giving a rather large middle finger to a certain level of the hierarchy.' She gave a little chortle. 'Which I shouldn't repeat, obviously.'

There was a sign-on sheet on a little card table at the front door, where volunteers would get colour-coded stickers onto which they'd write their name. An orange sticker meant the volunteer was in charge of intercepting the meals as they left the kitchen. This role soon became redundant as the kitchen staff were all on board and happy to bundle up meals themselves. Purple meant you were on look-out duty, green to chaperone the meals' recipients up through the carefully chosen clandestine route. Red meant you were on clean-up, and blue was float, doing any odd jobs Dolly saw fit.

One day she walked in, triumphant. 'Guess what's being delivered today,' she said to Marick. He had no idea.

'Chocolate,' she said. 'Barrel loads of it. All the broken blocks and bars the shops can't sell. Once you'd given me the idea, Father, I worked out that hospital meals weren't the only things going to waste.'

During the first week, Marick saw the doctor come in and collect a red sticker. She scribbled her name on it and stuck it to her scrubs. They smiled at each other. Marick had so much he wanted to ask but did not want to intrude.

'Purple today,' she said, indicating his sticker.

'Yes,' Marick laughed. 'It's my favourite role. But how do you have time to do this?'

'It's my lunch break. It's fine. It sometimes feels as though this might be the only good I do in a day.'

He wanted to protest, but she looked more rested than he'd seen her, more content, and he let it go.

Before he left to go to his position, to stand on a corner as sentinel, he saw her walk over and hug Dolly. The doctor's height made Dolly look like a child. He lingered, trying to listen to their conversation.

'Aren't you supposed to be using a walking stick after your operation, Dolly?' the doctor asked. Dolly just hooted, and Marick could not make out her reply.

Not once was the operation outed. Megsie was the ringleader under the fig tree, and ran an incredibly tight ship, despite the challenges.

⁘

Only once more did Marick venture down to the laundry. It remained unoccupied, with its broken latch still unmended and ignored. The room was nothing now. As he was about to leave, he caught sight of Lilyana at the end of the corridor, and he called out to her.

'Lilyana. I've been thinking about you. Did you still want help finding somewhere for confession?'

'No, Father,' she said. 'I good now.' And she beamed, that brilliant golden smile.

⁘

Marick and Hugo had dinner together every Friday night. They made it their mission to try every type of cuisine, booking small cheap restaurants that served authentic global dishes. International Fridays, they called it, and they liked to think of it as travelling together a little.

Hugo both spoke and asked questions. The marriage was over. His job was incredible. 'Private funding, Marick. You have no idea the possibilities that allows.' That night they were eating Mongolian. It was delicious and messy and tasted of dark, rich spice.

'So what have you found out?' Hugo asked.

Marick had to come clean. 'I'm too scared to ask.'

'Marick,' Hugo said, and no more.

Marick knew what he had to do.

There was a photo of Diane. She had a few more soft jowls and creases and looked a little yellowish in frame. No mention, no word of Claudia.

Marick debated endlessly with himself about the best way to contact her. Letter? Email? Phone? In the end he used the contact form on the website, dithered over it for an age, then finally laid it clean. He asked permission to talk after all these years.

Diane's response was unexpected. Uncoiling over the course of several weeks, with emails rolling back and forth, longer each time, she filled in gap after gap. She sent photos. And then there they were, standing together. There was Claudia. Curly-haired, tanned, smiling.

Yes, she's recovered, Diane wrote.

Marick's heart skipped so many beats he could feel a lightness within his chest as though his most important organ might float away.

As their correspondence went on – and it took some time for Marick to realise – it became clear Diane was apologising. She had missed him, missed the only person who had ever listened to her. She wrote that her guilt at cutting him off had grown so monstrously large she hadn't known how to go back and fix things. She'd talked it over with her parents, but they'd insisted it remain a clean break.

Does she ever ask about me? Marick wrote, almost in a whisper.

All the time, Diane replied. *I am so sorry. Forgive me.*

Can I write to her? Marick asked.

Even better, Diane responded, *come.*

And, with the low room at the hospital buzzing with meals and welcome and the laundry no longer, and a jewel of a sunrise, Marick buckled himself into the back of an aeroplane which took off and banked round like an albatross. The water was satin beneath him and the earth turned, magnificent in perpetual dawn. He had arranged a few weeks' leave. There would be time to talk through the ghosts. Time to tell them about a hospital and a basement and the tiny, temporary nuggets of gold. Time for grief to discover it has boundaries and time to traverse the plains of transformation. Every bone in Marick's body could be remade.

ACKNOWLEDGEMENTS

A book takes a village. Although it's my name on the front, it is the steadfast support and work and dogged belief of many that has transformed it from a scree of insistent words into miracle itself. My thanks, deeper than I am capable of expressing, go to:

Catherine Milne, who finally plucked the manuscript from her cyclonic inbox, and championed it from that moment onwards. A queen among publishers. My gratitude is fathomless.

Martin Shaw, the wizard, agent of the millennium, who has been unswerving in his support.

Kathryn Heyman, my mentor and role model, one of the finest writerly humans there is.

The supreme team at HarperCollins, the Bookwrights: Scott, Samantha, Hazel and a songsheet of others behind the scenes toiling away.

She who reads every word I ever write without complaint (well, only a little), my bestie, Anita.

My brother Wayne, whose scientific exploits and willing ear and lend of a lab coat to see what *E. coli* were capable of kick-started this rabbit-hole of a story.

While I'm at it, my other brother Anthony, just because. AND, since I'm there, Kathy and Jacqui and all the gorgeous children (and a special shout-out to Wendy and Andrew – you story-lovers).

My daughter, Isabelle, an artistic wunderkind, who inspires me to push beyond the ordinary.

My son, Jules, my rock. I cannot wait for your next chapter, and to watch where your star ascends.

My husband Richard, a quiet surgical hero, a saver of lives, a man of the utmost humility and grace, who has never wavered, not once, in his belief that I can keep sitting down, me and my words, and put them together in some sort of order.

Jen Hutchison, from Journeys to Words Publishing, who engaged in some flayed-skin-level editing. She taught me how to fish out the litter from each sentence and polish every one so they could find the light.

Those who read very early and very chaotic versions of the manuscript: Charlotte D., Amy N., Jacquie G.-S., Louise A. And Mario D. Very, very special.

A special thanks to Terri-ann White, now of the incendiary Upswell Publishing, for her advice and friendship.

The girls from the Australian Writers Mentoring Bali group, you gorgeous bunch: Susan M., Angela G., Alison L., Alice Y., Georgie M., Emma D., Sam L., Christie H., Emma D., Jak C., Kerry and the extraordinary Jill Dawson.

Varuna, Lamplight edition. The wonders of Zoom allowed a girl from the edge of the planet to sit among the genius of Carol Major, Gail Jones and Markus Zusak (who promised me that a 'Chernobyl of a novel' might be just the thing he likes to read).

On Carol Major, many thanks to her for discussing the denouement of this book, inspired by a tale of love she told herself, the love of her daughter, and a lone song in an ICU.

Every heroic person who dons scrubs to turn up to work at Royal Perth Hospital. Although the resemblance to that inner-city, labyrinthine mess of a place is PURELY COINCIDENTAL, the inspiration for much of *Tiny Uncertain Miracles* comes from those who go beneath, above and beyond, and then a little more.

The beautiful southern property to put the finishing touches, thank you Jon and Caroline.

My parents, those seriously good eggs. Judy and Ted. Thanks for being.

And you, dear reader, thank you. For reading not just this book, but all books. Books will save us somehow – books and stories and tales of lives other than our own, for how else can we nurture respect for all lives, if not by hearing about them from the inside?

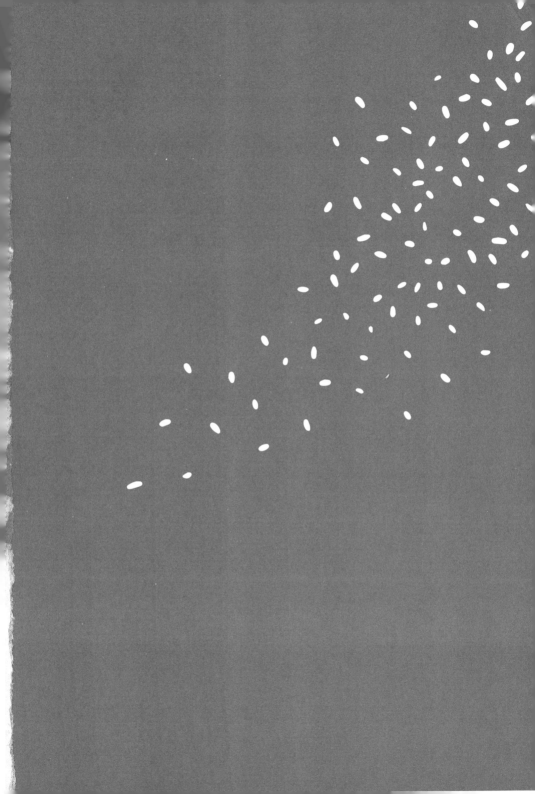